API

A

THE
China Garden

By the same author

EASY CONNECTIONS

EASY FREEDOM

MEL

THE China Garden

LIZ BERRY

Farrar, Straus and Giroux • New York

Copyright © 1996 by Liz Berry
All rights reserved
Published simultaneously in Canada by HarperCollins*CanadaLtd*
Printed in the United States of America
First published in Great Britain by Victor Gollancz Ltd., 1994
First American edition, 1996

Library of Congress Cataloging-in-Publication Data
Berry, Liz.
The China garden/Liz Berry.—1st American ed.
p.   cm.
[1. Mothers and daughters—Fiction. 2. Extrasensory perception—Fiction.
3. England—Fiction.]   I. Title.
Pz7.B46175Ch   1996   [Fic]—dc20   95-583 CIP AC

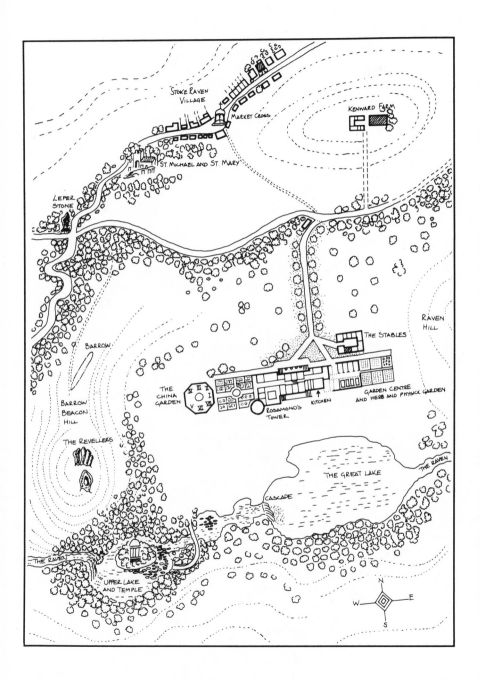

The Legend of Demeter and Persephone

Demeter, Goddess of Grain and Fertility, the Great Earth Mother, searched for nine days for her lost daughter Persephone, who had been carried off by Hades, God of the Underworld. Demeter, full of grief, wandered the Earth, pretending to be an old woman. When she came to Eleusis she cared for Demophoön, the infant son of the king. She was seen placing him in the sacred fire to make him immortal. She was recognized and a famous temple was erected to her at Eleusis.

Demeter, grieving for Persephone, made all the vegetation die—trees, plants, corn, rice, vegetables, everything died, and the earth lay desolate and barren. At last Hades promised Persephone that she could spend two-thirds of each year on Earth, and every year Persephone, Goddess of Spring and Rebirth, comes home to the light of the sun, the wind and the rain, and her mother bestows abundant food upon the Earth.

The legend symbolizes the cycle of human life—rebirth in Man as in nature. Human life is like corn: it grows with the season, ages, dies—and is reborn.

Chapter 1

Dark of the moon. Near dawn. Starlight shimmered along the dragon walls. Nothing stirred in the China Garden. No breeze. No night sound. The only waking creature was a tortoiseshell cat sitting on the step of the First Moon Gate like a creature from a pharaoh's tomb, watching and waiting.

It was many years since anyone had walked here, but now the grass was bending in the still air. Invisible feet were passing to and fro, leaving a winding track.

There was a drift of sound, ancient pipe music, then a strange shifting, something coming alive, and a whisper, like a breath, moving through the shadows, "She's coming . . . She's coming . . ."

On the great hill that rose above the Garden, a tall figure detached itself from the darkness of the ancient standing stone. The starlight gleamed on the wide shoulders of his leather jacket, as he stretched, stiff from his long wait. Sometimes it seemed he had been waiting for her for ever, but now at last he knew she was coming. He stared down at the darkened house. There was a light burning in a big window overlooking the terrace. Was the old man waiting too?

The clock clicked onto the hour loudly.

"Stop. Put down your pens *now*."

There was a muffled groan from the students.

Clare Meredith leaned back, added a final comma to the

sheets she had been reading, checked her name and clipped them together. *Finished.* Her last A-level paper. All over at last.

She could hear Sara behind her, muttering to herself and dropping her papers on the floor.

No more worry, panic and effort. So why was this ball of anxiety and tension in her chest getting bigger all the time, as though something unpleasant was about to happen?

"You all right, Clare? You look a bit odd." Sara tucked her arm through Clare's as they left the room.

"I'm fine." Impossible to explain this eerie feeling even to Sara.

"Listen—I've got *plans* for us this summer! Come on, I'll stand you a coffee and a burger. Let's live it up!"

"You're late, Clare. Where on earth have you been?"

Clare's fingers tightened on her house key. She glanced at the hall clock. "It's not half-five yet!"

"I've been waiting for you to get home. I've got to talk to you."

"We all went to McDonald's."

"With dear Adrian, I suppose."

"With *Sara*, actually."

Her mother's taut shoulders relaxed.

"Oh, Clare, I'm sorry. I forgot you had another exam today."

"The *last* one. We were *celebrating*."

"How did it go?"

"Okay," Clare said, shortly. "All topics I'd revised." She threw her book bag, strangely light now, into its usual corner by the front door, for the last time. She felt flattened, still hardly able to take it in.

"I can't believe it's finished."

"When will you get the results?"

"August sometime." Not quite out of the woods yet, she

8

reminded herself. Not enough to *pass*. She needed three good grades for university.

She watched her mother in the hall mirror. Frances was getting ready for work, stabbing pins nervously into her dark gold french pleat to go under her Ward Sister's cap.

"Well, it's done now, thank goodness," Frances said. "It's been a strain on both of us. You've been hard to live with, Clare."

"I know. I'm sorry." But it came out too stiffly. They both knew that the tension of the exams was only part of the trouble between them. There was her choice of career. And there was Adrian.

Until she had started to date Adrian they had always got on well together—joking, sharing, talking things over. They went shopping, poking about for bargains in the street markets, having a Chinese meal, wandering around the London museums on Sunday afternoons. They hadn't done that for a long time, Clare thought, with a sense of loss.

And it wasn't all on her side. Lately her mother had been unreasonably irritable and tense.

She said, embarrassed, "I . . . er . . . wanted to say thanks for everything. Letting me stay on into sixth-form college. Giving me a chance at university. I really do appreciate all you're doing for me. I wish you didn't have to work all the extra hours."

Frances looked at her in the mirror. "I haven't got anybody else, Clare. And, besides, you're worth it. You haven't wasted your chances, or taken them for granted. You've worked really hard."

Her mother was a good-looking woman, Clare thought. No, be honest. She was beautiful. High cheek bones, pale translucent skin. But there was something strange about her face that sometimes had people turning round in the street to take a second look.

They stood shoulder to shoulder staring into the mirror, feeling closer than they had for weeks. Clare was the same height as her mother, but she favoured her father's family. She had a mass of wiry black hair which she tamed by plaiting it back tightly from the crown of her head.

This afternoon, though, as they stood in a shaft of sunlight from the small window next to the front door, Clare was suddenly struck by their likeness. It's our eyes, she thought. Wide and silvery, tilting slightly upwards.

Her mother laughed aloud. "We're alike, Clare. Something weird about us. Look at those strange witchy eyes! You know they'd have burned both of us five hundred years ago."

Clare was not surprised Frances had picked up her own thought. Telepathy. It happened so frequently it wasn't worth mentioning.

Frances had stopped laughing and was staring into her own eyes in the mirror. The closed, shuttered look came over her face, her heavy eyelids drooped. "Perhaps they would have been right."

Clare felt a cold shiver run down her back. What was she seeing? Her mother's strange psychic ability disturbed and worried her. Although Frances rarely spoke of it, it was always *there*, ever present, a dimension of her mother's personality that Clare preferred not to think about.

She tried to draw away, but Frances' arm lay heavily on her shoulders. "I've got something to tell you, Clare. It's not the best time really, but I mustn't put it off any longer. I'm going . . . Well, I've got another job."

"You're leaving St Joseph's?" Clare was shocked. Her mother had worked at the hospital as far back as she could remember, even before her father died.

"It's a private nursing job. Looking after one elderly man. The salary is very good."

"B-but . . ." Her mother had often expressed her views on people who did private nursing in order to get a higher salary. "You said you might be in line for a Sister Tutor's job. I thought you liked it there."

"This job is residential, down in the West Country . . ."

"You mean we're *moving*!"

"Stoke Raven in Somerset."

"You mean we're leaving *London*? Leaving all our friends? Selling our house?"

"No-o. Not selling the house. Too difficult just now. But I've been incredibly lucky. I've been able to let it furnished to a bone specialist and his wife who are on exchange from the States for a year. It's just as if it was meant to be. They want to move in in two weeks."

Two weeks! Had her mother gone off her head? Clare said, dazed, "We're actually *leaving*, going to Somerset? Suppose I don't want to go? What about me? I was *born* here!"

"You're leaving home anyway. You'll be going to university in a few months. Until then I thought you'd want to stay in London. I've spoken to Sara's mother and she says she'll put you up in her spare room."

The significance of what Frances was saying hit Clare hard. She suddenly felt like a chick that had just been pushed out of its nest, cold and lonely and too frightened to fly yet. She wanted her freedom and independence, of course she did. She had looked forward to going to university. But this was too strange, too sudden. She wasn't prepared.

"I don't want to stay in London on my own."

"Hardly on your own. What about Sara and Adrian and . . ."

"I'd rather come with you," Clare said in a small voice. "Isn't there any room for me?"

"Well, there is, of course." Frances sounded reluctant and doubtful. "I'll have my own place. But I'm sure you wouldn't like it. There's nothing there, Clare. Just the big house, Ravensmere, and the village, Stoke Raven. It wouldn't suit you at all. I mean, there's no public library or swimming pool, or anything . . . There are no young people . . . And I'll be working all the time . . ."

"You don't want me," Clare said, blankly.

She couldn't believe that her mother was simply turning her out and going off to a new life in the country without her.

"Don't you have to give notice?"

"I already have."

"I don't understand what's gone wrong with us," Clare said desperately. "We always used to decide everything together, ever since Dad died. But you let our house without saying anything. You could have told me."

"I could—if I'd wanted endless rows and arguments. And upsetting you in the middle of the exams."

Her mother looked at her steadily, her eyes brilliant. "I've got to go back, Clare. I should have gone before. But you've been in the middle of all your exams the past few years, so I waited."

"*Back*? You mean you've been there before?"

"I lived there once. I went back for your grandfather's funeral three years ago."

"I don't remember that."

"You were in France."

The school holiday paid for by putting money weekly in the china cat on the kitchen shelf.

"I thought you'd always lived in London."

Clare was upset. She had thought they were so close that she knew everything about her mother. But a big part of her life had been missing. Not just missing—deliberately concealed. "What about relatives? My grandmother—is she still alive?"

"Of course not. I told you, my mother died when I was a child."

"But my grandfather was alive until three years ago, and you never said. Never let me see him." Clare's disappointment and sense of loss was so acute it was an actual pain in her chest. "You know I always wished we had some family and now it's too late. I'll never see him."

"He didn't want to know us, Clare. He wouldn't see me. He told me never to come back. It's no good digging up the past."

And yet she had cared enough to go back for his funeral, Clare thought.

The closed look was back on her mother's face, and Clare was convinced that there was a lot left out of what she was saying. Lying by omission they called it. She realized now just how little her mother had said about her early life.

"Look, we'll talk about it sometime. But I've got to go now. I'll be late." Frances avoided Clare's eyes. "You'd better start sorting out your things." She buttoned her navy cape, and started towards the door.

"So why go back *now?*"

The question sank into Frances' back like a knife and stopped her dead. There was a long silence. At last she said, "I haven't taken the decision lightly. I have to go back, Clare. I have no choice. I owe."

Clare's eyes widened. "*Money?*" Wild ideas of gambling and blackmail chased around her head.

Frances shook her head. "Big debts you can't repay with money."

Clare could hear the tiredness and strain in her voice, and knew suddenly that her mother was desperately worried, frightened even.

"There's something wrong, isn't there? You're not telling me the truth."

"I don't want to get you involved. You've got your own life ahead of you."

Clare stared at her, and suddenly heard her own voice sounding high and clear, echoing in her head, "I'm coming to Ravensmere with you."

13

Frances spun round. "Look, honestly, it's not a good idea, Clare. Oh, of course I want you with me! You're my daughter. I'm going to miss you dreadfully. We've gone through a lot together, but *no* . . ." Her hands were shaking. She said abruptly, hoarsely, "I can't protect you there."

"What absolute garbage! Protect me from what? I'm nearly eighteen. I can look after myself, thank you very much." Clare was furious. She said bitterly, "You're just trying to get rid of me. Making excuses. But don't worry, I won't stay. It's only for a few weeks and then I'll be gone. *Permanently*."

"I didn't mean it like that," said her mother helplessly. "It's just . . . Oh God, I can't explain now. I'm so late. We'll have to talk about it later. You'll change your mind when you think it over."

But Clare did not change her mind. Perversely, the more her mother tried to dissuade her, the more she knew that she would have to go.

She couldn't explain, even to herself, why the determination to go to Ravensmere with her mother had ceased to be a choice and become a compulsion. There was no logical reason.

She tried to tell herself that it was because her mother needed her support, but even that was not the reason. She only knew that deep down there was a driving urgency, a sort of *timing* that required her to go to Ravensmere—and be there as soon as possible. She felt it so strongly, there was no way she could think of opposing it. Curiosity, she thought uncomfortably. Just curiosity. But it was more than that. A lot more.

At last, after days of argument, when the books and packing cases were stacked around them on the dining room floor, Frances gave way, no match for Clare's steely determination.

"Oh very well, come if you must. But it's your own choice. Remember I tried to stop you. Don't blame me. Remember, I tried to *warn* you." Her eyes were wild, almost distraught.

Clare felt cold. She knew it was a serious warning. But why then had her mother somehow never managed to find the time to explain everything properly?

Chapter 2

"Why are we going this roundabout route?" asked Clare, impatiently. She had the road map book open on her lap. "We could have been in Somerset now, if we'd kept on the motorway."

They had started early, but it was already uncomfortably hot as they crawled around the M25 and out through the interminable western suburbs of London. They had been snapping at each other all the way like bad-tempered Yorkies, Clare thought, ashamed, but somehow unable to stop. Frances was edgy and strained, and Clare was hugging her resentment and anger to her like a baby blanket.

"There's no mad rush. I don't start until Monday."

"Anyone would think you didn't want to get there at all."

Frances rubbed the back of her neck and tried to relax her shoulders. "I thought you'd like to see something of the countryside. We've not been out of London much. Money too tight."

Clare shrugged, sliding down in her seat morosely. With every mile she felt more and more out of place. What on earth was she doing here?

The June countryside, laced with trees and flowering hedges, was like a single great green parkland beaded with ancient towns and villages. Every inch looked as though some-one or other had tended it lovingly for hundreds of years, ploughing and plastering, trimming and painting, and training up the clematis.

Picture postcard England, Clare thought disparagingly, feeling like a foreigner. It was all true—the pictures on the biscuit tins and the birthday cards, and none of it felt real.

It was a long way from gritty old London, with its rushing, shouting people, and broken houses, its grand buildings, and bags of spilling rubbish, the new offices glittering with glass and fax machines buzzing out information and news from every part of the world. The centre of everything, she had thought.

But all the while this other England had been going on without her knowing. The thatched cottages and timbered houses sat in their gardens, serene, *uncaring* about all the exciting, important things happening in London. A forgotten, permanent world, hardly changing, in a different time warp.

Adrian would hate it.

She wondered how his first day had gone. He'd be running the bank for them if they gave him half a chance.

"What are you grinning at?"

"Adrian started a job in the City today."

"On his way to his first million, no doubt," Frances said acidly.

Clare closed her mouth and looked out at the high open country of the Marlborough Downs, wishing she did not feel so miserable and flat. Exam reaction, maybe. Think of it as an adventure. Something new. If only her mother didn't dislike Adrian so much.

The first time Clare had taken him home he had got into an argument with Frances about some common land nearby where they wanted to build a six-lane motorway extension. Adrian had said you couldn't take the badgers and foxes into account when it was a question of economic profit. Frances was organizing the Save-the-Wildlife protest group.

"Patronizing fool!" said her mother, when he'd gone. "A greedy, conceited, male chauvinist. He's glib and specious, as smooth and hard as marble. I don't know what you see in him."

That was easy, Clare thought. He was the best-looking boy in the college, clever, a high-flier—and he was the only boy who had ever asked her out. Clare had been flattered and grateful. She knew she wasn't popular with boys. Too serious. A 'brain' who worked too hard. She was relieved to know she could find a boyfriend after all, like her friends who had all been dating for years.

Clare had been unsure about her choice of career. She was a good all-rounder, interested in all sorts of things, and in crisis about the subject she should read at university. She was glad to talk it over with Adrian.

You had to have money, Adrian believed. That was the first and most important thing. You had to have a career that would allow you to make big money and give lots of perks, like cars, mortgages and health and pension schemes.

Adrian had thought it pointless to read Social Sciences, Medicine or even History (Clare's vague long-term choices) because who in their right minds would want to be a social worker, a doctor or, worst of all, a *teacher*? You couldn't be a bleeding heart worrying about all the failures like the unemployed and sick. Why didn't Clare try for a business degree, he suggested, then she could go into a range of City jobs and get really good money.

As the time ran out, Clare, confused and finally desperate, had put in her application to read Economics and Computer Science at Sussex, and had been accepted, subject to her A-level results.

Her mother had been more angry than Clare had ever seen her.

"It's wrong for you, Clare. Economics is your weakest subject. Here you are, mad about History, brilliant at the Sciences, if Mr Syms is to be believed, yet you're forcing yourself into a business career. There's loads of things you could do that would give you a good career and where you could help people too."

"You're such a bleeding heart," Clare said angrily. "Always wanting to help everybody. I want to be well paid."

"Who doesn't? But I don't want you messing up your life just grabbing for money."

"There's nothing wrong with money."

"There is if it takes over, alters how you think about life. You've changed, Clare, since you've been with Adrian. All you think about is number one and getting on."

"But it's like that now. You have to be competitive if you want to get a job. Not like in your day."

"That's right. I'm the sixties' generation. I've got different values. I think the community matters too."

The disappointment and weariness in her voice stung Clare. "Other parents are pleased when their children have got ambition and sensible ideas that lead to a proper career."

"I'd love to see you make good and have an easier life than I've had. You know how much I want you to go to university. We planned it together. But there's more to life than money, Clare."

"Such as," said Clare, sceptically.

"Doing something you're interested in. Satisfaction. Self-fulfillment. Education isn't for getting a job. It's about developing yourself as a human being."

"Are you going to tell me that you can have a good life on family benefit? Adrian says . . ."

"I don't want to hear it. I've been hearing it for months. You're like a ventriloquist's dummy. Why don't you start thinking for yourself?"

And they had said hurtful, bitter things to each other— the worst quarrel they had ever had. The stiffness was still there between them.

Frances changed gears noisily, as they began to climb up a long hill.

Of course I don't agree with all Adrian's opinions, Clare thought. But had she been over-impressed with his ability to put words together cleverly, and perhaps a bit intimidated by his incisive, arrogant manner?

"What did Adrian say about the move?" Frances jabbed the window jet button viciously to sweep away the impacted flies and dust, as if she would like to sweep Adrian out of her life in the same way.

Clare glanced at her and shrugged. "That he'd write. Maybe."

In fact he had been very unpleasant, angry that she was not staying in London for the summer, and Clare had been angry too, at his lack of support and understanding. She was still hurt and angry.

Her mother looked at her sideways. "You don't sound too worried."

"I'm not a door mat. He can please himself."

After a moment Frances said, cautiously, "Plenty of fish."

"What about Chris Stevens?" *Doctor* Chris Stevens.

"What about him?"

"I thought . . . well, I mean he really likes you." An understatement. The poor fool was head over heels. He was continually underfoot whenever he was off duty.

"He's five years younger than me, Clare."

"So? He's not exactly a boy, is he?"

Frances shrugged, her lips tightening. "He'll get over it. They all do."

Clare said impatiently, "You're always so bitter about men. I can't understand you. Anyone would think Dad treated you badly, but you always say how great he was."

"Your father was one in a million. They're not all like that."

A thought struck Clare. "Did he live in Stoke Raven too?"

Her mother looked at her sharply. "You know very well

he didn't. He was Welsh. I met him when I was doing my nurse training."

Clare said, catching the undertones in her mother's voice, "There's a lot you haven't told me, isn't there?"

"About Ravensmere?" Frances purposely misunderstood, trying for a light cheerfulness and failing dismally. Clare could see the increasing tension in her tight mouth and across her shoulders as she gripped the steering wheel. "There's something in the guidebook. We're in the stables."

"The *stables*!"

Frances grinned reluctantly. "Don't worry, you won't be sharing your bed with a horse. They've been converted into apartments for the estate workers. But if you've changed your mind about staying, I can telephone Sara's mother." Her voice sounded hopeful. "You could catch the train back tomorrow. Maybe you could even get a holiday job."

Clare said, flatly, "There may be a job in the village."

"I shouldn't think so. It's a very small place."

"Or on a farm, fruit picking. Or maybe they need help at the House."

Frances said quickly, "The staff have all been with Mr Aylward for years. In any case, I don't want you working there."

Clare said, "I thought *I* was supposed to be the money-grabbing snob."

"I didn't mean ... Oh, *here* ..." Frances reached into the door compartment and tossed her a guidebook. "Read about it."

Clare found Stoke Raven in the index and read aloud: "*Stoke Raven. Remote, picturesque stone village, snuggled into one of the valleys of the Raven. Inn: Sun and Moon (no lunches/ dinners). P.O. Village stores (cl Wed.) Population: 920.*" She grinned involuntarily. "Sounds like a really wild place to live."

"I told you you'd be bored."

"*Church: St Michael and St Mary (C. of E.). Norman on Saxon foundation c. AD 700. Founded by St Aldhelm. One of the loveliest church interiors in an area abounding in splendid churches. Notable tombs: Sir Edward Aylward (1196); Edward John Aylward, Second Earl (1603). Memorial window by Burne-Jones, 'The Waters of Paradise' (1883).*

"Oh, here it is. *Ravensmere. (Occasional Summer opening only). The ancient Stoke Raven Abbey incorporated into a Tudor house, with extensive rebuilding in eighteenth century by Colen Campbell. Roman mosaic pavement (discovered 1896). Ravensmere Park includes one of the great eighteenth-century landscape gardens, the creation of James Edward Aylward, the Tenth Earl, with his son Edmund. Some work by Brown and Repton. Palladian bridge. Lake. Cascade. Follies. Grotto. Temples (Flitcroft 1765). Statuary attributed to Cheere and Rysbrack. Famous Herb Garden. Site of Holy Well, and ancient Maze (not open to the public).*"

Clare looked at her mother curiously. "Why did you say I wouldn't like it? It sounds wonderful. Very old. Historic."

"Everywhere's historic down here," Frances said, shortly. "We're coming up to Stonehenge. Do you want to stop?"

But there were too many cars and coaches and they drove on, following the road through the high, bare Salisbury Plain.

Without any apparent reason Clare began to feel a lightening of her depression, a growing excitement. She stared out at the great open uplands, with hills that seemed to move as the cloud shadows drifted across the land.

"What's that up there?"

"Barrows. Long barrows. Bell barrows. You know, ancient burial mounds made of earth and great stones."

"Before Stonehenge?"

Frances laughed. "Before the Pyramids. Long barrows are five thousand years old. We'll stop at Avebury for a meal. You'll find it interesting."

Avebury was bigger than Stonehenge, a massive circle of standing stones so big they had built a whole village inside it.

Fascinated Clare wandered down a broad avenue of alternate pillar and lozenge-shaped stones winding its way across country. She spread her hands over the ancient rock surfaces, thinking of the people who had erected them thousands of years before, and dug the fifteen-metre deep ditch that surrounded the whole place. Almost she imagined she could feel a tingling sensation, like a mild electric shock, spreading up her arm, gathering intensity. Hastily she took her hands away and shook them. This strange old country was beginning to get to her.

But when they started on their way again, she could still feel the tingling in the palms of her hands.

There was silence in the car. Clare stared out of the window. It was a long time since they had left the last town behind, some time even since they had left the last small village, and miles since they had turned off the A361.

There was fold upon fold of smaller hills. The lane was twisting and turning about, dipping and lifting. It narrowed, became single track, the hedges getting higher and brushing the sides of the car. The old trees grew closer and met overhead until it seemed they were driving through an endless green tunnel.

They turned into another lane, and then another and yet another, all unmarked by any signposts, threading a labyrinth of ever narrowing one-track lanes burrowing ever deeper into a lush secret country, overhung with tall trees, while above them the shoulders of great hills emerged from the hanging woods.

Clare said, "What happens if we meet a lorry coming the other way?"

She glanced sideways at her mother, suddenly aware of her growing tension. Frances was clutching the wheel tightly, her knuckles a tell-tale white, staring grimly ahead.

"You're driving too fast," Clare said.

The lane was rising up now along the side of a hill, bigger and higher than all the others in the surrounding country. Below, between the trees, there were panoramic views of the patchwork fields of the valley farms and the open moors spreading out into the blue distance.

"Barrow Beacon Hill," muttered Frances.

Clare found it on the map. 'Barrow Beacon, 303 metres', and looked up to see a road sign showing the twisting bends—'Gradient 1 in 5'—as they began to descend.

"You're driving too fast," she said again, sharply. "Slow down."

But Frances appeared not to hear. Her face was shuttered, her eyes fixed.

Clare put her feet on the dashboard and held on tightly. The trees flashed past, black bars of shadow against the gold road. The brilliant light flashed on and off. On-off. She began to feel giddy and light-headed, gripped with a kind of reckless euphoria as the lane switchbacked down and the car went even faster. For a strange moment it seemed that she had done this before, that she knew every twist and turn, every hump and hollow of the road.

She was laughing aloud, enjoying the wild sensation of speed, when Frances screamed "Bran!" and slammed on the brakes, narrowly missing the big motor bike that had appeared from the left and swung past them, blaring its horn.

Clare caught a glimpse of its leather-clad rider, his mane of black hair streaming behind him, as their car careered on over the concealed crossroads and came to a stop, its nose inches away from a huge mottled stone standing deep in the grass.

"Bloody road hog!" Frances shouted after the motor bike, her hands shaking.

Clare said, "Oh come on! You know you were driving too fast. Didn't you see the crossroads sign?" and realized that Frances hadn't heard. She was still gripping the wheel, staring straight ahead through the windscreen, her face a strange greeny-white.

"Oh my God!"

"What's the matter? What is it?"

"The Leper Stone."

"*Leper* Stone?" Clare turned her head and saw the big stone, glittering darkly, seeming to gather the intense afternoon light into itself.

"They used to leave food and water here in the old days for the lepers. Wouldn't let them into the village."

Clare shivered. She said. "Why the suicide bid? What's the matter with you?"

Frances took a deep, shuddering breath. "Sorry about that. I wasn't concentrating." She flexed her wrists. "This is a bad place. They had a gibbet here once, too."

She restarted the car and swung it up the right-hand fork of the crossroads. "Nearly there now." Clare could hear the effort she was making to sound normal.

"Who's Bran?"

Frances voice shook. "For a moment I thought . . . Please, Clare, just leave it."

Clare was peering out of the window. "This isn't the right way. It says, 'To Kenward Farm only'."

"Why don't you just shut up for a bit, Clare? I've had as much as I can take. You don't know bloody everything."

Clare went quiet. Guiltily she could hear her own voice going on and on in her head. "I didn't mean to nag," she said at last. "I just saw the sign. And this looks like a private road."

"I'm sorry. I'm too wound up."

"About the job?"

Frances shook her head. "Old hurts. Old memories. It's so difficult for me, Clare, coming back like this. Don't worry, we're on the right road. This is just one of the Aylwards' little ploys to keep people away from Ravensmere—make it difficult to find."

"You could drive around these lanes for hours. Why do they want to keep people away?"

Frances shrugged. "They have their reasons. And they're a family of recluses anyway."

The lane wound up and around the higher ground and a small closed valley dipped below them on the left. Half-way up on the rising land beyond, buried in a fold of the hill, Clare could see a collection of ancient buildings, so old they seemed part of the hill itself. For a moment she thought it must be Ravensmere, but Frances said, "This high stone wall on the right is the boundary wall of Ravensmere's park. If you look to the left you can just see St Michael and St Mary down in the valley in the trees."

"What's that over there? On the hill."

"An Iron Age hill fort."

"No, lower. The old grey buildings."

"A farm." Frances still sounded shaky, Clare thought. "Kenward Farm."

"It looks old. I'd like to go there."

"Twelve hundred and something. But there's always been people living there. Saxons. Romans . . ."

Clare glanced at her curiously. "You sound as though you know the place."

For a moment there was an odd silence. Clare thought her mother was not going to answer, and then she sighed and said casually, as though it didn't matter at all, "I was born there."

Chapter 3

"I thought you were born in London!" Clare exclaimed.

But her mother was turning between two pillars, set in the gold-lichened boundary wall. There was no name carved in the stone, no big triumphal arch suggesting a country mansion and powerful, important people, just iron gates standing open, and tucked away behind the wall, a small lodge cottage, buried in tassels of wisteria.

As they went past Clare caught a glimpse of a face looking at them between pink geraniums. Frances slowed and tooted the car horn, and then drove on without stopping.

"Who was that?"

"Mrs Anscomb, Mr Aylward's Housekeeper. Seventy-seven years old last birthday. She's worked here since she was fourteen."

"She was expecting us. The gates were already open. How did she know when we'd get here?" Clare craned round, and saw the woman walk out to close the gates. She was staring after the car. Then, as Clare watched, startled, she clasped her hands over her head and hopped about, shaking them like a triumphant footballer.

"Did you see that?" Clare said, amazed. "What was that all about? Are you sure they're not a bunch of loonies here?"

"Just pleased to see us." Frances was grinning.

An avenue of great lime trees lined the drive. With the orange afternoon sun glowing through them it was like driving into a cloudburst of golden light. Clare suddenly felt a tremendous lift of spirits, a surge of energy. For the first time in months she felt a loosening of the strain she had been under as she worked for her exams and tried to decide on her future.

The lime avenue snaked its way through rich parkland, dotted with huge oak trees, gnarled and twisted, spreading umbrellas of leaves over the sheep lying under them.

Clare sat forward. "I've never seen tree trunks this big. The trees are fantastic."

"Oaks mostly. And beech, ash, sweet chestnut, all sorts. Old Edward Richard Aylward planted forty thousand trees in the seventeen-thirties but the oaks were here before that. All the Aylwards have been great tree planters."

Clare said idly, without thinking, "To hide Ravensmere. Why do they want to keep people out? What are they guarding?"

The car swerved. Her mother shot a sideways glance at her. "What made you say that?"

But Clare had seen a flash of red behind a copse. "Look, *deer*. Red deer."

"There's been a herd here for four hundred years, maybe more. They're very tame. You can go right up to them."

Clare felt a tingling sense of excitement. There was a magic in this place that she hadn't expected, an atmosphere which it seemed she had once known and could recognize, like a remembered perfume.

"How big is this place exactly?" she asked, when they were still driving after a few minutes. "It's much larger than I thought."

There was a fork in the drive with a black iron signpost with gold letters. The right arm said 'House,' the others said 'Garden Shop, Stables, Herb and Physick Garden, Refreshments'.

Clare said, "Refreshments?"

"We have a café in the Orangery when the House is open to the public on Thursday afternoons."

"*We?*"

Colour stained Frances' cheeks and she didn't answer.

Clare said, "Why only Thursday afternoons?"

"I told you, the Aylwards like their privacy. I suppose they don't want too many visitors."

"Why open at all, then?"

"Clare, there are a lot of ancient and . . . well, strange . . . things at Ravensmere. Mr Aylward gets pestered by anti-quarian societies, archaeologists, all sorts of people, for special visits. It would look odd if he didn't let them in at all."

"People might start to ask awkward questions?"

Frances took the left turn with relief.

Clare said, "The proles go to the left. With all this you'd think he'd be more than just a mister—a 'Sir' at least."

"He is. Edward Eldon Aylward, Seventeenth Earl of Ravensmere, KCBE, VC, DSC, DFC."

"An *earl*! You didn't tell me that! What on earth do I call him?"

"You don't call him anything. You stay strictly away from him. Is that clear, Clare? He's a sick man. He won't want to be bothered with visitors. Anyway, he doesn't use his title. He prefers to be called Mr Aylward."

"That's odd. Why doesn't he use his title?"

"You'll come across a lot of odd things here. Better not to ask too many questions."

They were driving through a brilliant display of azaleas and flowering shrubs. On a slight rise of ground there was a grand building made of golden stone, with a wide archway in the centre.

Frances turned in under the arch and drew up at the second door along. She leaned on the steering wheel and turned to Clare, her mouth twitching with laughter. "Well, here we are. The stables."

"You're joking!"

"Built for the Eighth Earl in 1728. They did their horses proud in those days."

"Better than their villagers."

"Oh much!"

Clare got out of the car slowly, staring around the cobbled courtyard. It was quiet and empty. Grass grew between the cobbles and it looked as though it had been there for a long time.

"No horses."

"There aren't any now. Mr Aylward keeps his cars here." Her mother's voice sounded tinny and far away.

Clare suddenly felt very odd, light-headed. She knew the place well, as though she had been here before. She held on to the car door tightly. The air seemed to waver around her.

Surely there should be a row of stable doors on this side instead of the neat Georgian-style front doors? And where was the forge where the horses were shod and the carriages mended? And the tack room and the carriage house itself? She saw with relief that the carriage house was still there at the end, although the great doors were closed and she could see only the barouche through the side window . . .

Barouche? What on earth was a barouche?

"You're looking very pale, Clare. Are you all right?" Frances' voice penetrated. She was looking at her intently and Clare pulled herself together.

"A bit car sick, maybe."

"You'll feel better when you've had something to eat. Come on, let's get the car unpacked and I'll cook something."

Frances unlocked the door and carried in a load of groceries.

For a moment Clare lingered, still shaken. She stared around. The row of garage doors opposite was new too.

But there was something else. She realized she was waiting for something to happen.

The yard was deserted, the stone glowing golden in the early evening light. The place should be filled with the sound of horses' hooves on cobbles, comfortable West Country voices calling out and joking. But it was absolutely quiet. Much too quiet.

Into the silence came a whirring sound, followed by a clear sweet chime. Clare looked up at the clock over the stable arch. It had a black face with elaborate golden figures, surrounded by an enamelled blue band showing the sun, moon and stars, and the signs of the zodiac. There were two doors above the clock. As she watched, one door opened and a figure of a white-robed man framed in a sunburst of gold glided out. His beard and hair curled away from his face and turned into golden leaves. He was holding a long staff, which he raised slowly and jerkily in blessing as the chimes of the hour rang out. Five. Five blessings, she thought, that's what I was waiting for, and at the same moment she felt a soft furriness brushing her legs.

A tortoiseshell cat was circling her, butting its head against her ankles. Clare squatted down, delighted, and stretched out her hand to let the cat smell her fingers. It looked up at her and began to purr loudly.

Clare laughed, and the cat allowed her to rub its ears.

"Nice puss. Have you come to say hello to us?"

The cat put its paws on her knee and stretched up, looking earnestly into her face, as though it had something urgent to tell her.

Clare murmured to it and stroked the small round head with one finger. It stretched again, imperiously patting her cheek, demanding to be picked up, and she straightened, holding the fragile, living body against her own, feeling the vibration of its purring. Its pads were cool, slightly abrasive on her supporting hand, and Clare felt the familiar rush of tenderness and love she felt for all small creatures. Especially she loved cats, but her mother was a dog person, and had never allowed her to have animals of her own because there was nobody at home during the day to look after them.

The cat loudly purred its approval of her quick understanding, and Clare rubbed her chin in its silky fur. Once, long ago, before Adrian, she had thought of being a vet or a doctor. Was her mother right—had she chosen the wrong career?

"I wonder what your name is?" she said to the cat.

"Filthy creature. Half-wild," a voice said behind her. "They're alive with fleas, you know."

Clare turned quickly. The man was in his fifties, his thick body carried with self-importance. He was wearing an expensive tweed suit, with the trousers tucked into leather riding boots. He had a heavy, smooth face with a small moustache neatly trimmed. His eyes were dark, but with none of the warmth associated with brown eyes. These were dark as slugs, crawling over her body, coldly assessing her, his full lips stretched in imitation of a jolly smile.

An enemy, Clare's brain told her instantly, and a moment later the cat had arched and sprang from her grasp, spitting at the man before it leapt away on to a water butt and up over the carriage house roof.

Clare wished she could do the same thing. Instead, she held down her anger and said evenly, "Cat fleas don't live on humans. Cats are very clean animals. Cleaner than some humans, especially their minds." She allowed a disparaging glance to slip over him from his boots to his hair as though she suspected a nasty stain on his underwear and was rewarded with a faint line of red showing along his cheek bones.

She turned away, satisfied. "Excuse me, I have to unpack the car."

He said, with a kind of menace, "Perhaps I should introduce myself. I am Roger Fletcher, Mr Aylward's cousin. I'm the Land Agent. I manage the whole Ravensmere estate."

Clare straightened. *A pompous bully*. She said, coolly polite, "How do you do, Mr Fletcher?" She held out her hand. "I'm Clare Meredith. My mother..."

He ignored her hand. "I know who you are. Frances' daughter. I hope you realize that we've made concessions, allowing you to come here. You'll have to look after yourself, you know. Your mother is being paid to look after Mr Aylward. Not *you*."

Clare seethed with dislike. "My mother is very conscientious, and *dedicated*, Mr Fletcher. Mr Aylward's lucky to get her."

His eyes moved away from her. "There is really no need for him to have a nurse. He has his man, Mr Bristow, and his Housekeeper. If I'd been consulted I'd have advised against it. Totally unnecessary expenditure."

Mean as well, Clare registered with disgust, and wondered who had sent for her mother. She frowned. "But isn't Mr Aylward ill and very old? It must be more comfortable for him to have a trained nurse looking after him."

"Bristow was managing. There was no need for Frances to come back so dramatically."

He sounded petulant, Clare thought, like a schoolboy who had been outwitted.

"By the way, a word of advice." He smiled with false affability. "Mr Aylward dislikes visitors. He won't want to see you about the House or gardens. Keep to the park and the stable block and you won't be trespassing."

Clare felt the tiny hairs on the back of her neck lift. What was going on here? First there was her mother warning her off, and now this bully. Why were they both so anxious that she shouldn't meet Mr Aylward?

She stared at him and he moved uneasily, brushing invisible dust from his trousers, avoiding her penetrating eyes. People often became uneasy when she looked at them for

33

any length of time, but she was sure, suddenly, that he was lying.

"You've arrived much later than I expected," he said fussily. "Where is your mother? I want a word with her."

On cue her mother came through the door, saying "Clare! What on earth are you . . ." and stopped dead.

Roger Fletcher said smoothly, smiling like a Rottweiler, "Good evening, Frances. You've managed to get here at last, then. A lot of traffic on the road, no doubt."

"Good afternoon, Mr Fletcher. There was, of course, but we took our time. We came early to settle in. I don't actually start work until *Monday*." She stretched her lips in a polite, false smile. Clare could feel the dislike radiating from her.

"Mr Fletcher, Frances? Surely there's no need for such formality? We know each other very well."

"We did. A long time ago. Clare, take in that . . ."

"Ah yes. *Clare*. I was just telling her that as a guest here she should avoid disturbing Mr Aylward. That she must keep to the park and the stables."

Clare watched them curiously. They were glaring at each other across the car like stiff-legged dogs about to start a fight. She could feel the tension rising between them. There was something more here than mere dislike.

"It would have been better, perhaps, if you hadn't thought fit to bring her here." Again there was that underlying menace in his voice.

Frances said tightly, "Clare will be going up to university in a few weeks. Mr Aylward knows that my daughter is here with me, Roger. In his letter to me, asking me to come, he particularly suggested she should come too."

This was news to Clare. She glanced at her mother curiously. Had she forgotten her own warning to stay away from Mr Aylward?

"If he wants to see her, Roger, I can't stop him."

The smile had gone from Roger Fletcher's face. The slug

eyes gleamed with something not far off violence. "Be careful, Frances. Everything is arranged very comfortably. I won't let you start any of your witch's tricks. I am in charge of the estate, and when Cousin Edward dies, four thousand five hundred acres of land will be sold for . . . development. It's all agreed. Unfortunately the development needs to be sited just where the House and the gardens now stand. You've come back, Frances, just in time to see the end of your beloved Ravensmere."

The gloating in his voice was unmistakable. Frances had gone bone white and her hands on the car had curled up like claws.

Clare was shaken too. She was upset that the beautiful, peaceful countryside they had just driven through could simply disappear. She stared at him, and suddenly a tiny point of light in her mind expanded like a lens into a nightmare vision of a dead land. Pits pocked the dead grey grass between the heaps of industrial waste, and puddles of water moved dully under sulphurous-green slime. Discoloured leaves fluttered on the few remaining trees like dying, pleading hands.

She heard her mother saying incredulously, "You're going to spoil all this with a rash of nasty little houses?" and her mind cleared. She was over-reacting. Of course the development would be houses and flats, and people had to live somewhere, didn't they?

"The country needs energy and new industry. We need to exploit our resources, develop economically, make wealth and profits. Move with the times, Frances. Move with the times." Roger Fletcher laughed patronizingly.

It was an argument familiar to Clare. Adrian had taught her to use it, but now faced with the reality behind the ideas, she was full of doubt. Surely there were plenty of more suitable places that really needed to be developed?

She tried to shake her vision away, feeling queasy. You

couldn't stop development. Adrian called it dinosaur thinking. But if you exploited the resources in pursuit of profit until there was nothing left, wasn't that just stupidity? Wasn't it like killing the goose that laid the golden eggs?

Clare felt a shift in her thinking, turning her ideas upside-down.

"Wealth and profits for *you*, Roger. You'll be a very rich man," Frances said. "Tell me, does Mr Aylward know that you are going to sell off Ravensmere?"

"I've discussed it with him. He's a broken man, Frances. Bitter, broken and dying. He doesn't care." Again that shaft of satisfaction in his voice.

"Then there's no more to be said." Frances' voice was dull. "Excuse us. We have to unload and unpack."

"I have to be on my way too. I'll see you at the estate office each Friday at nine o'clock, for your weekly report on Mr Aylward. Good evening."

He turned away to the stable block arch.

"Insufferable pig," Frances muttered furiously, and called after him, "Oh, Roger?" He turned and she smiled at him brilliantly. "How is your wife? I heard you had married out of the area. A woman from Manchester."

To Clare's surprise, a wave of red moved up his neck darkly. "That's right." She could see the suppressed rage mottling his face, wiping away the smiling complacency.

"That's right—from *Manchester*. Not Stoke Raven. And it doesn't matter a damn. It's all finished. All the rubbishy old customs. All the old legends and stories. All finished and destroyed. You destroyed them yourself, dear Frances. You and Vivienne and Brandon between you."

He strode through the archway and Frances stared after him. She looked suddenly ten years older, and close to tears.

Clare said, slowly, "He hates you. And he hates Ravensmere."

"Yes. I never realized. He asked me to marry him once.

He used to stay at Ravensmere in the holidays sometimes. But we never liked him. He was obsessed with money. Always trying to worm his way into Mr Aylward's good books. Telling tales about B—well, just telling tales. He was a greedy boy and now he's a greedy man. He's after the Aylward money I suppose."

"He's the heir? He gets Ravensmere?"

Frances stared at Clare. Her eyes widened and went slowly blank, and the strange look that made Clare so uneasy spread like a shadow over her pale skin.

"Only the Guardians inherit."

Clare said loudly, "What guardians? What are you talking about? He said it was all arranged."

A second later the stable clock chimed the half-hour, and Frances' eyes cleared, but she looked even paler, almost distraught. "I've been wrong, Clare. Roger Fletcher mustn't inherit. I didn't understand the extent of the danger. Oh God, it's all going to have to start again."

At some time during the night, a sound woke Clare from the deep exhausted sleep she had fallen into as soon as her head had touched the pillow—something unexpected, ripping up the night air. She lay for a moment, disorientated in the unfamiliar room, trying to identify the sound. Whatever it was had stopped now. She turned over to go back to sleep, and froze. There was somebody out there. Somebody was walking lightly, quietly, on the cobbles of the stable yard. As clearly as if she could see him, she knew he was staring up at her window.

Not Roger Fletcher. Not a burglar. She knew that too. She slid out of bed and padded to the window, almost as if she was drawn by some sort of power she did not understand.

He was there, dark and shadowy, very tall, leaning on the stable arch. He was staring directly at her. She could see the faint gleam of his eyes in his starlit face. For an endless moment she stared back, pushing the mass of her long dark hair slowly away from her face, then the stable clock began to chime midnight and he had gone.

She leaned against the wall away from the window, her heart pounding in her throat. He couldn't be real. She must be dreaming that dream again. He was the same dark figure who had been hunting her through her dreams before she decided to come to Ravensmere.

Chapter 4

Clare woke early. She stretched luxuriously, the health and strength pulsing through her muscles. She realized that she felt better than she had for a long time. Even the worry of the August results seemed less acute here.

I've been neglecting myself, crouched over that desk for months, she thought. I'll get fit now. Go for walks. Eat fresh salads. *Get my ideas sorted out.*

She pushed open the small circular window and leaned out, sniffing the clear air. It smelled of cut grass and hot stone, not the peculiar London mix of soot and cars and chemicals which she was used to.

The sun shone in the cobbled yard and the brilliant red geraniums in their stone trough outside the neighbouring door seemed to burn with unnatural intensity. The climbing plant on the stable arch glittered with spangles of early dew.

Had she really seen that dark figure under the arch last night, or had she dreamed him as she had dreamed him so many nights before?

This morning only the tortoiseshell cat was there, sitting in the exact centre, washing her back. As Clare watched, the cat paused, then turned her head and stared straight up at her. The pink mouth opened and closed in a soft miaow of greeting. The cat was saying 'good morning'. Clare laughed aloud. She pulled on her dressing gown and went swiftly down the open wooden stair, trying not to wake her mother.

Last night after they had unloaded the car, cooked eggs and chips, and made up the beds, Frances had looked absolutely exhausted, the skin stretched grey and taut over her cheek bones.

Clare felt a rush of concern. She hoped her mother had made the right decision to come back, that it would not, after all, be too much for her. What had she said? *Old hurts. Old memories. That she owed a debt?*

Pushing aside her apprehension, she unbolted and opened the door. The cat was sitting politely outside. She wound herself around Clare's ankles and led the way into the small kitchen like a hostess showing in a guest.

Amused, Clare said to the cat, "I don't know where you've come from, but I think you've adopted me."

The expression of love and adoration it turned on her made her catch her breath. She bent down and kissed the top of her smooth round head and the cat leapt up on to the pine fitment, where she sat purring loudly, watching Clare getting out the breakfast things.

Clare looked at her doubtfully as she poured a saucer of milk. "Just don't let my mother catch you, that's all. Very hot on the hygiene bit she is."

"I'm really pleased that you've understood that, Clare," said Frances dryly, coming in. She had showered, and was wearing her grey uniform dress. "The strain of those exams must have been more than I thought if you're talking to yourself."

Clare grinned, and waved her hand. "We have a visitor." Her mother seemed better this morning, she thought, less like she was going to snap into tiny pieces.

Frances turned her head and looked into the gold eyes which regarded her blandly. For a moment she was still.

"Henriette?" she said on an indrawn breath, incredulously. "Not Henriette?"

The cat blinked contemptuously and looked away.

"Tabitha, I think," said Clare, the name coming into her head.

Frances laughed shakily. "I just thought for a moment . . . There used to be a tortoiseshell cat just like her, but that was years ago. It couldn't be the same one."

"A descendant daughter, maybe," said Clare easily. "What do you want for breakfast?"

"Just toast, I think. I'm going up to the House. I won't wait until Monday. After Roger yesterday I'm not easy in my mind. Have we unpacked the toaster?"

"No need. There's one here already. Brand new, like everything else. Bought specially."

"Lap of luxury," Frances said wryly, looking around. "Better than our own house."

Their new home had turned out to be surprisingly comfortable. The old stables had been converted with great care using natural stone and wood, and Clare was willing to bet that Roger Fletcher had had no hand in it.

The front door opened straight into a wide living area, divided from the kitchen by a pine breakfast bar. An open staircase led to a balcony and the main bedroom, with a bathroom slotted into a space next to it. The stair continued on to an attic room, with a low ceiling, golden floorboards and the circular window overlooking the stable yard. Delighted, Clare had claimed this as her own.

To their amazement, all the furniture and fitted carpets were brand new—expensive too, Frances said—just as though the place had been specially furnished for them. Nothing had been forgotten: washing machine, dishwasher, television and video—and someone had put a magnificent vase of roses in the open stone fireplace as a welcoming present.

"What are you going to do today?" asked Frances, as they washed up. "I won't be back for lunch. I'll eat up at the House."

"May I come?"

The question hung in the sudden silence. Clare watched her mother carefully.

Frances put down her nursing bag, picked it up and moved it from one hand to the other, and finally put it down again. "I don't think . . . I mean, perhaps it would be better if you kept away from the House, as Roger said."

Clare said tartly, "I suppose Mr Aylward really does know I'm here? You haven't smuggled me in illegally?"

"Not funny," said Frances, coldly. "You're a guest here. I'm just trying to . . . to prevent any trouble."

Clare said, "I'll finish the unpacking and maybe take a walk down to the village."

Frances looked relieved. "You'll enjoy looking at the church."

"Riveting," Clare said ironically. "Good luck with the job. Have a nice day."

Clare knew exactly what she was going to do, but thought it better that her mother should be left in blissful ignorance. She would certainly take a quick trip down to the village. But today was Thursday, wasn't it? This afternoon the House was open to the public. She would take the tour. And if she should just happen to bump into the mysterious Mr Aylward, then it wouldn't be her fault, would it?

An hour later, unpacked, showered and changed into her second-best skirt and blouse, she was on her way, escorted across the stable yard by a purring Tabitha with her tail straight up. She miaowed, and darted away into the bushes, and Clare continued on along the drive, enjoying the sparkling freshness of the morning. There were no cars or people. A rabbit bobbed away under a tree, and in the distance she saw the red deer.

The great gate was locked, but Clare found there was a narrow wooden door in the wall next to it which was unlocked. She looked nervously at the lodge cottage, but there was no sign of the crazy old lady who had danced in the drive.

She closed the door carefully behind her and stood for a moment staring across the valley to Kenward Farm settled into its big hill. Had her grandfather lived there? It seemed strange to think of her mother growing up on the farm, perhaps running along this very lane to school. Clare could see that there was a rough track to the farm, which must lead off the lane further along.

There was a small fair girl, her plaits flying behind her, racing across the field opposite, where it said 'Public Footpath'. She was not alone. There were two other children—a small girl and an older boy running after her.

Clare blinked and the field was empty. Shaken, she stared incredulously. She could have sworn there were children. A herd of cows was moving in the next field, and a tractor crawled along a ridge in the distance but there was no other movement.

She took a deep breath, and tried to grin to herself. The exams, she thought, *stress*, all those E-additives.

She looked again at Kenward Farm, wanting to go there, wondering who lived there now. Instead, she turned reluctantly to the left, and made her way along to the crossroads, where the Leper Stone glittered in the morning sun, and took the steep, sunken lane down to the village.

The hedgerows banked high above her head were alive with bees and insects, and tiny blue flowers glowed like jewels among the buttercups, ferns and wild roses.

At first she was careful to keep close to the side of the road, expecting cars and vans at every moment. But there was no traffic. Only a deep quiet. Then, far away, down the valley, she could hear birds and the faint sound of water trickling over stone.

The village was strung out along the way. Golden stone cottages, with sagging lichen-covered roofs burrowed into a riot of roses and clematis. It was hot and still and no one stirred. Here and there a window stood open, curtains blowing in the breeze, but there was no human activity at all. Just a Sunday-like peace.

Clare felt uncomfortable. She wasn't used to such quiet. It was like the stable yard yesterday, as though the silence was waiting for something to happen, almost as if she was being observed, eyes boring into her back. She swung round quickly, but nobody was there.

The lane curved and curved back again, following the line of some long-forgotten track around the field edge. In a terrace of ancient cottages a teddy bear looked out of a trefoil-shaped window, and a tiny bird, a flash of blue, was surprised from a shrub beneath it with an indignant squeak, but otherwise nothing was moving. No dogs barked. The stillness and quiet began to seem uncanny. Where on earth were all the people?

The lane widened into a small triangular village green. A handsome Regency vicarage was set at right angles to an even older square-towered church deep in the turf amid ash and yew trees as tall as the tower itself. St Michael and St Mary, Clare remembered, and turned into the churchyard through the lich-gate.

To her surprise the church was unlocked. She pushed open its heavy door, and caught her breath.

The church was small and ancient, and every available surface seemed to be blooming with white and gold flowers. Every corner, every carved pew-end had its own exquisite arrangement. By the door stood a Christening font, banked with yellow daisies, and next to the simple stone altar there were two arrangements of great white arum lilies, with golden hearts, so perfect that Clare thought at first that they were made of silk. Someone must have sacrificed them from their garden or greenhouse for a very special occasion.

Even the old tombs had their flower decorations. Clare found stone Sir Edward (1196) in his Crusaders' gear, lying next to his lady, his feet on a beast that might have been his dog, half-smothered in yellow roses, and the tomb of another Edward Aylward, the Second Earl, on the wall behind a stately arrangement of white iris. Magnificent in black and gold, it showed his wife, Lady Rosamond, and their five sons and four daughters kneeling below, looking faintly comic. 'Born 1509, died 1603', read Clare. Goodness, he was, what? *Ninety-four* when he died. That must have been an extraordinary age in those days.

She wandered on, reading the memorial stones. The Aylwards seemed to feature most, usually dying at a great age or violently when young.

There was a modest bronze plaque showing a soldier, his head bent over his reversed rifle: Edmund Albert Aylward, VC, who had died at Ypres in 1914, aged thirty-one. A hero.

The Burne-Jones window, *The Waters of Paradise* mentioned by the guidebook, showed not a river but a powerful waterfall and a pool, and was dedicated to Rosamond Aylward, Beloved Wife, who had died in childbirth in 1883, aged twenty. Could they be the current Mr Aylward's father and grandmother?

There were so many Aylwards, the first names repeated over and over in different generations, that she began to lose track. She felt tired suddenly and vaguely depressed, longing for some human company.

She went out of the church into the sun-dappled churchyard. Somehow the graves here did not seem so gloomy. They were moss-grown, sunken deep into the turf, the stones tilted at strange angles.

She drifted along the path, reading names and dates. Kenwards mostly, who must have got their name from the farm, and a sprinkling of Bartons, Anscombs, and Boyds, most living to surprisingly great age. By the gate on a stone plinth there was a modern-looking stylized angel, its arms raised to the sun as though it was about to take off.

*   *   *

45

Mr Holmes, the vicar, paused under the tall yew trees, as he trod the path across the churchyard from his vicarage. For a moment he watched the girl thoughtfully.

She had none of the elusive fairness of her mother. This girl was much harder and stronger. Silver and steel perhaps, not thin gold. But she was too self-contained, too businesslike in her smart tight skirt and high-necked classic blouse, her hair drawn back, not a hair out of place. Too cool and controlled and closed-up for a young girl. Too much brain and not enough heart and soul? Had they all made a terrible mistake?

Then he saw her eyes, as she looked at him, their strange, luminous quality fixed on him like an X-ray, and knew that it was going to be all right. She was her mother's daughter.

"Good morning," he said, coming forward. "There's something very comforting I always think, looking at the resting place of one's ancestors. Continuity, you know."

"Er, yes, I should think so," said Clare, surprised. "I don't know where my ancestors are buried, though. In Wales, I suppose."

Mr Holmes looked puzzled, his eyes going to the drunken gravestones and returning to her. "These are nearly all Kenwards and Aylwards."

"Oh yes, I noticed. All the names keep repeating. Edward and Eldon and Edmund . . ."

"And Rosamond, James, Frances, Sarah. All Kenwards and Aylwards. The two families have intermarried for generations."

"Is everybody in the village related to everybody else?"

He smiled. "It's not as bad as it looks. Everyone had large families in those days, and although the names are the same they were often cousins three or four times removed. You saw our Epstein? The angel by the gate. The Earl commissioned Sir Jacob in 1927, when his first wife Caroline

46

died. She was only eighteen. Very sad. They had been married only a year."

"The Earl? Oh, you mean Mr Aylward. I didn't know he had been married twice."

Mr Holmes pushed back his pale hair which had flopped over his eyes. "She was a Kenward, of course. The eldest Aylward son and heir always marries a Kenward daughter. It's the tradition."

"Even though they were lords and earls?"

He smiled. "The Kenwards are the older family. Back in the mists of time they owned the whole valley. The name means 'royal guardian'. The Aylwards are descended from a Norman overlord."

"But the tradition is finished now, isn't it? Mr Aylward hasn't got a son. Mr Fletcher is going to inherit, and he is married to someone from Manchester, so I suppose there aren't any Kenward daughters at the farm."

"Mrs Carlton-Winters is living there."

"So, no son and no daughter."

He stared at her, his pale blue eyes intense. "There's always a son, always a daughter. Always two are chosen. Always two Guardians."

Ice crept down Clare's back. She said, "What do you mean? I don't understand. Guardians of what?"

He smiled, his eyes clearing. "Did I say guardians? What on earth was I thinking of? Clare, I must be on my way. You've looked around the church?"

Clare was relieved. "Oh yes. The flowers are wonderful. Are they for something special?"

He beamed. "A celebration. Yes, I think you could say a celebration. And a thanksgiving. I'll pass on your comments to the village ladies. The whole village contributed, you know. They will be delighted you liked them."

"They will?" said Clare, dazed.

He hesitated and said gravely, "We would like you to know

47

that we are all very pleased that your mother has brought you home, Clare. Please give my regards to your mother. Tell her I am here if she needs to talk to me."

Clare said slowly, "My mother knows you?"

He grinned, suddenly charming. "Of course. I went to school with her. My name is Trevor Holmes. I'm the vicar here, of course. I'm a Kenward—on my mother's side."

"I'll give her your message," Clare said, guardedly, and watched him go into the church. He had been calling her Clare. How had he known her name? How had he known that she too felt she had come home?

Chapter 5

Clare continued on along the lane into the centre of the village, where old overhanging houses jostled around the Sun and Moon Inn. But this morning even the Inn was closed and quiet. Where the road widened there was a great tithe barn, and a Market Cross set on an island in the centre. Back from the road, with room in front for a couple of cars, was the village shop.

Like a camel scenting water, Clare headed towards it. It had the familiar post office sign, and an 'open' card, hanging on its door, but when she pushed open the door, and took the two steps down, she found it deserted.

She could see that the shop stocked practically everything. There was a refrigerated display of food, groceries, boxes of apples and oranges, sweets, stationery, magazines, even children's plastic wellies. At the back the post office counter was also unattended. A mug of tea steamed on the counter. A wasp buzzed against the window.

Clare was thinking wildly of the Marie Celeste, when the bead curtain behind the counter parted and a tall, bald man with tattooed arms panted into the shop hugging a sack of potatoes, chivvied by a small woman with a sharp voice.

"See there, you great lump! Didn't I tell you she'd be along this morning? And you poking about in the cellar. What sort of state be your shirt in now?"

The big man winked at Clare and dumped the sack next to the apples. A cloud of dust rose, followed by an anguished cry from his wife. He brushed his T-shirt down, banged the dust off his hands and stuck one out to Clare.

"Dave Gregg. And my wife, Betty, Village Postmistress."

Startled Clare shook his hand. Betty Gregg smiled at her warmly. "I'm a Barton, m'dear. Or Barleycorn as it used to be in the old days. Born in the village of course. But this'n here be a foreigner."

"That's right," said Dave Gregg, cheerfully. "Only been here fifteen years. I'm an ex-pat Londoner."

"I'm Clare. I'm from London too. Wanstead."

"Know it well. Went fishing there often enough as a boy."

Betty Gregg said, disapprovingly, "Clare? *Clare?* That's not right. It ought to be . . ."

Dave Gregg said quickly, "You're staying at Ravensmere, I hear. Betty said you'd be in this morning."

"But . . ." Clare swallowed. How could Betty Gregg have known, when she hadn't made up her mind where she was going until she had left Ravensmere? And how did they know she was staying there anyway?

Dave Gregg grinned at her expression. "Betty always knows. Women's intuition. Nothing much happens up at the House that we don't know. The whole village revolves around that place."

His wife snorted indignantly. "We just know to look after our own. 'God's in the ground at Ravensmere' my dear ma used to say. And there's the old rhyme too:

> "Guard Ravensmere well
> Its stones and its hollows,
> Health and prosperity
> Always doth follow.
>
> Let Ravensmere die,
> Let the land be torn open,
> The end of the world
> Is surely betokened."

Clare said, surprising herself, "Mr Fletcher seems to have plans to tear the land open. They're going to build a load of houses there."

Dave Gregg shook his head. "Factories, love, not houses."

"Lot of nasty rumours circulating, m'dear," Betty agreed.

"*A factory!*" Clare said, dismayed, and tried not to remember yesterday's vision.

Dave said gloomily. "More like an industrial estate. Be the end of the village, of course. And the farms. Beats me. Plenty of derelict industrial areas in the country that could be redeveloped for factories. No need to take good farming land."

Betty Gregg's smile had disappeared. She shook her head. "He's a wrong'n, that Fletcher. Always jealous and making trouble. But it won't do him no good. Not now. His time is over. They won't let it happen."

"Who won't?"

The woman smiled at her. "How are they up at the House? It'll be nice seeing Frances again. I always had a soft spot for her."

Clare stared at her. "How do you know who my mother is?"

The little woman raised her eyebrows. "Well, who else would you be, m'dear? It's the time. We've all been waiting."

"Waiting for what?"

"Why, for you to come, of course, m'dear. We knew your ma wouldn't keep you away."

Clare took a deep breath. She felt totally disorientated. Were all the people in this place a little crazy? She said quickly, "I just came in to buy some picture postcards and some stamps to send to my friends."

"Some nice ones of Wells and Bath."

"Haven't you got any of the village or Ravensmere?"

"Oh no, m'dear. We like to be private and quiet. If people

don't know we're here, they're not likely to want to come, are they?"

Clare stared into the dark eyes of Betty Gregg, who smiled back at her blandly.

Clare came out of the shop and wandered on up the deserted village street thinking. It must be all imagination. Of course there was nothing weird about this place. It was just that it was a weekday, and everybody was at work. And if Betty Gregg had heard there were new people staying at the House, she could have guessed they would walk down to the village this morning. She was making too much of it. Letting her imagination take over. Like seeing the children in the field. It was just overwork and stress and being in a new place . . . And what about the flowers in the church, and the vicar, her mind prompted, was that all imagination too?

Someone was watching her.

Once again she could feel eyes on her back. She spun round quickly and looked along the street. A figure in motorbike leathers was lounging on the shadowy stone seat under the Market Cross, his booted feet up on his motor bike. He was staring at her insolently, almost predatory. A lazy black tom watching a mouse he was going to eat.

Annoyed, Clare turned her back and walked on. At least he was a real person. Waiting for his mates probably. Nothing weird or strange about that. And then, suddenly, her heart was beating extra fast. She had identified the sound that had awoken her last night. The unexpected sound that had ripped apart the quiet had been a motor bike.

Clare looked back at the Market Cross. The motor bike was still there, but the stone bench was empty.

She took a deep breath and walked on quickly. She saw she was coming to the end of the village. After a terrace of eighteenth-century houses with sash windows and panelled doors, the houses began to spread out again. There were four

52

Victorian villas set in tree-shaded gardens. One had a brass plate on the gatepost: Dr S McKinnon, MRCS, LRCP, DCH, MFHom.

At least they have a doctor, Clare thought, relieved. They aren't still relying on a village witch! There were even two cars parked in the drive, a battered van and a bright red sports car that looked brand new.

Clare leaned on the low garden wall, admiring the car and the immaculate flower beds.

"Good morning." A very tall, thin woman unwound herself like a genie from behind a clump of ornamental pampas grass, and advanced briskly towards Clare. She transferred her gardening fork to her left hand and extended her right to Clare over the garden wall. "Sarah McKinnon. Thought you might be along today."

Clare put her fingers into the long bony hand.

"You're exhausted. Been working too hard. Burning the candle. Won't do, you know." She had a deep, gruff voice, but her eyes were kind, and Clare felt a sudden flow of warmth and energy moving up her arm.

"M-my A-levels. Are all the people in this village psychic?" Clare stammered, trying to joke.

"Quite a few of the women and some of the men," said Dr McKinnon, matter of fact. "Nothing to worry about. I've been in practice here for fifty years. It's a good place."

Clare was surprised. Dr McKinnon looked brown and fit and only in her fifties.

"Seventy-six years old," she said, reading Clare's mind. "They won't let me retire. Nobody to take my place." She opened the garden gate. "Come and have some coffee with us, Clare."

"Are you sure? I don't want to be a nuisance . . ." She stopped. "You know my name!"

"Know your mother. Matter of fact, brought her into the world. Have you met my great-nephew James Kenward yet?

53

He's chopping down a bramble for me this morning."

Clare followed her around the house to a beautiful Victorian conservatory where a cheerful young man with ginger hair was pouring coffee into some elderly cracked mugs.

"You must have smelled it," he said, grinning. "Aunt Sarah said you might be along soon."

Dr McKinnon said, "James is Mr Aylward's Assistant Land Agent. Assistant to Mr Fletcher, that is."

He sat down next to Clare, grinning at her expression. "I hear you had a run-in with him yesterday. He went off to London this morning in a very tetchy mood. Out of my hair for a few days, thank goodness. There's no love lost between Mr Fletcher and me. He'd get rid of me too, if he could."

"Why doesn't he?"

"Mr Aylward wouldn't hear of it. My gran was his wife Caroline's sister."

Clare's head spun with the web of family relationships. She gave up and said, "Do you live on the estate?"

"I've digs here, with Aunt Sarah. Until October. Then I'm getting married." He leaned back grinning and rubbed his hands. "*Hasta la vista*. No offence, Aunt."

"None taken, randy lad. They're moving into the stables cottage next to you, Clare. Have you settled in yet? How do you like it?"

"It's great. All the furniture is brand new, television. everything."

James was grinning complacently.

"It was *you*!" Clare exclaimed, staring at him. "I knew Mr Fletcher wouldn't have spent so much money."

"It was Mr Aylward. Sent for me nearly a year ago. Told me to sort out the best architect in Bath and get the block converted and furnished by the end of May. Fletcher was hopping mad. He was on holiday at the time and when he came back the work was already under way."

Clare said slowly, "Why the end of May?"

James shrugged. "The old man must have had a reason. He *always* has a reason, but sometimes it's years before you find out."

"Frances wouldn't stay in the House." Dr McKinnon poured herself another cup of coffee.

Clare looked startled. "You mean he converted the stables just for my mother?" For the first time she realized how odd it was that they weren't living in the House. There must be plenty of spare rooms there.

And then it hit her. "But how did he know she was coming? She only decided a few weeks ago."

Dr McKinnon shrugged. "How does he know anything? He just does."

Clare said, "Someone left us a beautiful vase of roses. Was that you too?"

"That was Mai, my fiancée. If you like I'll give you a lift back to Ravensmere and introduce you to her. I'm going back to work."

It turned out that the old van belonged to James and the sexy little sports car belonged to Dr McKinnon.

Clare got into the van chuckling, and waved her goodbye. "She's a fantastic person."

"The best," James agreed. "I sometimes think the whole place would fall apart if it wasn't for her. She knows everybody. Keeps things on an even keel. There's been a lot of bad feeling recently."

"Roger Fletcher?"

James hesitated. "And other things, maybe."

"Why don't you like him?"

"He's a great one for the nitrates and factory farming." He grimaced. "Likes to screw the last few pence out of the land."

"But isn't that right? I mean, good business practice?"

"Trouble is, he doesn't respect the land or the animals.

He takes everything and doesn't give anything back. In the long run it doesn't pay. If you look at the old records here everything is less productive at Ravensmere than it used to be in the last century. Yield per acre down. Livestock less fertile. His methods don't work. Or maybe it's something else I can't fathom."

Clare looked at him sideways. "Does it matter? Mr Fletcher said it's all going to be sold to developers when Mr Aylward dies."

James looked upset. "It matters to me. It matters to everyone here. It should matter to everybody in the country. It's not just about a rich man's private estate, Clare. A lot of the countryside is owned by big companies now anyway. It's about conservation and the environment. We're destroying the countryside. We can't go on ruining good land that can grow food.

"They've got up a protest group in the village. Mrs Carlton-Winters, of course. Always daggers drawn with Mr Aylward. Big feud."

He hesitated, then said abruptly, as though it was forced out of him, "They don't know Fletcher's been negotiating with Nuclear Energy. That's confidential, by the way. I've not told anyone. Not even Mai. I don't know why I'm telling you."

Nuclear Energy. Clare felt a strange sensation as though the bottom of her stomach had fallen away.

"You know there's a problem with the disposal of nuclear toxic waste? Nobody knows what to do with it. This country actually *imports* it. Ravensmere's off the beaten track, all nicely hidden away. They could take more waste from Japan and Europe."

"But I thought . . . I mean, I heard Sellafield's dangerous. That report about children with leukaemia and cancers in the area . . ."

"Exactly."

Clare felt ill. She looked out of the window as they turned through the gates into the golden lime walk, and the vision came again, clearer, more detailed. Devastation, pollution. A land poisoned for ever. The vision had been true.

"It mustn't happen," she heard her voice saying, hoarsely.

James glanced at her curiously. "How do we stop it?"

"Mr Aylward can't know what's going on. We have to tell him."

James looked uncomfortable. "He's ... well, he's a strange, man, Clare. He let Roger Fletcher take over. I don't think he cares about Ravensmere. Until a few years ago he only used to come down occasionally. He moved back permanently about three years ago."

"He *has* to care." Clare thumped the seat. "He has to understand what he's doing. He has to be told."

"Sooner you than me. He hardly sees anyone now, anyway."

"Perhaps he'll leave you the estate instead of Roger Fletcher," Clare suggested hopefully.

He shook his head. "There's no chance of that."

"But why not? He doesn't have a son and heir, does he?"

"His only son died years ago. But I've always known I wouldn't inherit. It's ... well, it's just not possible. There are other factors ... Only the Guardians ..." He stumbled to a halt looking flushed, and it was with obvious relief that he stopped the van abruptly and stuck his head out of the window.

"Hi, gorgeous. Want a lift?"

The tall young woman who had been striding up the drive ahead of them turned, laughing. She had a golden-brown skin, and short dark hair tapered into her neck. She was wearing a T-shirt and jeans, and mud-encrusted gum boots. She got into the van next to Clare. "Sorry about the squash. We wouldn't have this trouble of course if he got himself a Roller."

"Nowhere to put the ol' muckspreader," said James. "Clare, meet my intended, Mai Lee. She's Head Gardener here. And she never stops talking."

Mai leaned across and punched him on the shoulder, and grinned at Clare.

"Nurse Meredith's daughter, I presume."

"You're another Londoner," said Clare, surprised, hearing her accent.

"I'm from the Mystic East," said Mai, grinning. "East Ham, London, to be precise. My family are mixed Caribbean and Chinese. Lot of Chinese in the West Indies. I've been working here two years now."

"How did you get to be Head Gardener. That's important, isn't it? I mean Mr Fletcher didn't strike me as being exactly pro-women."

"The old man himself took her on," said James.

"True. I've only spoken to him twice. Thank God. Scary. And I mean, *scary*. I'll never forget my interview, Clare. He read through my application very slowly. Then he just looked at me, and went on looking, like he was X-raying my mind.

"Then he snapped, 'Herbs?' I was so nervous I just blurted out everything about my Chinese granddad, who was my hero and a great medical herbalist, and how I wanted to specialize in growing them. Perhaps develop a commercial supply."

"Then he barked, 'Maze?' And I yammered on about how one of the reasons I'd applied for the job was because someone had told me there was a famous maze here, and I was interested in mazes."

Clare said, "Oh, so am I. I love mazes. Where is it exactly?"

"I don't know. I haven't found it. One of the big disappointments. It must have been destroyed. Nobody knows where it was. Or won't say. There's a Chinese garden here that interests me too. I didn't tell him that but I bet he knew.

"Anyway, he just went on staring at me. Then he said, 'You'll be needed here. Start.' And that was that—I was

58

Ravensmere's Head Gardener. It was only when I got home I realized I hadn't said anything about herbs and mazes in my application."

She shivered. "Weirdsville. James says the old man has got second sight. The villagers think he's some sort of wizard incarnate. The whole thing was odd."

"Fate," said James, solemnly.

"Well, it really was," Mai agreed. "I fancied getting away from London, Clare. Saw the ad, but I couldn't find out anything about the place. Then I went to a party and started talking to this chap. And guess what? He came from Stoke Raven. *Up for one night only.* He told me all about the gardens, and of course, I was hooked. But I didn't think I'd get the job. No chance, I thought. They had over fifty applications. I don't know what made Mr A. pick me out."

"What about Roger Fletcher?"

"A right pain in the neck! He was furious when he met me. The Head Gardener—a Black and a *woman*, too. Unheard of. I pointed out that it was *Lady Clarissa* who'd made the Herb and Physick Garden here, that I'd done my training at Kew and worked in the Royal Parks, and that I'd got better qualifications and knew more about gardening than he did! Also he had no authority over me because I was to get my orders direct from Mr Aylward. After that he didn't tangle with me."

Clare laughed. Mai was a formidable young woman, and she was liking her more and more.

"Then she met me in the Number Four greenhouse," James said smugly, "and it was all up with both of us. Love at first sight."

Mai laughed. "He's absolutely right. Bowled over, first go. I didn't believe it really happened. You must come to the wedding."

"I'd love to," said Clare, pleased. "Oh wait, no, I can't. I'll be at university. What a shame." By October she would have left Ravensmere for ever. She felt a sharp pang of disappointment.

"Never mind. Maybe you'll be able to get back for the weekend. Come and see our cottage anyway. I'm camping there while we fix it up."

They pulled into the stable yard, and Mai and James proudly showed Clare over their cottage, identified by the tub of geraniums. Mai made sandwiches and coffee for lunch and Clare stayed chatting happily with them until James said he had to get back to the estate office. When Mai heard that Clare intended to take the tour, she said she would walk back with her.

"There's a lot of work here," she said, slamming the front door behind them. "The formal gardens on the other side of the House are marvellous, but they'd been badly neglected. I've got them in better shape now. And we supply all the vegetables and fruit for the House and the village, plus we're marketing a lot of herbs now to health food shops. I started the garden shop too, which is popular with the visitors and locals. Not bad for two years?"

"You must have been working your socks off. I want to see everything. It sounded wonderful in the guidebook. Temples and things. Did you say there was a Chinese garden?"

Mai nodded. "And it really bugs me. It's my other disappointment. The Maze has disappeared and the China Garden is locked up and *verboten*."

"The China Garden?" Clare felt an uneasy chill at the name.

"That's what they call it. It was fashionable in the eighteenth century to have gardens and pavilions, called China Houses, in the Chinese style. But I can't get in there, and Mr A. won't give me a key. I want to restore it. I've got a whole stack of books about Chinese gardens, and Moon Gates. But Mr A. wouldn't even discuss it. He told me to stick to my herbs. That was the last time I saw him. Somehow I didn't feel like arguing! Listen, Clare, if you ever get to see him yourself, maybe you could just mention it. He might have changed his mind."

It was unlikely she'd ever see him, Clare thought. But he ought to know about the nuclear waste. She must try to think of a way to make one last appeal to him.

Mai waved and strode off down the path to the Herb Garden, and Clare, with mounting excitement and curiosity, took the turn to the House. Roger Fletcher was in London, and her mother would be occupied in the private wing. She could see all she wanted, and with luck neither of them would know she had been there at all.

Chapter 6

The drive made a downward curve through tall trees and brilliant, banked azaleas, and Clare came to a halt, staring.

A great creamy stone pile rose from the lush turf. It was much bigger than she had imagined. The famous North Front of the House was very grand indeed. Rows of windows, two projecting wings, and four tall pillars like a Greek temple held up a portico over two flanking flights of steps.

For a moment she was bewildered. Why had she imagined that the House would look much older, with old weathered stones like a castle?

At the top of the stairs under the portico there were two large urns overflowing with flowers. Huddled nervously behind them outside the big entrance was a surprisingly small group of people waiting for the tour to begin. There were two smiling, middle-aged women, a younger couple and a small boy with glasses, a tall grey man with a notebook, and a young man, who might be a student, in trainers, jeans and T-shirt. Clare crunched across the gravel and climbed the stairs to join them.

The young man looked all over Clare and brightened up. "Hello, another intrepid traveller wins through."

"We got lost twice and then someone in the village gave us the wrong directions," said one of the middle-aged women.

"We had trouble too," said the boy's mother. "You'd think they'd put up some decent signs. But my son Darren is very good at map reading. How did you find the place?" she asked the student.

"Oh, I knew where it was. I'm on a dig the other side of Barrow Beacon Hill. You know, an archaeological dig," he explained to Clare kindly. "I'm Kevin. What about you?"

"I'm on holiday," Clare said warily, purposely misunderstanding.

"Staying locally?" he asked, too casually. And when she only nodded, he said, "Maybe you'd be interested to come over and I'll show you round the dig."

"Have you found anything?" Despite herself Clare was interested.

"A Roman farm. The places round here are incredible. You just uncover one layer after another back into pre-Roman times. The Prof even thinks there may be a Paleolithic—Stone Age you know—cave system in the limestone under Barrow Beacon Hill, like over at Wookey or Cheddar. But we can't get through. If we could do a bit of blasting we could open it up."

Involuntarily, Clare shivered.

> Let Ravensmere die,
> Let the land be torn open,
> The end of the world
> Is surely betokened.

"We're on Ravensmere land, and we only have permission to excavate the Roman site, and for this season only. Old man Aylward is difficult. It's taken years to persuade him. But Mr Fletcher seems a good chap. He let us come. The old man can't last much longer and when he goes Mr Fletcher has promised us that we can extend the dig this side of the hill. That's what we're really after. He says they're going to drive a tunnel through the hill to open up an access road for some scheme he's got on."

The cold feeling spread down to Clare's stomach. She said, "How do you know there's something to find?"

He grinned triumphantly. "Good old crop marks. You can tell from aerial photographs. The grass is a different colour." He looked at her sideways. "There's something to the west of the House, you know. We're dying to get at it. The Prof is pretty sure it's a sacred site of some kind. I thought I'd come on a recce—spy out the land." He grinned. "We might even find the Ravensmere Benison."

"Find *what*?"

Before he could answer, the main door was opened by an elderly man in a black suit. He was pale, and so shaky that Clare wondered how he had managed to make his way across the vast black and white tiled entrance hall.

He sat gratefully at the table by the door and issued their entrance tickets with careful concentration. "The tour will commence in a few minutes. Mrs Potts-Dyrham from the village will be your tour guide."

"The original ancient retainer," said Kevin sarcastically, in Clare's ear. "Half-dead."

She moved away from him, annoyed. She felt sorry for the old man and anyway hated people who made nasty comments about other people behind their backs.

She bought a printed sheet about Ravensmere and read it while she waited for the tour to begin.

People have been living in this fertile valley of the River Raven for perhaps as long as thirty thousand years. Human bones and tools have been found beneath Ice Age stalagmites. The long barrow on Barrow Beacon Hill was built five thousand years ago. Neolithic hunters also settled here, burying their dead in round barrows and erecting standing stones like the Leper Stone and the Revellers. They were followed by the Beaker people, the Bronze Age and the Iron Age peoples (Camp above Kenward Farm), all of whom left traces of their lives . . .

At this point Mrs Potts-Dyrham arrived, out of breath. She was a portly lady in a pink knitted suit, with an artificial orchid pinned to her splendid bosom.

"So sorry, Mr Bristow," she said breathily. "A tiny problem with my little car, just as I was setting out."

Mr Bristow? thought Clare, surprised. The Mr Bristow who was supposed to be looking after Mr Aylward according to Roger Fletcher? He looked as though he needed a nurse himself.

Mrs Potts-Dyrham rounded up her party briskly and urged them on through the Loggia, into the Great Hall.

"Welcome to Ravensmere. This is the modern part of the House, rebuilt in 1726 after the disastrous fire of 1724. Ravensmere has been a private residence only since Henry VIIIth's time."

"The Dissolution of the Monasteries," said Darren, pushing up his glasses. "Was it a monastery?"

"What a clever little man!" said Mrs Potts-Dyrham. "It was a nunnery. It was known as Raven Abbey. But Ravensmere is a very ancient site and has always been recognized as a special place of great power, a holy place. The Romans built a Temple to Cybele, or Demeter, Goddess of Agriculture and Fertility."

"There's no evidence for that," said Kevin. "At present."

Mrs Potts-Dyrham's bosom swelled indignantly.

"I assure you the evidence is quite irrefutable. Eldon Edgar, the Sixteenth Earl, the present Earl's grandfather and predecessor, was a great scholar, as indeed have been many of the Aylward family. After the tragic loss of his young wife he became reclusive and devoted all his time to archaeology and natural history. He uncovered slightly to the west of the House a Roman mosaic pavement showing a female wearing a garland of corn, a snake coiled about her arm, set in the centre of a complicated maze pattern. She has been identified as Demeter, or the Great Goddess. You may read the account of his excavations in his monumental work in ten volumes, *An Evolutionary History of Human Cultures*, published in 1911. Now . . ."

"He was a nut," said Kevin. "He thought he'd found evidence for the existence of Atlantis."

"He was a friend of General Pitt Rivers, the Father of British archaeology." Mrs Potts-Dyrham crushed him. "I am sure that if the Earl said that it was so, it was indeed so. Now if we may get on . . ."

"Excuse me," said Darren, "what's fertility?"

Mrs Potts-Dyrham took a deep breath, then smiled upon him sweetly. "I am sure your father will explain later, little boy."

Darren said indignantly, "I'm *not* a . . ."

Mrs Potts-Dyrham raised her voice. "After the departure of the Romans there was a prolonged struggle here in the West Country between the invading West Saxons, and the Romano-British under Arthur. We are not far from Glastonbury and Cadbury. How thrilling to think that the great King Arthur himself may once have drunk at our Holy Well."

Kevin said, exasperated, "Arthur was only an imaginary character, dreamed up by . . ."

"Many thousands of us know that Arthur lives!" thundered Mrs Potts-Dyrham magnificently, and Kevin subsided, muttering.

"By AD 658 central Somerset was the occupied frontier. By good luck Ravensmere appears to have escaped the dreadful massacres and fighting elsewhere, although there is evidence of burning and the Roman Temple disappeared. It seems that the Saxons settled peaceably on the site of Kenward Farm, integrating with the local people.

"St Aldhelm, the Apostle of Wessex, came here in 705 and converted the people to Christianity. He established a small Abbey on this already sacred site, with nine nuns of the Benedictine Order, under an Abbess called Rosamond.

The Benedictines were scholars and educators, important in preserving the ancient learning.

"If you will look towards the great fireplace you will see a stone carving brought we think from the old chapter house— one of the emblems of St Benedict—a *raven!* A delightful coincidence, I think you will agree."

"The Raven is also an important Celtic symbol of rebirth and renewal," the grey man said unexpectedly. "And the Roman soldiers worshipped a God of Light called Mithras. The Raven was one of their grades of initiation."

"How interesting," said Mrs Potts-Dyrham, coldly. "However, I am sure this is a *Christian* symbol. If I may continue?

"All through the Middle Ages the small Abbey remained peaceful and quiet, hidden in the folds of the hills. There were usually nine nuns with some lay sisters. Not all of them would have taken vows. Some girls would be here for their education, some women just came for sanctuary, or lived here while their husbands were away at the wars.

"The Abbey was extremely highly regarded. It was a healing centre and gave much help when there was distress in the countryside. Although it never sought riches and lands like some great abbeys, its benign influence was very great. There are many legends about the good nuns and their marvellous cures.

"It was one of the last religious houses to be suppressed by Henry VIII. The King's Commissioners visited the Abbey in 1539 and reported that the nuns were 'full of charitee, virtuous lyving and diligent'. Nevertheless, the elderly Abbess was beaten to make her reveal the whereabouts of the concealed treasure known as the Ravensmere Benison, one of the many great mysteries of this house." She paused dramatically, confident that she had caught their full attention at last.

"What's a Benison?" asked Darren, speaking for all of them.

"It means a *blessing*, of course. But no one knows quite

what the Ravensmere blessing was. It was always referred to simply as the Benison. We only know that it was the most precious thing in the whole of the Abbey. And King Henry went to extraordinary lengths to get hold of it." She lowered her voice confidentially. "*It has been suggested that Ravensmere might well have been the resting place of the Most Holy Grail.*"

She waited for their comments, but even Kevin was silent.

"The old Abbess was found dead, and eventually a large, ancient, marvellously decorated golden bowl was handed over to the King's Commissioners. It disappeared. We know that it never reached London with the rest of the gold plate and valuables from Ravensmere. A great search was made, both then and many times later, but it was never discovered."

"Load of cobblers," muttered Kevin, recovering, but Mrs Potts-Dyrham ignored him.

"The Abbey was sold off to a local nobleman. He was Edward John Aylward, the Second Earl—we call him the Great Founder to distinguish him from all the other Edwards. He bought the Abbey and its lands for £842, and began to turn it into a residence for a gentleman.

"He married Rosamond Kenward, who had been the last Abbess-Elect of the Abbey. The romantic legend is that he had always been in love with her, but she had chosen to be a nun. They had nine children, all of whom made important marriages which helped to protect Ravensmere through the next century of turmoil."

Clare remembered the extraordinary tomb in the church, with all the kneeling children, and wondered how Rosamond had felt having to get married after all.

"His fine portrait, attributed to Hans Holbein, the Younger, is there on the East Wall, together with that of his lady."

They all turned to look. The two portraits made an extraordinary contrast. Edward Aylward stood foursquare, a towering figure, in a pearl-embroidered velvet coat and a fur jerkin. He had the bold, ruthless face of a man who always got what he wanted and wasn't too particular how he went about it. Rosamond, on the other hand, was dressed in a plain black gown, and a white cap.

Clare lingered a moment as the others moved on. Rosamond's eyes looked directly at her, amused and luminous. Her mouth was full and looked as if it would begin to smile at any moment. The face seemed almost familiar, as though she had seen it before somewhere. Peeping from the folds of Rosamond's velvet skirt was a small cat—a tortoiseshell cat, that looked remarkably like Tabitha.

Clare caught up the rest of the party in the Dining Room, where they were looking at the Hepplewhite chairs ranged down a long table, with the second-best Wedgwood china and settings for thirty-six people.

"The silver needs a bit of a clean, don't you think, Joan?" Clare heard the jolly lady whisper to her friend. "And the china is dusty."

Clare wandered on through the great rooms, full of antique furniture, priceless carpets, paintings and porcelain; through the Great Drawing Room, the Lesser Drawing Room, the Ballroom with its painted ceiling, and tall mirrors carved by Grinling Gibbons, and the Music Room, with its painted cherubs flying around painted pillars and a harp and spinet in the corner.

"They need to get those curtains cleaned, Joan."

Clare followed the women, half-listening to their disapproving comments. She found herself sympathizing. There was a general air of dusty grandeur, a neglected beauty, things mouldering away like Sleeping Beauty's castle. If they didn't want them they should put them in a museum, she thought, surprised at how upset she felt. The whole place needed to be looked after and *loved*.

"When do we get to the historic part?" asked Darren, dissatisfied.

Mrs Potts-Dyrham smiled insincerely. "I'm afraid, little man, that the remains of the Abbey are not open to the public. Now, here we are in the West Gallery, which is devoted to the more important paintings—Rembrandt, Canaletto, Turner—and the Family Portraits.

"Here is Sir Edmund, the First Earl, ennobled by Henry VII on Bosworth field. And here the Third Earl, who was with Drake at Gravelines. He wrote sonnets and a book on the benefits of clean water, which he is holding."

It was clear that Mrs Potts-Dyrham regarded the Aylward family with a breathless awe, which Clare found very irritating. The portraits were interesting, though.

"He looks very sexy," giggled Darren's mum.

"They all do," Clare heard Joan mutter to her friend, and surprised, she let her eyes run down the line of portraits. It was true. The family likeness appeared again and again. Dark handsome faces with penetrating, uncomfortable eyes, often a disconcerting, brilliant green. The sensuous mouths suggesting a wild humour.

"Reckless and ruthless," said the grey man, disapprovingly, surprising them all.

Mrs Potts-Dyrham bridled. "It is true that the Third Earl was considered something of a womanizer, but his son Edmund, the Fourth Earl, was quite different. He was ascetic and a recluse. A Puritan, in fact. There was rioting in the village when he forbad the traditional Maze Dance which used to take place here each year. And the Fifth Earl sat in the Long Parliament. He was a soldier and a politician, and was killed at the Battle of Worcester."

"He was a Roundhead?" said Clare, surprised. He had a hard poker face, but in the green eyes there was an ironic gleam, and something suspiciously like a quirk in the corner of his mouth. "I thought the Aylwards would have been Cavaliers."

"There has always been a strange streak of radicalism in the family," said Mrs Potts-Dyrham, disapprovingly. "Over there, James Arthur, the Revolutionary Earl, who refused the Trust and was drowned."

"What's the Trust?" asked Darren.

Mrs Potts-Dyrham became red and flustered. "Why, er, I meant his inheritance, of course. Here is the wonderful portrait of another Rosamond, the Fifth Earl's wife, by Sir Peter Lely. As you have seen, ever since the Abbey became their home the Aylwards have traditionally married Kenwards. The eldest daughter is often called Rosamond. This is Rosamond the Strong. She protected Ravensmere and the village throughout the Civil War. She rebuilt the Muniment Tower. And she was obliged after the death of her husband to go on running the estate—very successfully by all accounts—until her grandson came of age. There are many legends about her."

"I don't see her son's picture," said Darren, pushing up his glasses. "The . . . um . . . Sixth Earl."

"There is no portrait," said Mrs Potts-Dyrham, shortly. "He was a black sheep. He also refused the Trust, and was found dead a few months later."

Clare looked at Rosamond's portrait. Most of the women in the portraits had been fair-haired and beautiful. They looked from strange, tilted eyes, as though they were seeing things that most people could not see, faery women, despite their grand clothes.

But this Rosamond was quite different. Her dark eyes stared from under strongly marked eyebrows with a frightening intelligence. She had a mass of dark hair heaped up under a tiny lace cap, which looked as if it might easily fall off. Her lips lifted in a smile full of mischief. Leaning against her knee affectionately was a handsome boy in a violet silk suit.

71

Once again Clare had a strong feeling of recognition. Could she have seen the portrait reproduced in a book?

Mrs Potts-Dyrham said, "Notice the beautiful tortoiseshell pussy reclining on her lap. That's Selene, after the Goddess of the moon. It is said they were never apart. When she died the cat disappeared and was never seen again."

"Ahhhh," said all the ladies. The grey man coughed irritably. Kevin said, "Who's the boy?"

"That's her grandson, James Edmund. We call him the Restoration Earl. Here he is at nineteen, and here again in this splendid portrait by Sir Godfrey Kneller. He was a member of the famous Whig Kit Kat Club, and was one of the few who made a vast fortune out of the South Sea Bubble enterprise.

"He loved Ravensmere, and was very happily married to Clarissa Kenward, who had been his childhood sweetheart. It is said that he died of a broken heart when his wife was killed in the fire of 1724, which destroyed part of the Abbey. Clarissa was famous for her great knowledge of herbal remedies. We are indebted to her for our famous Herb and Physick Garden."

Clarissa was tall and thin, with a look of Dr McKinnon, Clare thought.

"The Ninth Earl, here in the corner, refused to return to Ravensmere. He ran away with Lady Henrietta Orrery instead. He was killed in a duel only two months later."

"They didn't have much luck when they married outside the Kenward family, did they?" commented Joan.

"Very true. It is a strange thing that while in general the Aylwards are exceptionally healthy and long-lived, those who have left Ravensmere once they inherit, refusing to accept their responsibilities, die soon afterwards."

"How weird," said Darren's mum, shivering.

They trailed after Mrs Potts-Dyrham through the heavy mahogany door at the end of the Gallery.

"This is Lord Edward's room, named for the Eighth Earl,

Edward Richard, nicknamed The Builder by the family. He rebuilt the House after the fire, which killed his grandmother Clarissa. Henry Hoare was building Stourhead over near Mere at the time and he introduced him to the architect Colen Campbell, who was Deputy Surveyor-General, successor to Sir Christopher Wren.

"Here in his portrait you can see that he has a rolled-up drawing of the North Front in his hand, and on the table is the plan of the new Palladian House, which incorporated the remaining parts of the old Abbey."

The painting showed a tall man in a plain brown coat and white stock, leaning on a table. His face, thin and bony under a heavy wig, was dominated by his glittering green eyes, sharp, intense, and never missing a trick, thought Clare.

"He was noted for his foresight and political acumen. His letters are full of surprisingly accurate predictions about the future including the industrial revolution. He reorganized the estate and the farming practice.

"Before the work was completed the Earl was thrown from his horse and killed. As you have heard his son died in the same year, and the succession went to his second son, James Edward, whom we call the Travelling Earl.

"Before he accepted the Trust . . . Before he came into his inheritance he had been a great traveller. He brought back many of Ravensmere's treasures, which we will see in the Etruscan Gallery.

"It is to him and his son Edmund, the Eleventh Earl, nicknamed The Gardener, that we are indebted for our wonderful landscape park and garden. The very fine joint portrait here of father and son is by Sir Joshua Reynolds."

An older, elegant man was leaning on a classical pillar in a garden. He had inherited his father's green eyes, but here they looked amused, almost cynical, with some secret joke. His son stood beside him, dark-eyed, alert and wary, unsmiling, dangerous even, carrying a sporting gun. He didn't look at all the sort of young man to be interested in gardens, Clare thought, and heard her voice from a long distance, saying, "What is that wall behind him, that circular hole like an arch?"

Mrs Potts-Dyrham looked at her sharply. "That is the wall of the China Garden to the west of the House."

"I'd like to see that," said Darren, rubbing his nose. "Is it made of cups and saucers?"

Mrs Potts-Dyrham tittered. "Oh no, little man. The Travelling Earl admired the Chinese gardens he had seen on his travels so much that when he returned he had one built here. It is simply a walled garden that he called the China Garden. The circular openings are very common in China. They are called Moon Gates, and they are used as we would use an archway, to frame a special view. The so-called Chinoiserie style had become very fashionable in England and many landowners put China houses into their parks."

"How very interesting," said Joan's friend. "We must see that before we go. We love gardens."

"I'm afraid that the China Garden is not open to the public." Mrs Potts-Dyrham smiled.

"This place is no good, Dad," said Darren. "All the interesting places are shut up."

Clare went on staring at the painting as the others moved on into the Library next door. Behind the figures on the left side there was a lake and a classical Temple on an island reflected in the water.

She had seen the view before. She had seen the Moon Gate before. She knew what she would see if she stepped through the opening in the wall. There would be other Moon Gates—six, no, *seven* of them. And she knew the Temple in the painting too.

Inside it had a high curved roof and marble steps that led down to a pool, where a beautiful statue of Demeter, Earth Mother, was bending, arms outstretched welcoming back her daughter Persephone, Goddess of Spring and Rebirth, who was stepping from the dark of Hades, through a crystal cascade of water . . .

Clare felt her stomach clenching in fear. It couldn't be true. How could she possibly know? She had never been here before.

Chapter 7

The Library was the most beautiful room Clare had ever been in. Not dark with oak and mustiness, but all white and gold, with arched bookshelves decorated with gilded swags of fruit and flowers. It was an immense room, bigger by far than her old public library.

". . . built by the Thirteenth Earl to house his great collection of books. The painted ceiling shows the Muses, and the long tables were made on the estate by my great-great-grandfather, Elihu Kenward."

Another Kenward, thought Clare, resigned.

"Pity there's such a nasty scratch in the polish there, Joan."

"Why haven't we seen the Fourteenth Earl," said Darren, pushing up his spectacles.

Mrs Potts-Dyrham sighed. "He was a dissolute young man, resident in London. He was not willing to live at Ravensmere, and was killed a month after his accession when his carriage overturned on the turnpike."

"Not another one!" exclaimed Darren's mum. "Is there some sort of family curse?"

"Certainly not," Mrs Potts-Dyrham said, affronted.

"Does the present Earl live here?" asked Joan.

"He lived in London for many years, only visiting us occasionally, but he returned to live here permanently a few years ago. He is in his eighties and has his own apartments overlooking the South Terrace."

"Will you tell us about the *books*," said the grey man with a barely suppressed impatience.

Mrs Potts-Dyrham tightened her lips. "There are approximately thirty thousand books here, as well as many historical documents and maps relating to the House and this part of the country.

"The Aylwards have been great collectors of books of all kinds. The Library has many rare books, some collected by Edmund Edward during his residence in Italy before he became the Thirteenth Earl, and here in this small anteroom is one of the very few chained libraries in the country. It is thought to date back to the earliest days of Raven Abbey."

Clare saw a heavy oak seat and ledge, like a long old-fashioned school desk, below three shelves of huge books which appeared to be back to front, with chains hanging from their front edges, all linked together by a rod so they could be pulled down and opened, but not taken away.

"The earliest book is an illuminated manuscript, the *Liber Somnium Sanctus, Book of the Sacred Dream*, made by one of the nuns here in the year 910."

"I'd like to see that," Darren said, keenly.

"I would too," said his father.

Mrs Potts-Dyrham was flustered. "I'm afraid it's never on display. It is so precious it is always kept under lock and key."

There were rebellious murmurs of disappointment.

The grey man surprisingly joined in. He sounded annoyed. "Surely it would be possible to put it on display in the security of a special display case. Even the Crown Jewels are on display."

Mrs Potts-Dyrham's cheeks were bright red. "It's an *illuminated* script. It has to be protected from the light."

"You could speak with the British Museum about the problem," the grey man said, stubbornly. "I understood I would be able to make an extended study of it today. I am interested in buying it."

"*Buying it!*" Mrs Potts-Dyrham's voice rose in outraged astonishment.

"I represent several well-known libraries in the States and Japan."

"Mr Aylward would *never* dispose of the manuscript. It has been at Ravensmere for over a thousand years. It's absolutely *unthinkable . . .*"

"I have already been in correspondence with his representative, Mr Fletcher."

"Well, I'm sure I don't know anything about it," said Mrs Potts-Dyrham, affronted. "I am only a voluntary guide. I suggest you write to Mr Aylward's solicitors in Bath. They are dealing with most of his business, *not* Mr Fletcher, who is merely his Land Agent. Now, if we can get on . . ."

She rounded up the rest of her party, and indignantly led them off to the Etruscan Gallery.

So Mrs Potts-Dyrham was no friend of Mr Fletcher either, Clare thought. She lingered a moment, watching the grey man examining the chained library with frustrated irritation.

"It really is too bad bringing me all this way on a fool's errand," he said, angrily.

"Mr Fletcher actually said that Mr Aylward wanted to sell?"

"He assured me that the greater part of the collection would be coming on the market shortly, including the *Liber Somnium Sanctus.* I came at once, of course."

"It's that important?"

He stared at her. "The Ravensmere collection is a legend. No one has even been allowed to examine it since 1893. And the *Liber Somnium Sanctus* is unique. Many of the hand-written illuminated books of that time were copies of the Gospels, or the lives of the Saints, but the *Liber* is quite special—a personal account of a sacred dream or a vision that the nun herself had. Worth a fortune if only I could get

78

my hands on it. The whole of the rare book trade will be in a furore when the word gets out."

Clare said, brightly, "But, of course, the Earl's still alive, isn't he? Funny he doesn't seem to know about the sale. Are you sure this Mr Fletcher is quite, er, trustworthy? Not trying to sell you something he doesn't . . . um . . . actually own?"

She sauntered away, casually, badly wanting to laugh at the expression of dawning horror on the grey man's face.

The Etruscan Gallery was stuffed full of Greek goddesses, Roman busts, Chinese vases, Indian Buddhas, Italian inlaid cabinets, Japanese screens, and display cases full of fascinating things from every period of history, but Clare suddenly felt too exhausted to appreciate them properly.

The rest of the party were looking tired too, she thought, except for Darren, still pursuing Mrs Potts-Dyrham with awkward questions. He had to be dragged, protesting, from an Egyptian mummified cat, as they were all ushered back briskly to the main entrance, and the tour was over, much to Mrs Potts-Dyrham's obvious relief.

"Light refreshments are available in the Orangery. Down the stairs and through the gateway to the right, madam. Yes, it is signposted. Yes, the Herb and Physick Garden is there as well. And the garden centre. Thank you for your interest. We hope you have enjoyed your visit."

They all trooped out, most of the party making hastily for the café. The grey man strode angrily down the steps and away towards the car-park.

"I've got an old banger. Give you a lift somewhere?" suggested Kevin. "I'm parked over there under the tree."

Clare glanced where he was pointing, and stiffened, her heart beginning to pound. Next to Kevin's old Ford, in the deep shade of an old oak, a dark figure was sitting astride a powerful motor bike. She took an involuntary step backwards.

"No. No thanks. I think I'll have a look at the Herb Garden," Clare said.

79

"Righto. See you at the dig. By the way, you didn't tell me your name."

"Clare Meredith," Clare said reluctantly, her eyes still on the motor bike.

Kevin hurried down the steps. It occurred to her that they might know each other. Spies or vultures? She had no intention of going anywhere near the dig. Who was the motor bike rider? Was it coincidence he was here, or was he following her?

There was a dismayed squeak behind her.

"*Clare Meredith*! Oh dear! Oh dear! I really didn't know." Mrs Potts-Dyrham was wringing her hands. "*Clare.* What must you be thinking of me? I never *guessed* you would . . . Why didn't you speak?"

Clare flushed guiltily. "I'm sorry. I just wanted to have a look round. I didn't think there would be any harm. I did pay my entrance fee. My mother is . . ."

But Mrs Potts-Dyrham's face was beaming and joyful, not accusing. She said, roguishly, "Of course I know who your mother is. We are all so glad that she has come home and that Mr Aylward will be properly looked after now. Poor dear gentleman, so neglected. If it hadn't been for Mrs Anscomb smuggling out his letter begging her to come, I really don't know what might have happened. All the same I never really believed she would come back—and bring you *too*! We're all absolutely *thrilled*.

"I can't tell you what it means to the village. The dear vicar has arranged a thanksgiving service, and the village ladies have been decorating . . ."

Clare gaped at her. "You mean all those flowers in the church are for a thanksgiving that *my mother* has come back?"

"A thanksgiving for *you*, my dear. Now you've come, I'm sure everything will be all right." She took in Clare's astonishment, and her face fell. "Oh dear, you *don't know*, do you? I've spoken too soon."

She looked genuinely distressed and Clare felt uncomfortable and alarmed. What on earth was going on? What didn't she know? They were all trying to involve her in something she didn't understand.

"I'm only here temporarily," she said, firmly. "I go to university in the autumn."

Mrs Potts-Dyrham's face fell into even deeper folds. "Oh dear! We did so *hope*. And in three years' time it will be too late. What are we going to do?" Her deep contralto rose almost to a wail.

"I'm sorry you're upset. I really don't know what you want me to do."

"No, no, *of course* you don't. Oh how disappointing. You have no idea how difficult everything has been. There's so much to do here, with Mr Fletcher cutting down the staff all the time. And poor Mr Bristow so ill, that we hardly know how to go on.

"That dreadful woman, making comments about the dusty curtains and tarnished silver . . . Of course, she was quite right. It was only a matter of time before it was noticed. Mrs Anscomb will be so upset. We try so hard to keep this great place in the condition it should be in, but we can't even keep the State Rooms clean now. I hardly dare wonder what the rest of the House is like. And there's the garden centre and the refreshments in the Orangery on Open Days . . ."

Clare said, doubtfully, "If you are short of staff I'll be glad to help out while I'm here, but I think I ought to tell you that I shouldn't really be in the House. I met Mr Fletcher yesterday and he told me to keep away. So perhaps I shouldn't . . ."

Mrs Potts-Dyrham went a dark, angry red. "It's not up to Mr Fletcher to say who comes into this house. Not yet it isn't. You must come and meet the staff, and have a cup of tea with us. Mrs Anscomb will be so pleased."

She swept Clare through an unobtrusive baize door to the left of the great staircase, and along narrow corridors with closed doors opening from them.

"This is the Service Wing," she said. "The Still Rooms, the Butler's Room, the Servants' Hall, all of them shut up now, of course. We only use the Great Kitchen. My great-grandmother was Housekeeper here, and in those days there were thirty-five people employed in the house alone. Now there's only Mr Bristow, Mr Aylward's man, and Mrs Anscomb, the Cook-Housekeeper, and a few of us from the village who come in to help out or to clean. Mr Fletcher would get rid of both of them if he could, I'm sure, but they've been with Mr Aylward for years and he wouldn't hear of it."

"There's not enough money to run the place?" Clare said, sympathetically.

"Money!" Mrs Potts-Dyrham snorted. "Why, Mr Aylward is one of the richest men in the country. He's made a fortune on the Stock Exchange. Not to mention the family money and the income from the estate. It's Mr Fletcher, running everything down. Cuts. Cuts. As though there won't be more than enough for him when Mr Aylward goes."

"Look," said Clare, hurrying along behind her, and wondering where her mother was, "I really don't think this is a good idea. I'm not supposed to be here."

But Mrs Potts-Dyrham had already pushed open a door. The kitchen was a huge room, lined with cupboards, drawers and open dressers laden with china, and two bulky kitchen ranges, straight out of the last century. The only evidence of the twentieth century was a large modern cooker and a walk-in freezer.

The two people sitting at the big scrubbed table in the centre of the room drinking tea looked up startled. One was Mr Bristow, the other was a pretty, elderly woman with bobbing curls. Clare recognized her at once. She was the crazy lady who had been dancing triumphantly in the drive yesterday—Mrs Anscomb, Mr Aylward's Housekeeper.

"I have brought Clare to meet you," said Mrs Potts-

82

Dyrham, complacently, a conjuror who had produced a particularly fine rabbit.

Mr Bristow, beaming, struggled to his feet to clasp her hand tightly. Mrs Anscomb, exclaiming joyfully, was hugging and kissing her with tears in her eyes, as though she was a prodigal daughter of the House, just come home, when the door opened again and her mother came through, carrying a tray.

Chapter 8

Bad timing, Clare admitted to herself, stretching out on the grass and watching a large bird hovering way up in the golden heat haze of the afternoon sky. A kestrel? A hawk of some kind. She knew next to nothing about birds, but there was something predatory and worrying about that dark shadow.

She might have known that her mother would appear at the crucial moment. Hadn't she always done so?

Clare had got out of the kitchen as soon as she could, promising to come back next day and help with the chores. Of course, her mother hadn't said anything in front of the others, but her tight lips and cold eyes had promised a reckoning this evening. Another row. Clare sighed. Why couldn't they get on together now?

Generally her mother appeared calm and even-tempered. But Clare was aware of strong feelings buried deep, and seldom expressed. Frances could be inflexible and unforgiving when something mattered deeply to her. And there was something here that kept welling up, breaking through the wall of her control, like water through a sea wall, no matter how much she scurried round blocking the holes.

Clare turned over and propped her head on her hands, chewing a stem of grass. She had climbed the steep rise to the east of the House, Raven Hill, with its crown of trees, and was looking down on Ravensmere.

It lay on a terrace of level ground against the guardian bulk of Barrow Beacon Hill, cupped in a ring of lesser hills and hanging woods. Its lawns sloped down to the River Raven winding through the centre of the bowl. The river had been dammed to create a great irregular lake, like a glimmering mirror several miles around, before curving away below her along the base of a wooded, secret valley.

At the other end of the lake she could see an elegant bridge and a Cascade, and a series of smaller pools. Each was lush with waterlilies and had a marble statue. There was a glimpse of the Upper Lake with its island, green and secret, hidden in the oak and beech woods which clustered closely here and covered the lower steep slopes of Barrow Beacon Hill. Above the trees rose the white dome of the Temple of Demeter, a romantic vision of another time, just like the painting in the House. Clare felt the same uncomfortable jolt of recognition and looked hastily away.

From the hill it was easy to see the great age of the House. No ordered design on this side. It lay spread out like a tom cat basking in the sunlight, a jumbled collection of walls and towers. An E-shaped building with a long terrace and rows of big mullioned windows faced the lake, next to an even older wing, with pointed windows and narrow doors, which must be the remains of the original Abbey. And there was Rosamond's Tower, comically tacked on to the corner like an afterthought. Everything was built of weathered stone, just as she had imagined.

The sides of the House were flanked by gardens. On the east side, below her, were the vegetable and herb gardens, divided into walled squares like a chessboard. The light was so clear and sharp she could even see Mai and a youth walking towards the greenhouses of the garden centre.

On the west side there were formal gardens, flower-beds and rose gardens and, surely somewhere beyond, there would be the China Garden. Suddenly, for no reason, her heart was beating heavily against the walls of her chest. Even the name made her feel frightened and excited at the same time.

Tomorrow, she thought. Tomorrow I'll go and look for it. The lambent sunlight of the afternoon seemed to deepen and expand, washing over the golden stone, illuminating every detail like the pictures in old painted manuscripts. She could see the mossy cobbles of the courtyard, the lichened-covered walls of the dovecote, the carved stone of the windows and lintels. A prancing dragon looked down from a corner of Rosamond's Tower.

It was a house built over the centuries by craftsmen with loving care, paying attention to the exact and proper detail, Clare thought. No shoddy materials. Nothing make do, or bodged-up like today. Nothing tricky or done to show off. Just care and love and the best they could do.

Generations of people had worked here and loved this place. They had worshipped here. There was an almost tangible atmosphere of peace. A sacred place, Mrs Potts-Dyrham had said.

There was energy too—a tingling sense of aliveness . . . *something else*. She had felt that from the first, as they drove through the gates. She wasn't imagining *that*. There was something immensely important here for everyone. Peace? Healing? *Something*.

But it was all to be destroyed. Turned into a nuclear dumping ground.

Pain moved inside her chest and diaphragm, clenching her stomach until she thought she was going to be sick. She closed her eyes. She couldn't bear it to happen. The very idea had become agonizing. Ravensmere had reached out somehow and claimed her for its own.

When she opened her eyes again there was a change. The air wavered. The edges of the building seemed to be softening and blurring. The House looked smaller, older, different somehow. Rosamond's Tower had gone, and then all the stone buildings faded. There was a sturdy church made of wood, and huts surrounded by a high fence, then they too were gone, and there was a spacious single-storey white building with a courtyard and a fountain. The water in the fountain flashed in the sunlight, and then there were no buildings at all in the secret green bowl in the hills, just women dancing, a snaking line of nine dancers weaving a spiral knot with their bodies.

Despite the warm sun on her shoulders, a slow shiver ran the length of Clare's spine. There was no church, no white temple, no women.

She rolled over on to her back and pressed the back of her arm against her eyes. The sun sent golden sequins spinning behind her eyelids.

Of course, it could just have been the heat bouncing off the stone, or maybe it was the way she was staring. If you looked at things hard enough . . .

No good inventing excuses. Her stomach bunched up again. She was hallucinating. There were the children in the field this morning, and the picture, and the stable yard yesterday. That was when it had started. And all the time it was getting clearer, more intense.

She would have to see a doctor. I'm absolutely spooked, she thought. There were goosebumps on her skin and her hair prickled with electricity. The sun had gone behind a cloud and the shadow spread a chill all over her.

Time to go. She moved her arm, curiously reluctant, and opened her eyes.

No cloud. He was standing over her, blotting out the sun. A tall bulky figure in black leathers, staring down at her. She looked into the darkest coldest eyes she had ever seen. The kind of cold that burned. She stared back hypnotized, and for a moment the bird sounds faded and there was only the sound of the breeze in the tall grass.

How had he got there, Clare wondered, dazed. She hadn't heard a sound. He was just there, like a wizard. Conjured up. Another hallucination. *Or a ghost?*

On that thought, in one fluid movement, she was on her feet and running, leaping down the hill, her legs aching, her lungs bursting. She swung over the low stone wall of the outer field and glanced back briefly. He wasn't following. But she could hear his wild laughter.

She made for the House, forcing herself to drop into a walk, and turned quickly into the Orangery. All the visitors were gone, and it was empty now except for Mrs Anscomb counting the takings.

"What's up, m'dear?" she said, alarmed, staring at Clare. "You look like you've seen a ghost."

Clare pulled in a few deep breaths and propped herself against the counter. She felt ashamed of her wild flight. She hadn't run away like that since her junior school days.

"There's a man up there. A young man. He startled me. I don't know how he got into the park. I don't think he's a visitor."

Mrs Anscomb looked at her narrowly. "Where did you say he was?"

"Up on the hill. Raven Hill. I didn't hear a thing. He just sort of appeared like a ghost. Very tall. All in black leathers, on a day like this. He was kind of shadowy . . ."

Mrs Anscomb dropped the pile of coins. They ran around bumping over the old uneven tiles. Clare chased them and piled them back on the counter, but Mrs Anscomb wasn't looking at them. She was staring at Clare, her cheeks mottled an unhealthy red.

"Joseph Barton swore he'd seen him up there. Disappeared, he said, just disappeared."

Clare gaped at her. "You don't mean it really *was* a ghost?"

Mrs Anscomb looked away uncomfortably. "Could be," she muttered.

"But he was wearing motor-cycle gear! You know, leathers and stuff. He didn't seem like a ghost to me, he blotted out the sun. I thought you could see through ghosts. I thought they had armour and clanking chains."

She tried to laugh, but Mrs Anscomb picked up the coins and fingered them uneasily. "Not that one. It's not an old ghost."

"But who is it supposed to be?"

"Likely Brandon Aylward, Mr Aylward's son."

"Mr Aylward's *son*? But why . . ."

"Better not to talk about him."

"But . . ."

"Look, m'dear, we none of us talk about Brandon. Mr Aylward don't like it. He had an accident and died sudden like, and Mr Aylward never got over it." She smiled comfortingly. "Don't worry, Clare m'dear, you'll probably never see him again. Nobody ever seen him twice."

Clare devoutly hoped not. It was not that she actually believed Mrs Anscomb. The figure had been too solid, too *alive*, somehow, to be a ghost. It was the memory of those ice-dark eyes which gave her the shivers, that and the feeling of danger and the wild laughter.

Chapter 9

"Clare, you promised!" Frances closed the front door with a snap, and walked angrily into the kitchen where Clare had started to prepare a salad for their evening meal.

"No I didn't." Clare turned. She was in no mood to be conciliatory; she had several bones to pick with her mother. "I said I would go to the village, and I did. There's no sensible reason why I shouldn't take the tour of the House. It's open to the public, isn't it? And if you're worried about your precious job—Roger Fletcher has gone to London for a few days, James Kenward said so. Nobody in the House will tell him. They don't like him."

"You've met James?" Her mother dropped into a chair drawn up at the kitchen table.

"And Mai Lee, and Dr McKinnon, and a whole lot of other people. Oh, and I've got a message for you from the vicar. He said to tell you that he's there if you need to talk to him."

Frances said warily. "Trevor Holmes. What else did he say?"

"Did you know they've filled the church with flowers *because we've come here*? Flowers everywhere. Now isn't that weird?"

The colour crept up Frances' cheeks, and suddenly there were tears in her eyes. She got up, took eggs from the fridge and set them to boil on the cooker, keeping her back turned to Clare.

Clare said grimly, "What's going on?"

"I don't know what you mean."

"Oh no, you're not getting away with that. I want some answers. Everybody here knows something that I don't know, and they expect me to know it too. I feel a complete idiot. This place, the village, is . . . strange. You know, don't you? You know all about it."

"Don't push things, Clare. You'll understand everything—at the right time."

"That's not good enough. You could have warned me. You could have told me that everybody knows you. Mrs Gregg at the shop, Mrs Potts-Dyrham—they've all been waiting for you to come back. Why? And how come they knew my name, and who I was—*before I told them?*"

"I . . . well, it's a small village. Gossip gets around. Your grandfather . . . our family is . . . was respected."

"And you were born at Kenward Farm," said Clare slowly. She leaned on the kitchen units and watched her mother's back, and part of the puzzle slotted into place.

"You're a Kenward, aren't you. One of the old families here. Of course they would know you. No wonder the vicar was telling me about the Kenwards in the churchyard. He must have thought I was half-witted."

Frances ran the eggs under the cold tap, and began to peel them. At last she said reluctantly, "Kenward was my maiden name."

"Weston. That's what you always said."

The icy accusation in Clare's voice brought her mother to the table. "Please, Clare, you've got to understand. This is very difficult for me."

"So tell me. Explain. How can I understand if you don't clear up all this stupid mystery?"

"There's no mystery. When I went to London I changed my name. There's nothing wrong with that. Lots of people do. I'd . . . well, I'd run away from home and I didn't want to be found." She took a deep breath. "There was a terrible quarrel here and I—left. My father told me he wanted nothing more to do with me and I swore I'd never come back."

"But you came back for his funeral. You must have kept in touch with someone here."

"Sarah McKinnon. She's my mother's cousin. I needed a reference for the hospital. And she wrote me from time to time, telling me how Father was. I knew she could be trusted. I loved him very much, Clare." Her voice broke and she hastily turned back to the chopping board.

"Did my dad know your real name?"

"Of course he did. He knew all about it. I met him at the hospital. He supported me through it all and then I married him."

"Supported you through what?"

"Bad times. And I had a nervous breakdown."

She put the knife down, and rinsed her hands under the tap. They were shaking. "Clare, I really can't face any food just now. You go ahead and eat. I want to go back to the House. I'm worried about Mr Aylward. I need to check on him."

Clare watched her. "You're just putting it off. There's a lot you're not telling me."

"Honestly, Clare, I do need to go back. I don't know what they've been doing here, but Mr Aylward has been terribly neglected. He's got *bed sores*, apart from all his other troubles." She was outraged. "I suppose they've done their best, but Mr Bristow has been in hospital himself, and can't lift him. They should have got in a proper nurse long before this. I know he's a difficult man, but really, *bed sores!*"

"Trying to save money," Clare said.

Frances looked at her sharply. "Why do you say that? There's no lack of money here."

"But Roger Fletcher doesn't want to waste any of it, does

he? He's already thinking that it's all his. He doesn't want to waste it on keeping Mr Aylward alive."

"That's monstrous! Honestly, Clare, you've been watching too much television."

"That letter you had, asking you to come—did you know they had to smuggle it out? Mr Fletcher wasn't exactly pleased to see you yesterday, was he? And it's just a guess, but when did Mr Aylward last see a doctor? I don't say Roger Fletcher is a murderer, but there's a lot of money at stake here and he'd certainly not worry too much if the old man died tomorrow."

Frances looked at her indecisively. "I can't believe . . . But perhaps you're right. I'll call in Sarah McKinnon tomorrow morning. If she'll come."

"You said Roger Fletcher was greedy," Clare thought aloud. "But I think he's crooked. Have you noticed how run down everything is? All the cleaning staff were sacked last year. Everything is dusty and neglected. There's just a handful of elderly people trying to keep it all together. It's not fair."

"How on earth did you find all this out?"

"There's more. A man on the tour had come to *buy* an extremely valuable book in the collection. The *Sanctus* something. Mr Fletcher had written to him. I just wonder if Mr Aylward knows the Ravensmere collection is about to be sold."

Frances looked horrified. "Not the *Liber Somnium Sanctus*? He can't sell that!"

"He can do a lot worse. He's going to allow the archaeology people to dig here. And there's to be an access road through Barrow Beacon Hill. Remember he told us that he was going to sell the estate to 'developers'? Guess who he's negotiating with?"

Frances shook her head. She sat down shakily.

"Nuclear Energy. You know they've had trouble with the Hinckley Point site which has to close in a few years. And there's a need to find somewhere to dump nuclear waste."

"He can't do it!" Frances jumped up. "He can't. It's unthinkable. What about the Benison? Mr Aylward can't know about it."

"They say he doesn't care. They say he's a bitter man. His wife died young or something. What it amounts to," said Clare, spelling it out, "is that this place, the whole area even, is on its last gasp. When Mr Aylward goes, Stoke Raven, Ravensmere, and the whole valley will go too. The archaeologists, the dealers, and the nuclear energy people will move in for the kill. They're not going to develop this place, they're going to destroy it."

Saying the words she felt again the pain, the profound sense of misery and horror that she'd felt on the hill.

"I've seen it. They'll pull up the hedgerows, and knock down the cottages, and build their concrete boxes. They'll poison the land and pollute the waters. I can see the fields blighted, the trees brown and dying, the Abbey roofless and decaying in the weeds and nettles . . ."

She heard the high keening note in her voice and stopped dead, staring at her mother, who was staring back, her hand over her mouth.

"*Clare?*"

Clare swallowed. She said, trying to make her voice normal and casual, as though nothing had happened, "And there's nothing we can do about it, is there?"

Frances' eyes dug into her. She'd guessed, Clare thought, waiting, but Frances was silent, just looking at her.

"There isn't anything, is there?" Clare repeated. "There's no one to protect Ravensmere."

"I don't know, Clare," Frances said slowly. "Maybe it isn't too late. I'll have to think about it." She stood up shakily and pulled on her woollen jacket. "Don't wait up for me."

When she opened the front door, the dark gold evening sky had burned into amethyst, rose and lilac. Clare followed her and leaned on the door frame. "By the way, there was something else I wanted to ask you. Did you have an older sister?"

Frances halted, surprised. "What makes you ask?"

"The tradition. The oldest Kenward daughter marries the oldest Aylward son. You should have married Brandon Aylward, Mr Aylward's son."

Clare had expected her mother to laugh, or even exclaim with annoyance. Instead, all the colour drained from her skin. The face she turned on Clare had been wiped of all expression, the bones prominent like a skull.

"Yes, that's right. I was engaged to Brandon Aylward. I was the Kenward bride."

"But you never married him. Or did you?" Nothing would surprise her about her mother now.

"I never married him in church."

"What does that mean?"

"It means he died before our wedding day. He *died*." Her voice was flat, dead, but Clare saw the tears standing in her eyes before she turned and walked hurriedly away.

Clare could not sleep. She had heard her mother come in late and go to bed several hours ago. She had heard the stable clock chime twelve.

The room felt hot and airless, and the events of the day chased themselves around her brain in endless succession. The church full of flowers, the people, the portraits in the house, and especially the black figure in leathers slid through her mind like a pack of holiday snapshots. Face replaced face and always there were those icy eyes drawing her in. She knew that there was an emerging pattern. But the fear inside was forbidding her mind to recognize it.

The bright moonlight shone through the small window, pooling on the floor beneath, and suddenly she could bear the heat no longer. She got up and pushed the window wider, to let in the air. Outside, the stable yard was flooded with light, as bright as day. The granite paving between the cobbles glittered like diamonds, and even the shadows seemed luminous.

She felt a sudden longing to be out of doors. There was no reason why she shouldn't go out and walk for a while. This wasn't London and there were no wild animals, nothing more sinister than the odd fox.

What about wild *people*—in black leathers?

But she could see no sign of the shadowy figure lurking under the stable arch and somehow she knew he was far away tonight. She could go safely and look at the garden she had seen from the hill. The air there would be cool and perfumed with the scent of roses and night stocks.

She pulled on jogging pants and a T-shirt, and holding her trainers in her hand so as not to disturb her mother, she crept down the stairs.

As she closed the front door, the stable clock began to chime. She looked up, waiting to see the white-robed man, but instead the other door opened and a maiden appeared. No golden sun around her, but a full moon and stars, and instead of a staff she was holding a leafy branch.

Delighted Clare stared upward, and received her single blessing. One o'clock. Of course there was a Moon and a Sun figure. A male and female. Yin and Yang. One for the day, one for the night.

Tabitha, the cat, was waiting for her under the archway. She chirruped a greeting and wound herself around Clare's ankles.

"All right," Clare said laughing. "Where shall we go?"

To her amusement, Tabitha, her tail straight up, moved off briskly, as though she had been waiting for some time and wanted to be on her way.

Intrigued, Clare followed where she led, slipping across the drive, choosing the shadows of the trees in the park, down past the front of the House, with its blind, shuttered windows and its great portico, ghostly in the brilliant moonlight.

Tabitha was actually taking her to the rose gardens, Clare realized, surprised. The cat stopped, waiting for Clare to catch up, and then without hesitation slipped through the entrance in the yew hedge.

The beauty of the formal gardens in the moonlight took Clare's breath away. This part of the garden was a series of terraces and walks, gardens enclosed in tall hedges like rooms, each with its own special plants and character. There were waterlily pools and a pergola hung with roses, white clematis and honeysuckle, great urns foaming with flowers, and marble nymphs hiding in secret arbours.

Under the moon it looked frozen into stillness by an enchanter, waiting for someone to come along to release it from its spell.

Clare wandered down the central walk dreamily, almost floating on a cloud of fragrance. Every flower, every rose bush seemed to have its own exquisite perfume, poured out on the warm, still air.

At the end of the walk Tabitha was sitting motionless, like a small statue, on top of a sundial, watching her closely. When Clare reached her she jumped down and set off again, along the further path, shadowy with trees.

Clare paused at the sundial to decipher the lettering set in brass around its base, but it was in Latin—*dies natalis solis invicti*. Something about the birth of the sun? Clare wondered, and then followed Tabitha beneath the trees. Tiny white petals drifted down over her like confetti at a wedding and Clare lifted her face to them, her eyes closed, breathing their perfume.

When she opened her eyes, she came to an abrupt halt. Facing her across a grassy path was a very high wall. Cut into the wall was a circular opening, about six feet high, its bottom curve forming a step about eighteen inches from the ground. Inside the opening, two semi-circular iron gates interlaced in a beautiful Chinese design barred the way. *A Moon Gate.*

The air seemed to leave Clare's lungs. She had found the China Garden. She knew it immediately. Knew that all the time she had been wandering, losing track of time, it had been waiting for her here. If there had been any doubt, Tabitha, small and dignified, was sitting before the Gate between two stone, snarling creatures which could have been dogs or lions guarding the entrance.

Clare smiled, although her heart was banging in her chest. The China Garden was making her feel frightened and excited at the same time. She knew that she must go in. There was something that she must do, something urgent and important.

Reluctantly, she crossed to the Gate. Above it was a scroll with Chinese letters and a number—one—elaborately carved and gilded. Taking courage she tried to turn the big iron handle. It was stiff and rusty, too big for her hands, and no amount of rattling would shift it. The iron gates were locked and clearly nobody had opened them for years. They were boarded up inside, so she could not even see through.

But perhaps she could get in through another Gate. There were six of them, weren't there? No, seven.

She turned and followed the heavily overgrown path around the outside of the walled garden. Once, long ago, it had been a properly paved path, but it was a long time since anyone had walked there. The weeds pushed up between the paving and small bushes and saplings had planted themselves against the wall. After a few minutes she came to another Moon Gate, but it was totally blocked by a stack of logs piled against the inner wall.

Undaunted, determined to get in somehow, she continued on around the wall. One of the Gates at least must be open. The garden was large, octagonal in shape, its thick, confining wall at least four metres high. But when, sometime later, she found herself back again at the first Gate, she had discovered only five other Gates and all of them were impassable, blocked with masonry or overgrown with rambling plants.

Clare was puzzled. Why was she so sure there ought to be *seven* Moon Gates?

Frustrated, she shook the Chinese-patterned ironwork. She was surprised how upset and anxious she felt that she couldn't get in. She poked hopelessly at the wooden backing through the iron lattice. There was a sudden cracking sound as two of the boards gave way, and thumped on to the ground, and at last she could see in through the narrow space.

It was a disappointment. No trace remained of the original Garden. No beautiful secret garden. It looked like a field of hay. In the centre on a mound, spectral in the moonlight, was a small Chinese pavilion, like those on a willow pattern plate, with a curly roof and a key pattern balustrade.

She felt a surge of anger. Why had Mr Aylward allowed the China Garden to die like this? Why leave it to rot away behind its locked and blocked Moon Gates? No wonder Mai was annoyed.

One thing was certain, tomorrow she would try to get the key for her. If they could get in, it might be possible to give it at least a few more years of life, before it was all swept away for ever.

Chapter 10

The next morning, in the clear light of day, Clare wondered what on earth she had been thinking of last night. She must be crazy to imagine she could have any effect on events at Ravensmere. She was here for only a few weeks.

When she left the stables, Mai fell into step beside her. "You're going up to the House?"

"I promised to help out."

"If you've got some time, how does packing herbs grab you?"

Clare grinned. "Okay, but I'm helping Mrs Anscomb first. Listen, Mai, at the end of the rose gardens there are big iron gates with two dogs outside."

Mai looked at her alertly. "The China Garden. You found it then?"

"Last night. But the Gate was locked. Isn't there any way in?"

"I haven't found one. And there's only one key—which Mr A. looks after. Even Roger Fletcher doesn't have a key. Neither of them want it opened up."

"But why? I mean what does it matter to them if it's open or not?"

Mai shrugged. "James says Mr A. always has his reasons. But he doesn't have to give us any explanations."

"It's all overgrown," Clare said, depressed. "And the Pavilion must be falling down."

"What pavilion?"

"Why, the one in the centre of the Garden."

"Do you mean you could actually see in?"

Clare said, shamefaced, "A couple of boards fell off the inside of the Gate. I'm sorry."

Mai laughed. "Well I don't know how you managed that, it never worked for me! I'll get down there as soon as I can. I can't wait to have a look. I want to get that garden back into cultivation. I want to make a real Chinese garden. I don't like bits of my gardens going to waste. Clare, if you do get anywhere near Mr A, you will ask him about the Garden, won't you?"

"But I'm only a visitor. Why don't you ask him yourself?"

Mai grinned. "I'm a natural-born coward. Besides I've got this weird idea that he might just listen to you more than me."

They parted at the Orangery, Mai heading into the garden centre and Clare towards the kitchen entrance of the House.

Dr McKinnon's racy sports car was parked in the service yard, and Dr McKinnon herself was coming out of the staff entrance with Mr Bristow beaming behind her.

Impulsively she called, "Dr McKinnon!" and regretted it at once when she saw how grim and upset the doctor looked.

"I'm sorry, I'm interrupting. Mr Aylward—he's worse?"

"Not well and very uncomfortable. I don't know if his condition has deteriorated recently. I haven't been in this house for over twenty years. Stupid to keep up old quarrels. All over now. I've made my peace, but I feel guilty."

"My mother called you then?"

"I should have come before. He needs medical treatment, but I thought he was seeing his London doctor. What can I do for you?"

"It doesn't matter now. I can see you're upset."

"Nonsense." She pulled a large cotton handkerchief from her pocket and blew her nose. "I've known Edward Aylward since I was five. I always rather fancied him—he was a handsome young man—but, of course, we all knew he would marry Caroline Kenward. Never mind, all done with now. Come along, walk me to my car."

She extended her long thin hand to Clare. Clare put her own into it and Dr McKinnon tucked it companionably under her arm. Clare felt the deep warmth spreading up her arm and across her shoulders, a feeling of well-being.

"You're nervous and wound up still, Clare. Won't do, you know. Got to conserve your strength. Important events ahead for you."

Clare said shyly, "I . . . er . . . I'm not one of your regular patients, but I wondered if I could come and see you? Consult you, I mean. Do you have surgery hours?"

"Not necessary. We're a pretty healthy lot here. I know everyone who's ill and I visit. What's the matter? Speak up."

Clare swallowed. "I hope you won't laugh. It's a bit embarrassing. I'm . . . Well, I'm seeing things. Hallucinating. I'm frightened I'm having a breakdown."

The doctor stared at her. Her eyes were pale, almost translucent. "What things?"

Hesitating, Clare told her about all the strange incidents, from the children running across the fields, to the visions of the House, appearing and disappearing.

To her relief Dr McKinnon listened without laughing or disbelief. There was a moment's silence, then she said, "Do you remember I told you that most of the women in the village are psychic to some degree? Some outstandingly so. My late husband used to call it the second sight, but he came from Scotland."

"And some of the men, you said."

"You thought I was joking."

Clare's eyes widened. "You mean, *I'm* . . ."

"Your mother is. It passes through the female line here. Has she told you yet?"

"About being a Kenward?"

"Ah, I see she hasn't."

"She never talks about being psychic, if that's what you mean. But you're a doctor. Surely you don't believe all that stuff!"

"Clare, I'm a doctor, but I'm also a psychic healer. Like you, I have to accept that I've inherited certain . . . abilities, just as I know that my eyes are grey."

Clare was embarrassed. "I don't know what to say. I just can't believe . . ."

"They're natural abilities, you know. My theory is that we all had them in the early days. Gradually we stopped using them or didn't need them. But some people have them still. Dowsing. Telepathy. A good sense of direction, even. It's just the same as being good at sport or maths or art. You know that we only use a tiny part of our brain capacity?"

Clare laughed uneasily. "I know I do!"

"There's nothing to be worried about."

"But wouldn't I have known before? It's only since I came here."

"Perhaps something about the place woke old inherited memory in the genes, or latent abilities which you had blocked before. Are you sure you didn't have any odd experiences as a child?"

Clare was staring at her, remembering now a number of tiny incidents—of people seeming to disappear suddenly, of knowing what her friends were thinking, of looking down at herself far below in bed—all of them forgotten until now.

She felt shaken, as though a door had opened in her mind, revealing a whole new part of herself she had never even suspected was there.

"I'm all right? Not ill?"

Dr McKinnon smiled. She had the kind of smile that made you feel better just looking at her, Clare thought.

"Tired. Stressed. A bit anaemic. Not mad. Not ill. Not

hallucinating. Just more than you thought you were. Rejoice. You'll soon get used to it."

Stunned, Clare watched Dr McKinnon fold herself into her car. She leaned out. "For hundreds of years the Abbess here was chosen in a peculiar way. Come down and see me one day when you're ready. I'm writing a local history of Ravensmere. I think you'd be interested."

"Very partial Mr A. is to a bit of fish," Mrs Anscomb was saying, chopping parsley for a fish casserole. "Only eats fish and chicken. No meat since the War, you see. A great hero he was, m'dear. Though you'd not think it, him sitting so miserable now. One of the Few he was, flying them old Hurricanes in the War. There's a painting of him in his uniform."

"Sorry?" said Clare. She was sitting at the big scrubbed table in the kitchen, picking the tops off raspberries, half her mind following the flowing stream of Mrs Anscomb's comments, the other half trying to think of a way of getting to see Mr Aylward. It was not something she was looking forward to, but her conscience would not let her remain comfortably silent. Somehow she must speak to him personally. All her instincts were telling her it was vitally important, not just to ask him to let Mai open the China Garden, but also to make a last-ditch effort to stop the destruction of Ravensmere. She must tell him what Roger Fletcher was doing. He might tell her to mind her own business, but at least she would have done what she could.

"Sorry?" Clare said again.

"The painting," Mrs Anscomb repeated patiently. She was used to only half the attention of her listeners.

"I didn't see it on the tour."

"It's in the South Drawing Room. My mother always said he were such a sad little fellow. Only had his Grandpa Eldon, and a strange one *he* was, always digging about for old bones."

Clare grinned. It was a good thing Mrs Potts-Dyrham

couldn't hear her disrespectful comments about the author of the ten-volume *Evolutionary History*.

"What happened to his father and mother?"

"His father fell at Ypres in the First World War. There's his memorial in the church. Another hero, they say, but if you ask me it was a lucky escape for Ravensmere." She looked sideways at Clare. "Women. And gambling in the south of France with the Prince of Wales set. He had a vicious temper. When he went off to France his wife ran away to London, and refused to come back although the old Earl begged her to for the boy's sake. She died sudden in the great flu epidemic after the War."

"Mr Aylward lost his wife, too, didn't he?"

"He's never been lucky in love, poor man. He married his childhood sweetheart, and she died only a year after they were married. It changed him, my mother always said. Got very bitter. His second marriage didn't do nothing for him neither. That were a funny business. Very *sudden*.

"We never thought he would marry again. But his cousin was killed at Dunkirk, and he up and married Cecily Carlton-Winters the following week, and went off to the War two days later. All the village thought he'd, like, got her in the family way, but t'werent so—Brandon weren't born till a good few years after the War.

"A very posh lady, she were. Foreigner to these parts, you know, came from Westbury way. Didn't care for the House or the village. Didn't understand our ways."

Mrs Anscomb slammed the oven door on her casserole, and began to assemble the ingredients for pastry-making.

Clare watched her. Maybe she could speak to Mr Aylward in the garden—if he ever went in the garden, of course. Roger Fletcher would be back soon and it would be even more difficult to get to see him.

Clare washed the raspberries under the clear, icy water. Spring water. Even the water was different here. She drained them and stood the bowl on the table. There must be some way she could get to see Mr Aylward and introduce herself. Maybe she should write a letter to him. But how good was his eyesight? Did somebody read his letters to him? Probably her mother. She'd never get a letter past her mother.

"She weren't liked, you know," Mrs Anscomb was saying. "Very unhappy they were. Rows could be heard in the kitchen. You'd see her galloping away up on the old moor. Wild blood in the Carlton family, they say. Broke her neck she did, out with the Hunt, and no one surprised about that or regretting her, to be truthful."

Clare felt a twinge of sympathy for Cecily Carlton-Winters. It couldn't have been easy, trying to fill the place of an adored childhood sweetheart. Second-best and hated by all the staff.

Mrs Anscomb shook her head. "Marry in haste." She sprinkled flour on to her board and swiftly rolled out the pastry, tipped it over and rolled again.

"It was the succession, I should think," Clare said, getting interested. "His cousin was probably his heir. If he was going off to the War he maybe thought he might get killed himself. He needed a son."

Mrs Anscomb nodded sagely. "That'll be the way of it. But you can't change fate, I always say."

"But he did have a son. What happened to him?"

Mrs Anscomb seemed to be concentrating on her pastry. She lifted it, filled the base of the dish, tipped in the raspberries, and covered them, deftly pinching and shaping the pastry into flowers and fluting the edge.

"That's fantastic," Clare said, admiringly.

Mrs Anscomb laughed. "Sixty years' practice makes perfect."

"What happened to Brandon Aylward?" Clare asked again, gathering up the pastry things, determined to get an answer this time.

Mrs Anscomb hesitated. "I told you, Mr A. don't like him

106

mentioned. Very angry he was when he died. He had an accident."

"He was *angry*!"

"I've never known him so angry." She shivered. "Oh well, it's all water under the bridge now. I shouldn't talk to your mother about Brandon either, Clare m'dear. Very painful subject it is to a lot of people."

"But why . . . ?"

Mrs Anscomb glanced up at the big clock on the wall. "Well, well, it's nearly eleven o'clock. How time do fly. Time for elevenses."

Rapidly she began to lay out a silver tray with a lacy cloth, cups and teapot.

"Very partial to a cup of tea is Mr A. Never liked coffee. Always the China tea and a couple of my oatcakes. Lapsang Souchong. Tastes funny to me, but it wouldn't do if we were all the same."

She poured steaming water into the pot. "You could help me by taking the tray up to him, m'dear, if you don't mind. He'll be out on the terrace in his wheelchair, taking the sun."

Clare gaped at her, unable to believe she had heard right. "Take Mr Aylward his tea?"

"You don't mind, m'dear? I want to finish off here. It's easy to find. There's a service lift at the end of the corridor, direct to Mr A's own dining room. And there's a door on to the terrace. It won't take you a few minutes."

"No, that's all right. No problem." Clare could have kissed her. She couldn't believe it was going to be so easy, after all.

Chapter 11

The door of the lift opened on to a small service area and Clare went through into Mr Aylward's private dining room. The room was smaller than the Great Dining Room she had seen yesterday, but not much.

It had a big oval table in the exact centre, on a Persian carpet woven to the same shape, but its chairs were set back against the gold-damask covered walls, and the bare top of the table had a film of dust. It was a long time since there had been a dinner party here, Clare thought.

She could hear raised voices. She rested the heavy tray on the table, and saw that the french doors at the end were open to the terrace. She hesitated nervously. Should she knock on the window or something, or wait until the shouting match was finished? She moved forward cautiously.

"Bring the girl to me here!" The voice was bell-like and strong, modulated like a great actor's.

She could see him clearly through the door. Mr Aylward was sitting in his wheelchair next to an ornamental iron table, newspapers and books scattered around him on the stone paving, as though he had thrown them down impatiently.

"Bring her here! *Here* I say." He thumped the paving with his stick, frustrated, like a child. "I want to see her."

He was a big man. Even huddled under the rugs he was tall, broad shouldered, with long arms and legs folded into the wheelchair, which seemed too small for him. Once upon a time he must have been huge, Clare thought. His face was

strongly boned, hawkish, handsome even now in old age.
There was a strong family likeness to the paintings she had
seen yesterday. He had the same arrogance, the same sar-
donic amusement, but there was a bitterness about the mouth,
not softened by the heavy white hair almost to his shoulders.

Clare had expected someone withered and very old, but
he hardly looked his age. A powerful and angry man, she
thought, swallowing. Did she really need to speak to him?
Wasn't there any other way? It was absurd to be afraid of a
sick old man of eighty-seven, but she was afraid, all the same.

Her mother was standing next to him, looking strained,
her hands clenched on a chairback.

"Mr Aylward, I don't think that's a good idea."

"Did I ask you to think? Just fetch the girl. You brought
her with you. I know she's here."

Clare realized, with a shock, that he was talking about *her*.
She moved back quickly behind the thick brocade curtains
that framed the windows.

Frances said sourly, "I didn't bring her. She came of her
own accord."

Mr Aylward grunted with satisfaction. "I thought so. It
goes on."

"I'm not having her involved. She's going to university in
October. That's what she wants."

"She was sniffing around the China Garden last night."

Clare flushed. How on earth did he know that? You
couldn't see the Garden from this wing. It looked south to
the lake, not west to the gardens.

Frances was clearly shaken. "I don't believe you. She was
in her room all night."

"Trying to get through the First Gate. She's ready. It's
the time. The cycle begins again."

"No!" Frances' voice rose. "I won't have her involved."

"You have no choice. Surely you understand that after all
these years?"

"She's going to university," Frances said obstinately. "She has a right to her own life."

"She's the Kenward daughter. The Chosen."

"Over my dead body," said Frances wildly. "She's not to be told."

There was a tense silence and then Edward Aylward said in a low strange voice that made Clare's blood freeze in her veins. "If you obstruct them, Frances, it may well be over your dead body. You know that. Haven't you learned your lesson?"

"She's not to be told," said Frances again. "It's all a lot of nonsense."

Clare could hear the note of hysteria in her voice. She was close to breaking point. Clare was suddenly furious. This dreadful man was actually threatening her mother.

She retreated silently, picked up the tea tray and carried it swiftly out to the terrace. She banged it down on the table by Edward Aylward's side, and straightened, pushing the hair back from her face, so that her accusing eyes met his fiercely, and got a shock of surprise. His eyes were bright green, as brilliant as emeralds, astonishingly young in the networked folds of his dark old skin.

"Clare!" Her mother exploded angrily. "You have no right to be here."

"Mrs Anscomb sent me."

There was a series of strange, croaking sounds coming from Mr Aylward. Clare moved forward, alarmed, but Frances put out her arm, her face icy. "Mr Aylward is amused. Since you're here, you'd better pour the tea."

Clare stared at him, the angry colour high on her cheeks. "Why are you threatening my mother? Why are you laughing at me?"

"Not you, young woman," he said, recovering. "The irony of fate, destiny, call it what you will. You laugh or you cry. I've always laughed. Where did you get that dark red hair?"

"It's black, not red," Clare said, her colour deepening. She felt uncomfortable with red-haired people. They always seemed so extrovert and free—not at all like herself.

"It's black with dark-red lights. Do you think I'm blind? What's your name?"

Clare swallowed. There was a frightening aura of power about him, and a strangeness which she could not identify. The brilliant green eyes stared at her, sharply alive and penetrating.

Frances said tightly, "This is my daughter, Mr Aylward. She seems to be helping Mrs Anscomb today."

"What's the matter with her? Can't she answer for herself?" He hadn't taken his eyes off Clare and she stared back, half-hypnotized. "Well?"

"I'm Clare, sir. Clare Meredith." She swallowed again, annoyed with herself for speaking to him as though he was her old headmaster.

An odd expression shadowed his face and was gone. His eyes moved sideways to Frances, blandly. "Clare . . . *Meredith?*"

Frances said angrily, "My husband's name. As you know. Clare is only seventeen, Mr Aylward."

"What's your second name, girl?" Once again, the question shot at her, caught her off-guard. There was a queer note in his voice and he was sitting forward gripping the arms of his chair.

"Clare. Just Clare."

He looked at Frances and waited, like a judge, pinning her with dagger green eyes.

Her mother shifted uncomfortably and said reluctantly, "She's Clare Rosamond."

"Ah!" He sank back in his chair.

Clare stared at her mother, and could hardly believe she had heard correctly. *She had another name.* Rosamond. It made her feel very odd. A different person. A stranger to

III

herself. She felt very upset. No wonder her birth certificate had always been unavailable, locked in the bank with the other family papers.

"*Why?*" she said to her mother, but Frances turned her head away.

"After your mother. It's a family name. It's the tradition." Edward Aylward sounded amused.

"You're Rosamond too?" Clare said to her mother.

Frances said bleakly, "I left Rosamond behind. I changed my name."

"You should have told me my real name," said Clare trying to keep the hurt out of her voice, but her mother was looking at Edward Aylward angrily.

"I hope you're satisfied. You're so clever, but don't think it makes any difference. She's only staying here until she goes to university. She's not getting involved. Do you hear? I won't have it. She's free and she's staying that way."

He smiled, ruefully, charmingly. "Dear Frances, you still can't accept, can you? I tell you that we are not able to choose."

The smile transformed his face. Clare blinked and saw a much younger Edward Aylward looking at her with a handsome, hard face, reckless and laughing, with those strange magnetic eyes. The image faded and the older man was there again instantly, smiling at her as though he knew.

Frances said bitterly, "Well, *you've* changed your tune, Mr Aylward. When did *you* accept?"

"I learned by experience. I came back—eventually."

"Well, I got free," Frances said proudly. "I made my own choice. I made a good life." The colour was flaming in her high cheek bones, the emotion sizzling off her like electricity.

Edward Aylward smiled derisively. "Did you, Frances Rosamond Kenward, Guardian of the Benison? What then are you doing here?"

"You know why. I came because you needed me," she said wildly. "I came to help you."

His eyes seemed to be glimmering with light. He shook his head. "To expiate. To atone. You broke the sacred Trust, Frances."

For a moment Frances held her ground, her eyes locked in battle with his, and then tears spilled over and ran down her face. She turned swiftly and ran through the dining room.

"What have you done to her?" Clare cried and turned to go after her.

His raised voice stopped her. "Let her go. She needs to cry. She needs to accept and to mourn. It's been a long time. Bring that chair here and sit down."

Clare hesitated, then moved the chair forward.

"I don't understand any of this," she said wearily, sitting down. "I never even knew I had another name. Why keep it secret?"

"It's a special name. One Rosamond in every generation. It means 'famous protectress'. You may pour me a cup of tea. No sugar."

Clare had forgotten the elevenses. She thought the tea was probably cold by now, but she hastily filled one of the fine bone china cups and handed it to him. His fingers were long, and seemingly all bones and skin. The cup and saucer trembled. He crunched one of Mrs Anscomb's oat cakes, and stared out over the balustrade to the Great Lake laying below the curve of the lawn, shining like a mirror in the morning sunlight.

Clare wondered if now was a good time to introduce the subject of the China Garden, and make her appeal to save Ravensmere.

She said, instead, putting off the difficult moment, "What is that tower, up on the hill, the other side of the lake?"

The green eyes swivelled back to her, gleaming with humour. "The Tower of Freedom and Justice. Erected by the Twelfth Earl to commemorate the American and French Revolutions—and to irritate his neighbours, no doubt. He was an interesting character. He had to marry hastily at seventeen, but his wife died in childbirth soon after. He ran away to America in 1785, leaving his son behind. Then he eloped to France with a wealthy Dutch heiress, Hannah Van Buren, was active in the French Revolution, became a member of the National Assembly of 1791, which issued the Declaration of the Rights of Man, and finally joined Napoleon in Italy. He refused the Trust, of course. Didn't believe in hereditary titles. Came back for his father's funeral, stayed for six weeks and was drowned in the Channel in a freak storm on his way back to France. An eventful life, you might say."

Clare smiled. "Mrs Potts-Dyrham didn't tell us about him yesterday."

"His son Edmund Edward was responsible for the Library. He built it to house his father's collection of revolutionary writings, but he was a great collector of paintings and books himself."

The green eyes watched her speculatively.

"So. What subject are you reading at university?"

"Economics and Computer Science."

He shook his head. "Not for you."

"I worked hard for my A-levels. I think I've passed."

"You've passed, but you won't take up that place." His voice was even, certain.

Clare stared at him and could not look away from the brilliant eyes which seemed to widen and deepen.

"What were you doing at the China Garden last night?"

"I . . . How did you know I was there?"

He said, cryptically, "I haven't lost all my faculties yet."

"But you can't see the China Garden from here."

He smiled. "There are more than five senses, Clare."

She shivered. "I wasn't doing any harm, just wandering around. I wanted to go in, but it was locked and all the Moon

Gates are blocked." She took a deep breath and plunged in, "It's awful to see it so overgrown. I was talking to Mai Lee, your Head Gardener, and . . . well, we'd like to open it up and restore it. Make it look beautiful again, like the rest of the gardens. I said I would . . . ask you for the key."

There was a long silence. He seemed to have shrunk in on himself, his eyes hooded, like a very old roosting bird. Clare waited uneasily.

Eventually he said, "When they took my Caroline I swore I would have my revenge. I would let it all go."

Clare said, groping, "Your first wife?"

"My life ended when she died. Whatever I did, nothing but emptiness."

"But you were in the War. You had a son."

"The son of my second wife. She was a Kenward on her grandmother's side, so I thought it would serve. But she was no use. And Brandon refused the Trust and died. All waste and devastation. A wasted life."

Clare wondered if he meant his own life or his son's life.

"I closed the China Garden, bricked up the Fourth Moon Gate, and I let it fall into ruin deliberately."

Clare said, slowly, absolutely sure now, "You know about Roger Fletcher, don't you? About what he's doing? Letting things run down. Sacking the staff. Trying to sell off your books. Bringing in the archaeologists. Do you know what he intends to do with Ravensmere and the village when he inherits?"

"I believe he intends to sell it to Nuclear Energy."

"You do know! It will destroy everything here. The farms. The countryside. Everything. They'll use it for a nuclear dumping ground. Don't you care?"

His eyes were fixed on her. "He says we must move with the times. Capitalize on resources. The days of the estates are over."

Clare felt the terrible despair wash over her. It was what

she would have said herself before she came here. "Please, please, don't do it. It's all wrong. Evil. Please think again."

"What's it to you? You don't live here. You're going away."

Clare stared at him. She didn't know why she cared so much. She said at last, "I . . . just know it's dreadfully wrong. I'm only a visitor, but I can't bear to think of all this beauty . . . broken . . . ruined." She gestured at the great bowl of hills, with the tree-fringed lake lying at its heart. "How can you want to destroy so much? Just because your wife died. Thousands of people lose the people they love, but they don't try to destroy the Earth for revenge."

"No, they destroy for less creditable reasons—money, power, nationalism, greed. You think that's better?"

"No. Well, I don't think so. I've not begun to think about all that yet. But once it's destroyed, it's destroyed, isn't it, whatever the reason? I only know that Ravensmere is a special place. You can feel it. You'll laugh, but I think it is a sacred place. You can't let it happen."

"A place of beauty, and power. And terror. You do not know yet the great burden."

His eyes seemed to have filmed over. He sat hunched and unmoving, deep in his mind, in a time and place long ago.

Clare was silent too, hardly daring to breathe.

Suddenly he was struggling with the rugs, trying to push them away. He thrust his hand into an inner pocket of his jacket, and pulled out a key.

"Here!" He tossed it across the table. It slid over the wrought iron top on to the paving stones of the terrace and skittered to her feet. Clare picked it up and stood holding it, turning it hesitantly. It was a beautiful key, brass, intricately patterned with a double spiral at the top.

There was a difference in the air, a silence, a holding back. Clare looked up and saw that he was watching her.

"You're sure?" She was frightened, knowing that whatever he said she wouldn't be able to give the key back to him. It clung to her fingers, heavy and warm, a powerful force holding her. Whatever happened she must keep the key and open the China Garden.

"The cycle is starting again. I have no choice. They are too strong for me."

He closed his eyes and lay back in his wheelchair. His skin was an unhealthy grey and violet. He suddenly looked tired and very old.

Clare said, alarmed, "Are you all right, sir? Can I get you anything?"

"You can fetch your mother. I'm ready to go in."

Feeling guilty, Clare quickly collected the tray and made for the door. Then she hesitated.

"My mother—you said she'd come to expiate, to atone. What for? What did she do wrong?"

For a moment she thought he was not going to answer, then he said, slowly, "She killed my son."

Clare wanted to laugh. She said disbelieving, "You're not trying to tell me my mother is a murderess? She can't even kill a moth, let alone a person. Mrs Anscomb said your son died in an accident."

Clare thought, he's old. He's wandering in his mind.

He opened his eyes, and there was no sign of madness or weakness, only the inimical green glitter. "I may have phrased that badly. My son Brandon died by his own hand. He committed suicide. Your mother was responsible for his death."

Chapter 12

Her mother was in the big kitchen, her eyes red, sitting at the table drinking coffee, with Mrs Anscomb fussing around her.

Clare said coldly, "He's not well. He wants to come in."

Frances got up quickly, avoiding Clare's eyes. "He's exhausted himself. I told him he wasn't well enough to be up."

"He said you killed his son," Clare said evenly.

There was silence in the kitchen. After an exclamation even Mrs Anscomb didn't speak. Clare could hear a blackbird singing outside the open window.

Frances pulled herself up, her face stony. "Bran killed himself. He was the next Guardian. He knew what he had to do. But he couldn't accept it. He tried to leave Ravensmere for good. And he died. It was his own fault. Not my fault. *Not.*"

She sounded desperate, as though she was repeating stubbornly something she had told herself many times for her own sanity but didn't quite believe any more.

There was a long silence, then she spoke again, the words forced out of her at last. "But he left because of me. It was my fault he left. I suppose . . . in that way . . . I killed him. I failed the Trust too."

She walked out of the kitchen, very pale, but somehow more impressive than Clare had ever seen her before.

"She were more sinned against than sinning," said Mrs

Anscomb, angrily banging the coffee cups in the sink. "T'weren't her fault. Not any of it!"

Clare stared after her. "This Trust they keep talking about, what is it?"

"She was to have been the Guardian. Her and Brandon Aylward together. The two new Guardians, after Mr Aylward, of course."

"But what were they supposed to be guarding?"

"Why, the Benison, of course. For hundreds of years there've always been the two Guardians looking after it. The two families, Aylwards and Kenwards. And before that they do say t'was they old nuns in the Abbey."

"But I thought Henry VIII had the Benison taken to London, where it disappeared."

Mrs Anscomb looked sly. "Depends what the Benison is, don't it? We say, 'God's in the ground at Ravensmere'. They'd never have let it leave the Abbey."

"Do you mean it's still here? That people have seen it and know where it is? Mrs Potts-Dyrham said it was a golden bowl."

Mrs Anscomb laughed. "Bless you, how would we know if it's a bowl? Only the Guardians know what the Benison is. They say they tell the Aylward heir when he's twenty-one, you know, like the secret of Glamis Castle, and he tells his bride, the other Guardian."

"So only the Aylwards and Kenwards know? No one in the village?"

"That's their job. That's what the names mean—awe-inspiring guardian and royal guardian. They guard the Benison. In the village . . . well, we look after Ravensmere and guard the Guardians. That's *our* job. And the Benison looks after all of us."

Clare said, incredulously, "But it's just an old bowl you've never seen and which may not even exist."

The smile disappeared from Mrs Anscomb's face. She

looked at Clare, her bright blue eyes very intense. "Oh, it exists, m'dear, the Benison. Never doubt it. A most sacred and holy Trust, passed on from generation to generation and we have to look after it. There's not a soul in the village who'd disagree."

"You don't really think it's the Holy Grail?" Clare tried to keep the disbelief out of her voice. Mrs Anscomb turned, putting the china away on the huge dresser.

"A most sacred and holy Trust," she repeated stubbornly. "That's what my old granny told me. And that's what we all believe."

"And that's why my mother feels so bad? She said she failed the Trust."

"T'were none of her doing." Mrs Anscomb sat down. "He tried to go away. The Guardians have to stay. Oh, they can go away for a while, but they have to come back. They have to *accept*. If they try to go for good . . . if they refuse to accept the Trust, well, they don't seem to last long if you see what I mean. They all know that, but some of them don't believe it until it's too late."

The goosebumps rose on Clare's arms. She remembered the Sixth Earl, running away and dying in a ditch; the Ninth Earl refusing to marry his Kenward bride and dying in a duel; the Revolutionary Earl drowning in the Channel . . . and Darren's mum asking if there was a family curse.

"B-but that's superstition. Just co-incidence," she stammered. "My mother left. She didn't die."

Mrs Anscomb shrugged. "She weren't married. Didn't know the secret of the Benison. Brandon never told her before he died. It all happened too quick. I tell you, m'dear, I wouldn't like to chance it myself."

As Clare crossed the service yard Mai pounced on her, laughing and jubilant. "You got the key to the China Garden then. That was really fast work."

Clare stared at her. "Yes, but how did you know?"

"Because it was unlocked, of course, dumbo."

Clare opened her hand slowly and showed Mai the key. "Mr Aylward only just gave it me."

"But it was already open when I went along earlier," Mai said, mystified. "The boards were off as you said and one of the iron gates was half open. I thought *you* . . ."

Clare shook her head. "I did everything I could to open it, but it was all rusted up."

"Weirdsville," said Mai. "Maybe you loosened it, or one of the boys had a go. I'll ask around. Anyway it doesn't matter if Mr A. himself has given you the key. We can start cutting down the hayfield."

Clare's excitement surged back. "You've been in?"

"Only a quick look. I'll get John and Billy started in there this afternoon with the strimmers, and we'll see what we've got under all that lot. James will be pleased. Do you want to have lunch with us? Only cheese sandwiches, I'm afraid, but you're welcome."

"No, no thanks. I think I'll take a look at the China Garden first. I'll see you later."

Clare could not have explained, but suddenly the need to see the Garden, the need actually to go in, was so great that she could think of nothing else.

She made her way along the gravelled forecourt and through the rose garden, a blaze of colour today, alive with bees, under the noon-day heat. Even the fearsome guardian dogs looked almost benign. One of the two iron gates that had been rusted together last night was partially open. She took the shallow step up into the circle and went through the First Moon Gate.

Inside the huge space, the grass grew waist high, full of poppies, buttercups and dandelions. There had been no rain for several weeks and the grass was tawny and parched.

The ground was irregular, full of humps like miniature

hills and valleys. Around the tall walls there was a raised bank, and in the centre on a higher mound was the octagonal Chinese Pavilion. She could see now that it was badly in need of repair. Spars had fallen from the roof, the trellised sides were hanging loose, and the steps up to it were splintered. Once it had been painted red and gold, turquoise and blue, but most of the paint had peeled away. Cautiously Clare picked her way to it, along what appeared to be a raised path over a sunken area, and sat down on the lower of its two steps.

She looked around, angry again with Mr Aylward. There seemed to be nothing left of the original Garden.

The tall walls were almost obscured by rambling roses and clematis, and small trees and bushes woven with ivy and bindweed. Above them the top of the wall, curiously tiled, curled up and down like a serpent. Her eyes followed the wall around, and stopped, delighted. Not a snake—a *dragon*. Two dragons. There they were, curled around the top of the wall, with their splendid heads meeting either side of the First Moon Gate.

She could see the other Moon Gates more clearly now. Each of them was framed with smooth dark marble, set into the creamy pink stone of the wall. But as she had found last night they were all blocked or overgrown.

The midday sun burned down, bouncing off the walls and the golden grass. It was like being inside a great bubble of light, cut off from the rest of the world, she thought, and felt suddenly drowsy. It was so hot there seemed to be a thrumming in the air.

She leaned back and looked again at the Moon Gates. There were three on one side of the octagon, and three on the other with one blank wall opposite the First Moon Gate. Each had its scroll of Chinese letters over it, and its carved and gilded number.

The Second Moon Gate was to the right, half-hidden

behind a pile of logs and small tree trunks. A rambling rose with thorns at least an inch long rioted over the Third Moon Gate. The deep red roses were huge, and she could smell their glorious perfume even from where she was sitting.

The Fourth Moon Gate had been completely bricked up. Mr Aylward's orders, she remembered. But why only that Gate? Why not all of them?

Then there was the blank section of the wall. An ancient fig tree as thick as a python twisted through the Fifth Moon Gate.

The Sixth Moon Gate was blocked by a pile of rubble, chunks of marble and huge stones like crumbling holed cheese. Something had been knocked down. Could there have been a fountain or a stone basin there?

The next Gate, in the wall to the left of the First Moon Gate, was the strangest of all. It was only an imitation Gate. It had its dark marble surround, and its inscription, but there had never been a real opening. The centre of the circle was the pinkish surface of the original wall itself. 'Seven', Clare read. *The Seventh Moon Gate.* She had been right. There were seven Gates. Six real Moon Gates and one pretend one.

She got up and moved slowly around the Pavilion over the uneven ground, pushing her way through the long grass. It was so quiet, suddenly, even the birds and bees seemed to be taking a siesta. She walked around again, trying to see clearly, dazzled in the white blaze of sunlight, an expanding arc of light.

The Third Moon Gate was not blocked after all.

She could have sworn that this one had the red roses with the big thorns. How could she have made such a mistake?

The Gate was open. Framed in its circle she could see Stoke Raven village, with its ancient buildings and the Market Cross set in the centre. It seemed very close. She could see the dew damping the cobbles and the early morning heat mist just lifting. Lounging on motor bikes on the steps of the

Cross was a group of leather-clad bikers. They were laughing, ribbing each other, *waiting*. As Clare watched, another motorcyclist appeared, swooped around them, shouting, and accelerated away. In a moment the others, whooping, were streaming after him.

Her head was banging, her brain swimming in the intense heat. She rubbed her forehead and stared at the Third Moon Gate.

There was no opening. The rambler rose was there, blocking it completely.

She drew in a slow breath. Even if the Gate was clear, she could not have seen Stoke Raven. The village was deep in the valley. Between the China Garden and the village lay the whole of Ravensmere's park, and the boundary wall.

She felt sick with fear. It was happening again, the hallucinating. All very well for Dr McKinnon to say it was a natural ability and nothing to worry about, but she couldn't stop shaking. Maybe it was just the heat. Maybe she had dropped off to sleep for a moment and dreamed. Maybe.

Chapter 13

"Do you fancy a day out tomorrow?" Frances asked
that evening. "I need some nursing supplies, and Sarah
McKinnon left prescriptions for Mr Aylward."

"Where would I go?" asked Clare, surprised.

"Well, there are buses to Wells and Bath, but if you want
to go further, there's a special bus from the village tomorrow
to Salisbury for market-day. You'd like Salisbury, it's an interesting city."

"All right," said Clare, without enthusiasm.

She had been intending to help Mai in the China Garden,
and she felt cool towards her mother, and disinclined to help.
They had hardly spoken to each other over the evening meal.
Clare was finding it difficult to forgive Frances for not telling
her the truth about her name. She felt uncomfortable with
her too. It was as though her mother had turned into a
stranger, with whole areas of her life and experience a
mystery.

But for Mr Aylward she was prepared to put herself out
quite considerably. It surprised her that she liked him so
much. Despite their differences and his autocratic manner
she wanted to talk to him again.

The next day there were four women waiting to board the
Salisbury bus outside the Sun and Moon Inn. They greeted
Clare politely, and said what a fine day it promised to be
when the morning heat mist lifted.

She was uneasily aware that there was a strange note in

their voices—respect, reverence almost—and when the bus came she went quickly to the back seat and looked out of the window.

It was a long and interesting drive. The bus threaded the narrow lanes and wound in and out of villages and small towns, picking up cheerful, chattering shoppers.

The bustle and crowded liveliness of Salisbury's market-day came as a shock to her after the tranquility of Ravensmere. Clare grimaced. She had always thought of herself as a big-city girl, but only a few days at Ravensmere had turned her into a hayseed.

"Four o'clock return, ladies," said the bus driver. "Not a moment later. I'm off sharp, remember. Last bus back, four o'clock."

She saw the chemist almost at once, and handed in the medical prescriptions with her mother's list of urgently required nursing supplies and they promised to have them ready for her to collect after lunch.

The market-place was alive with traders and stalls, and Clare wandered around the shops, enjoying the timbered fronts leaning over the pavements, the narrow alleys full of ancient shops stocked with modern goods.

She tried on a pair of spectacular jeans which fitted her like a dream. But every penny she had saved from her Saturday job at the bakers was needed for university. Besides, she didn't wear jeans now, did she? Adrian didn't like them. He thought she should sharpen up her image as a future businesswoman with smart dark suits.

She looked at herself in the mirror wistfully. The jeans felt so comfortable and free after her tight skirt, and Adrian wasn't here anyway. Now that she was away from him she realized that she had often felt uneasy about his opinions. She was fed up with his sulkiness, and having her own ideas derided and dismissed. There was nothing to stop her deciding for herself now. She could be herself. She wouldn't be

seeing Adrian again. If he wrote to her she wouldn't answer.
"I'll take them," she said to the assistant.

"They look good on you. Long legs. They're a good buy."

"I'll keep them on," said Clare. "But could you give me a bag for my skirt?"

She sauntered out of the shop and caught a glimpse of herself in another shop window with satisfaction. She looked good and felt free and alive. No more being pushed around like a timid mouse, because she was afraid he would dump her. She was the one doing the dumping, and never again would she allow any boy to tell her what to think and what to do, no matter how good-looking and popular he was.

Down a narrow street under an ancient town gate Clare discovered a sign which said 'Museum'. It was irresistible. As a history buff—her best friend said history *nut*—she had always loved museums.

She followed the path, staring at the splendid old mansions surrounding the Close until she became conscious of something behind her and, turning, lost her breath. Across the grass was the gigantic cathedral, with its towering spire like a spaceship rearing up into the space above it. She stared at it disbelievingly. She had forgotten that Salisbury had a cathedral. There it was, just like the print of the Constable painting on the school library wall. But in real life it was so much bigger and higher and grander, almost frightening.

Inside it seemed empty and vast, the space spreading and soaring upwards. Her eyes were drawn higher and higher. Incredible to think that this place had been built nearly eight hundred years ago, without any of the modern building technology, all the stones cut by hand, carved and built up piece by piece. The sun shone through the great window, pooling the floor with coloured light. She felt surrounded by the space, ever expanding space, and she was a tiny atom, not separate, but part of a whole, a glistening three-dimensional web, full of movement and energy.

She closed her eyes and was suddenly moving upwards, flowing in a silvery substance, not air, not water, but something between the two. She felt the movement, the slow turn of herself in the air, like a dance. She opened her eyes and saw her body far below, tiny, with a woman in a scarlet jacket coming across the floor to stand next to her. Panic swept over her and the next instant she was in her body again, standing on the stone floor and the woman in the scarlet jacket was smiling at her.

"Beautiful, isn't it?"

Speechless, Clare nodded.

"Are you all right? You look a bit peaky."

"Giddy," Clare croaked. "Think I'd better get some fresh air." She walked away stiffly, gratefully feeling the strength coming back into her wobbly knees.

Outside she gulped in the clear air, with its hint of flowers and grass cuttings, and almost in a trance she crossed the green, and found the museum opposite in another old mansion, the King's House.

Salisbury Museum was just the sort Clare enjoyed most, full of every-day things that people had made and used. As she wandered around the galleries, smiling at the pageant figure of the Salisbury Giant and his companion, a huge cross-looking chicken-like creature called Hob Nob, admiring the costumes, and staring at the stuffed Great Bustards, she began to come to terms with what had happened to her in the cathedral.

If Dr McKinnon was right she must begin to expect these strange happenings. They were uncomfortable, but they didn't actually harm her, did they? In a way they were even interesting.

She found she was looking at a display of archaeological exhibits, the Pitt Rivers Collection. Where had she heard that name recently? Obediently her mind clicked up the information. Mr Aylward's grandfather who had written the ten volumes, had been a friend of General Pitt Rivers.

The wooden painted models of excavations done throughout Wessex fascinated her.

On an impulse, Clare asked the attendant about the excavation at Ravensmere.

"In the other gallery. Try in the corner."

It was there with its photographs and details. 'Barrow Beacon Hill Excavation, Long Barrow, 1895', Clare read avidly, amused at the pictures of Victorian gentlemen in their shirt sleeves and waist coats and long moustaches, staring sternly at the camera from a deep trench of gleaming mud. The caption said, 'Lieutenant-General Pitt Rivers with Eldon Edgar Aylward, Sixteenth Earl of Ravensmere, Site Foreman Silas Kenward and estate workers'.

Two of the five burial chambers in the long barrow had been excavated for the first time, revealing seven burials with grave goods, including pottery of a hitherto unknown kind, and astonishingly a large goblet finely carved from quartz crystal, an object which could not possibly have been made by people living at that period. The Earl had then stopped the excavation.

"Inclement weather," said the letter in the glass case. But the dig never started again. The site had been filled in and despite the General's appeals, it had never been re-opened. The pottery and the goblet had been retained in the Earl's private collection, said the display label.

They might be somewhere in the Etruscan Gallery, thought Clare. She would ask about them. Why had the Earl stopped the dig? Was the quartz crystal goblet the famous Benison?

Clare looked at the carved wooden model again, and saw to her surprise that Ravensmere itself was not shown. According to this model, the House didn't even exist!

Somewhere a clock chimed musically. Clare looked at her

watch. If she hurried she just had time to grab a coffee and a bun before she picked up the supplies at the chemist and caught the bus home.

But back in the town centre a small second-hand bookshop tucked away in a narrow street tempted her. She picked out a couple of romantic paperbacks from the box outside—she was entitled to a little fun reading after all that studying. Adrian had jeered at her reading romances. In a dusty corner upstairs she came across a very old dog-eared pamphlet, *An Account of a Visit to the Pleasure Gardens of Ravensmere, lately completed by Edmund Aylward, Eleventh Earl of Ravensmere*, which the owner sold to her for a pound.

Three doors away Clare found a café. It was small, with a dirty window and a smeared board outside. She looked at her watch again. It was too late to look for somewhere else. The place was empty, and at least she would be served quickly.

The hostile girl behind the counter gave her a cup of scalding, near-black coffee and a piece of wrapped fruitcake, and Clare took them to a table in the corner by the window.

The cake was stale. But even this was not enough to dent Clare's feeling of cheerful well-being as she sat staring out of the window. It was a long time since she'd enjoyed a day as much, even though she had been on her own. Perhaps it was because she *was* alone, with no critical Adrian following her around. She could just imagine him looking at the cathedral and saying loftily, "Well, of course, it's not bad—if you haven't seen Rheims or Chartres, that is . . ." Grinning, she wondered what he would say about her recent psychic experiences, and realized that a heavy weight had gone from her life. It had all been a mistake. She could admit that now.

The door swung back, bashed against the wall, and five huge bikers boiled into the café, a frightening mass of black leather and silver studs. They were laughing and shouting at the girl for cans of Coke and hamburgers.

Clare slid down in her seat, her heart jerking unpleasantly, annoyed with herself. Of all the cafés in Salisbury, why on earth had she picked a bikers' hang out? She quickly swallowed her piece of cake and pushed the coffee away. She would get out now, before they noticed her and started something.

It was too late. Even as she reached for her carrier bag, they spread themselves over the surrounding tables, penning her into her corner.

"Well, well, see who I've found."

Clare's heart sank. She looked around for help, but the girl behind the counter was giggling and being chatted-up by the bikers' leader, and wouldn't help anyway.

She pretended to look out of the window. Perhaps if she ignored them they might find something else to interest them, but the next moment one of them leaned across her line of vision and said in a posh falsetto, "Excuse me, darling. Can you tell me the time?" and started to laugh like a maniac.

Clare was forced to look round. They were all staring at her, grinning. She stood up. "Excuse me, I've got to catch a bus."

"You're a long way from home, darling," he said and stretched one leg across the space between the tables, blocking her exit. He was a burly youth, with a red face, a button nose and a thatch of tow-coloured hair.

"There you are, Pete, I told you it was her," said one of the others. He was the shortest, with a sharp nose and too-close eyes.

"I said I've got to get a bus. Are you going to let me pass?" Clare said tersely.

But Pete didn't move. He just continued to stare at her, mocking and grinning. A wave of anger flowed over Clare. She tried to step over his leg and then tripped as he moved his other foot swiftly to curl round her ankle. He caught her shoulder and tipped her back into her chair.

"Careful, darling. You're not leaving us already? Not without saying hello."

"Don't want to know us peasants," sneered the foxy-faced one. "Stuck up."

"What are you on about?" Clare said, furiously. "I've got to catch the bus. And I *don't* know you. I've never seen you be . . ." Her voice died away. It wasn't true. She had seen them before. Yesterday. *Through the Third Moon Gate.* She could feel her hands trembling.

"You know my gran," said Pete. "Mrs Anscomb up at the House. We're all from Stoke Raven. That's Foxy. That's Zonk, because that's what he says all the time—'I'm zonked out'—and that's Blackhead. You can see why. And," he jerked his thumb over his shoulder to his leader at the counter, "that's Mark. Mark the Bastard, because that's what he is." He raised his voice, "Hey, Mark, look who I found."

Their leader finished his conversation and sauntered casually over to their table. He was very tall, well over six feet, with wide, powerful shoulders, and dark hair nearly touching his shoulders.

There was a pause. A tense silence. Clare lifted her head slowly, reluctantly, and looked into the darkest, coldest eyes she had ever seen. Except that now she could see they were a dark emerald, and they weren't cold, but glowing with a darker fire, burning like ice.

Her first thought was relief that the figure on the hill had not been a ghost after all. And then the deeper recognition came. *She knew him.* She had an age-long, bone-deep knowledge of him. She had never spoken to him before, but she knew the way he thought, his impatience, his recklessness, his humour, his courage, and that dark, secret, closed part of him.

And physically she knew him too. The way his hair grew round his ears, the shape of his long hands, his great strength and energy. She had lain in his arms and felt the imprint of his body on hers.

The blush flooded scalding up her neck into her face.

"What's your name?" His voice was unexpected. Clear, deep, a beautiful voice.

She said, reluctantly, half-hypnotized, "Clare."

"*Clare?* What's your other name?"

"Clare Meredith, if it's any business of yours." The blush had begun to fade.

"No second name? Like Rosie, for instance?"

She stared into his eyes, startled, then after a moment she said, firmly, "No second name." And knew he knew she was lying. She got up and found herself too close to him.

He continued to stare deep into her eyes, not letting her look away. He said, so softly she could hardly hear, "Hello, Rosie. You took your time getting here."

She swallowed. "I don't know what you mean."

He smiled, slowly, allowing his eyes to move over her face, down her neck to her breasts.

Clare said, huskily. "I've got to go. I've got to pick up something from the chemist."

He stroked his knuckle gently down the side of her face, and touched her bottom lip lightly with his thumb. Clare felt the whole of her body react.

"You haven't drunk your coffee." His voice sounded slurred, drugged.

"No . . . It's too strong."

Without looking around he said to the girl behind the counter, "Give her another coffee. More milk."

Clare said, desperately, "No! I mean, no thanks. Honestly, it's all right. I don't want any more. I've got to go. I've got to get something. I've got to catch the bus . . ."

He moved his head slowly from side to side, pulling down the corners of his mouth, mournfully mocking. "Nowhere to run now, Rosie."

"But it's the last one. Besides, I've got to . . ."

They were all shaking their heads now, solemnly, trying not to laugh.

"You've missed the bus, darling," said Pete, and Mark held his wrist-watch under her nose. The bus had gone five minutes ago.

"Oh no, what'll I do?" She was dismayed and then furious with them. They had delayed her deliberately.

"I'll give you a ride on my bike, of course. I'll take you back to Ravensmere."

The idea appalled her. "Oh . . . *no*. No thanks." She backed towards the door, desperate to get away from him, desperate to get herself under some sort of control and back to normal. "I'll make my own way home. Thanks for the offer." She felt shaky and unreal. In the space of a few minutes her whole life had been turned inside out.

"Not very friendly, is she?" said Foxy.

"Miss Black Ice," sneered Zonk.

"Trouble is, Mark, she don't like you," Pete said, judicially. "You'd rather come along with me, darling, wouldn't you. You don't want to truck with Mark the Bastard."

Clare glanced quickly at Mark, and saw his eyes narrow. He went on smiling, but his eyes glittered dangerously. He said mildly, "The name is Winters."

"Don't trust him," Pete said confidentially. "He's a Bad Man. Come on, darling, I'll give you a good time."

"She don't like you, Mark," said Foxy.

"She's just shy," said Mark. "You're shy, aren't you, love?" He put his fingers under her chin and forced her to look up. He smiled down at her. She felt herself blushing and jerked her head away. "Leave me alone!"

"Don't sound as though she's shy. Sounds as though she don't like you." Foxy's voice goaded him. The other bikers laughed. "Maybe she likes Pete better."

134

"Yeah," Pete said. "That's right! You come along with me, darling. I'll show you Barton Quarry."

Their laughter rose again.

Clare swallowed and looked around. There was no break in the circle. They were all on their feet, towering above her. There was no chance of walking away.

"But she's coming with me," Mark said, very gently. "*Aren't* you, Rosie?" The underlying menace in his voice made her shiver. She realized suddenly that under the banter and joking his status in the group was being questioned. He was into some sort of trial of strength with Pete and she was just a pawn in the game.

"But I've got to pick up . . ."

"*Aren't you?*"

"Look, I just want to go home." Her voice shook.

He stared at her and for a moment she thought that he would let her go.

"There you are, she don't like you. She just wants to go home," growled Blackhead.

Mark stiffened and she knew it was no good. He would not listen to any appeal now.

"The bikes are just outside. Come on, Rosie." He put his arm around her and propelled her out of the café.

Chapter 14

The motor bikes were lined up in the side street, huge chrome-covered monsters with powerful engines. Suddenly Clare was shaking with terror. She would never be able to stay on.

Mark bumped the largest of them off its stand and got on. Clare looked around desperately. *Now* was the time to get away, to run. But the others had crowded together behind her and there was no way she could push through them. No passerby would think anything was wrong. Just a group of bikers and a girlfriend outside a café.

Mark looked at her. "Ever done this before?"

She shook her head, dumbly, trying not to let him see how much she was shaking.

"Keep close against me. Let your body go with the bike and hang on tight. If you come off, it's raspberry jam all over the road. Get on."

She froze, unable to move or speak.

"I said, *get on.*"

Pete, grinning, picked her up easily, dumped her on the seat and shoved her feet onto the foot rests.

Mark said, "Give her Foxy's spare lid, Pete, and take her bag like a nice little gentleman."

The helmet was crammed over her head none too gently and done up. Pete's big red face grinned down at her. "You look beeeautiful, darlink," he said in a sexy European accent, kissed her on the nose and wrested from her hand the plastic carrier bag containing her shopping and shoulder bag.

"*Don't . . .* You can't . . ."

Mark, annoyed, said, "Put your arms around me," and set the bike in motion, not waiting for his mates.

Clare, taken unawares, was jerked backwards and nearly fell off. She clutched his jacket terrified, and felt the leather slide away under her numb fingers.

He stopped the bike and looked over his shoulder. "Watch my lips. I said put your arms around me. Around my waist. I'm not contagious."

"I heard, but I can't . . ."

"*Under* the jacket." He grinned wolfishly. "Keep your hands warm. Give you a thrill. You'll be able to feel my . . . er . . . muscles moving up and down." He laughed aloud, watching the scarlet flood up under her clear skin, and turning pulled both her arms around his waist, tugging her along the seat so that she rested against his back as snug as a postage stamp.

The next moment they were away, weaving dangerously along the narrow crowded streets, and then out on to the main road that ringed the town. On a curve she caught sight of the other bikes a long way behind, trying to catch up.

The turning for Ravensmere came up. Mark slowed, hesitated for a split second, then, making up his mind, accelerated past. He grinned recklessly, wondering if Clare had noticed. A cacophony of hooting and loud whoops far back told him that he was on his own.

Mark could feel that Clare was responding to the sway of the bike. Suddenly he felt good. The girl behind him, the sun-bronzed road, the bike running well, the feeling of coming out on top—so Pete fancied her as well, did he? Too bad!—everything came together and he felt a powerful surge of exhilaration. He drove the speed up and forgot everything else.

It was a glorious summer afternoon, the sun lower in the

sky gilding the edges of the leaves and trees, lying in great swathes of brilliant gold across the open plain and along the shoulders of the steep hills.

Clare kept her head down, sheltering against the width of his shoulders, holding on grimly and concentrating on staying on the bike.

The villages and towns flashed by, a blur of old stone and flowering gardens. A line of uplands with a huge white horse cut into them. Wide open hill country with small remote farms nestling in the folds of the valleys below. Then, far away a strange-shaped hill with a tower on top standing alone in a land spread out in the sun like a quilt of green and gold patches. She saw a sign which said 'Glastonbury', and took a quick breath. King Arthur country.

There was a road arrowing into the lush green countryside, so straight it must surely be a Roman road. She heard Mark give a great shout and the bike leapt forward under them. She closed her eyes and briefly there was nothing but the wild rush of the speed and air through the glowing countryside.

If she hadn't been so terrified and full of rage and humiliation Clare might have enjoyed it, but nobody had ever forced her to do anything like this, totally against her will. She was incoherent with fury.

Mark was in a very good mood. He slowed, drove down a steep hill, over a narrow bridge and into the market square of a small town. There was an empty parking place by the bank and he pulled into it and cut the engine. He turned to her with a flourish. "There you are. A tourist trip through Somerset and a bit of Wiltshire."

"Where are we?" She could hardly get the words out.

"Frome. There's a place here that sells good fish and chips."

"Fish and chips!"

She slid off the bike and stood shaking with rage. Rage at

him for humiliating and coercing her, and at herself too. For a while there on the road, despite everything, she had actually enjoyed the freedom, the wind and sun and speed and the feeling of his body moving under her hands. Was she crazy? Hadn't she decided that she wasn't going to allow anyone to tell her what to do? He was even worse than Adrian.

He took off his helmet and ran his fingers through his thick dark hair and grinned at her triumphantly. "See. I knew you'd like it."

She slapped his face then, with all the force of her arm and body. And felt the shame of it immediately. Never before in her whole life had she hit anybody. There was a wild storm of emotion, driving her before it, out of control.

He laughed. Amused. Mocking. As though he understood the explosion of rage and sex and excitement and helplessness in her.

He picked her up with no effort at all, her feet inches off the ground, kissed her, put her down and kissed her again, pulling her against his body, sliding his hands in her hair so she couldn't pull away. He was experienced and sure, knowing how to hold and handle and kiss. His mouth was warm, slightly moist. His tongue parted her lips.

When he let her go she turned her back abruptly and walked away, half-blinded by tears.

Mark watched her without expression. "Where do you think you're going?"

"Home."

"How?"

"Mind your own business."

He called after her, laughing, "I'll go and get us some fish and chips and then we'll go back." He sounded as though he was talking to a sulky child. "I'll be here in ten minutes. Don't go away. I won't wait." He was still laughing as he stalked away down a narrow alley nearby.

Clare didn't answer. She crossed the road to a bus stop

outside the post office, narrowly missed being knocked down by a hooting car which swung down unexpectedly from a steep hill on her left, and stared at the bus timetables feverishly. His last comment had acted like a whiplash on an open cut. She wouldn't go back with him if she had to walk the whole way.

"Where do you want to go, m'dear?" asked an elderly woman, passing the bus stop, recognizing a stranger.

"Stoke Raven."

The woman shook her head. "Not from here, m'dear. No buses from here. Not even part of the way at this time of an evening."

"Oh no!" Clare stared at her in horror. She had just remembered that she had no money to pay her fare anyway. Her purse was in the bag that Pete had taken off her.

She turned away, her shoulders slumped. She would have to sink her pride and go back to the bike and wait tamely until he turned up with his rotten fish and chips. She would have to wait until he felt like driving her home. No wonder he had been laughing. She felt the frustrated rage leap up again.

The woman watched her sympathetically. "Pity they stop so early, the buses. Stranded, are you? You'll have to have a car. There's a taxi rank by the new shopping precinct if you want one."

Clare stared at her. She felt like hugging her. A *taxi*. She could borrow the money off her mother to pay the taxi when she got home. She drew a deep breath of relief. "That's a marvellous idea! How do I get to the shopping precinct?"

"But fourteen pounds!" her mother said, outraged. "Fourteen pounds for a taxi! Are you out of your mind? You know we can't afford that kind of money."

They had gone over the same ground several times since Frances had paid off the driver of the cab.

"I didn't know it was going to cost that much, did I?" Clare said desperately. "I had to get back somehow, didn't I? I told you—they took my bag and my purse. But don't worry, I'll pay you back. Every penny."

"You should have stayed with him and let him bring you home."

"I should have walked into the police station and laid charges against him," Clare snapped. "Kidnapping. Robbery. He *mugged* me."

And he'd kissed her. Kissed her in the middle of Frome market-place with everybody looking. Kissed her in such a way that for the first time she had lost control of her mind and body to somebody else, returning kiss for frantic kiss, shuddering and moving helplessly against him, with her mouth open under his. She had hung on to him and it was as though she had kissed him like this through all eternity. And then he had laughed.

"And to forget the prescriptions and the medical supplies . . . Honestly, Clare, I don't know what came over you. It's not like you to be so thoughtless and irresponsible. Poor Mr Aylward is really uncomfortable. His bed sores . . ."

"I told you! I didn't forget the stuff. They wouldn't let me go. They made me miss the bus and get on this motor bike and . . ."

"You could have refused the lift . . ."

Clare said, despairingly, "You don't understand. Look, I'll go back tomorrow and pick up . . ."

"It's *Sunday* tomorrow, and this isn't London. The bus only goes on Tuesdays and Saturdays for market-day."

Clare groaned. "Oh no!" She clapped her hand to her forehead. "Look, I'm sorry, sorry, *sorry*."

"Oh forget it," Frances said wearily. "I'll drive over Monday afternoon, while he's resting."

"I could borrow the car and . . ."

"Not on your life. You've not passed your driving test yet.

I thought you wanted to go to university, not end up in gaol."

"Look, I'm just trying to help . . ." Clare's voice rose and wobbled dangerously.

Frances suddenly took in her daughter's state. Under the beginnings of a tan she was strained and pale, her eyes wide, shining with unshed tears. Her hair, always severely braided, had lost its confining band, and waved in a dishevelled mane around her shoulders. There was a rip in the shoulder sleeve of her best shirt, and a long dark grease stain on her jeans. *Jeans?* Frances looked again. Clare looked wild and angry, the cool control and sophistication which she had imposed on herself since she had dated Adrian broken away. For the first time in months she looked fully alive, her mother thought, relieved. Like her old self, full of energy and emotion.

She said, concerned, "Clare, are you all right? What's the matter?"

"No, I'm not *all right*," Clare choked. "And *everything's* the matter. But don't let it worry *you!*" She stormed out and slammed the door behind her.

"So you got back."

He was standing over her, his hands on his hips. A dark figure against the fiery sky, his shadow stretching huge and black down Raven Hill like the great hill figure in Dorset. He was furious. No patronizing mockery now, Clare noted with vicious satisfaction. She turned her back.

"I spent an hour looking all round Frome for you. I must have been down every damn road and alley in the place."

"Worried about me, were you?" Clare sneered her disbelief.

"What do you think? You just disappeared. I thought someone might have picked you up."

"Like *you*, you mean?"

"Like some bloody rapist. It was getting late and I knew you hadn't got any money . . ."

"Of course I hadn't. You took it away. Why don't you just clear off? I don't want to talk to you."

"Here." He tossed her plastic carrier bag on to her lap. She took out her shoulder bag and looked in her purse. All the money was there.

"Not very trusting, are you? Pete Anscomb's honest. He wouldn't touch a thing."

She shrugged and got up. "How would I know that? You're lucky I didn't walk into the police station at Frome and swear charges against you."

He laughed. "Such as?"

"Try mugging." She suddenly felt cold and tired, *disappointed*.

"Or assault?" He was smiling, looking at her mouth. "Don't I get any thanks for bringing your bag back?"

"*Thanks*, you stupid oaf?" The anger surged back. "You made an awful scene with everybody looking. You made me look a fool. You made me do something I didn't want to do. You cost me fourteen pounds which I need for university. And I'm in terrible trouble with my mother. I was supposed to be picking up urgent prescriptions and nursing stuff from the chemist. But you didn't listen, did you? And now my mother will have to drive all the way to Salisbury on Monday, when she's supposed to be here. Mr Aylward is ill and really needs . . ."

To her fury, the tears came then, rolling helplessly down her cheeks. She was exhausted and thrown badly off balance. Her defences had gone.

He put his arms around her and pulled her close, stroking her back. He was so tall she only came to his shoulders, and he seemed to surround her with a wall of strength and safety, but she knew it was only an illusion. He was dangerous, reckless and hard.

"Look, I'm sorry, it was just a joke. I thought you'd like a ride on my bike."

143

"Don't lie," Clare said, sniffing. "You got into a power struggle with Pete, and I was just a pawn, a non-person."

"You didn't really think we'd hurt you? You're one of us. Even Blackhead wouldn't touch you. Wouldn't dare. A Ravensmere *Guardian?*"

Clare went still. "What are you talking about?"

"Poor little Rosie. You're really done up, aren't you? Not thinking straight." He was kissing her forehead, soft light kisses where her hair curled into tendrils. "Surely you realize they've got you earmarked as the next Guardian?"

She pushed him away. "Don't call me Rosie. I'm not Rosie. And you're talking a load of rubbish."

He put his arm around her shoulders and kissed her neck under her ear, laughing. "Clare *Rosamond Kenward* Meredith. The daughter. Rosie. *My* little Rosie, and don't you forget it. See you Monday."

Then he was leaping away down the hill with giant strides, towards the main gate and the lane that led to Kenward Farm.

Chapter 15

On Monday Clare slept late into the morning. It was nearly eleven before she was ready to go over to the House. Sunday she had spent with a book down by the lake, feeling totally exhausted, and had finally fallen into her bed and into a deep pit of dreamless sleep.

This morning, surfacing slowly, she felt strange, almost light-headed, *different*. It was as though something in her had been changed completely and she was a new person, rainwashed after a great storm. Something that had kept her closed-in, made her unsure and anxious, had let go. She felt healthy and carefree.

Even the sunlight seemed brighter, the air clearer. She shook loose her silky newly-washed hair. She wondered why she had kept it dragged back all these months.

As she came through the arch into the service yard she could hear the shouting.

Mai, with John and Billy, the under-gardeners, were staring across the cobbled yard to where Roger Fletcher, puce, was raging up and down, shouting at Mark Winters, who was leaning insolently against his motor bike outside the kitchen entrance. He was a powerful figure in his leathers, his head thrown back in arrogant amusement.

Clare's heart gave a great leap and settled down to a heavy thud. She ought still to be angry and offended, but it was joy she was feeling. She put her hands in her jeans to stop them shaking. Even the sight of him affected her physically. What was he doing here?

"... trespassing on the estate. You're not allowed here. It's forbidden, absolutely forbidden, for you to set foot here, as you well know." Roger Fletcher was almost dancing with fury. "Mr Aylward gave strict orders ..."

"He can stuff his orders. Get this straight, Mr Fletcher. I come and go as I please. No one tells me what to do, or where to go."

"You'll stay out, or by God I'll have you thrown out."

"You and whose army?"

"Me and my staff. Billy, John—*here!*"

But to Clare's amusement both the boys had hastily melted away seconds before Roger Fletcher looked around for them.

Mark laughed, and Clare thought the older man was going to fly at him.

"Don't be a fool, Fletcher," Mark said. "Do you want to get badly hurt? I'm a stone heavier and thirty-five years younger. And I haven't got a beer belly either."

Roger Fletcher stopped. There was a dribble of spittle running down his chin and he was a dark heavy red. Clare thought that he was heading for a stroke if he didn't calm down.

"Next time I see you here I'll take my shotgun to you, you stable yard rat."

Clare took a quick, anxious breath. She could see Mark's hands, the knuckles shining white, but he only said, evenly, "Three witnesses, Fletcher. You'll go to gaol."

Roger Fletcher took in Mai and Clare, and James Kenward who had just come through the arch. He said, contemptuously, "They'll do as I tell them. Kenward—get rid of this excrement. Throw him off the Estate."

"Who, *me?*" James said, amazed. Clare could see his lips twitching. "He could pick me up with one hand. He's a big boy, Mr Fletcher. I couldn't shift him."

Mark, grinning, said, "Don't worry, James. I'm going. I was only waiting for Clare."

Clare thought Roger Fletcher was going to explode. Instead he spun round and glared at her viciously. "*You.* I told you to stay away from the House. You can clear out. Get your cases packed. You're on your way."

Clare looked at him with contempt. The bullying swine. "You're having a disappointing morning, Mr Fletcher. Mr Aylward wants me to stay here."

The colour drained away suddenly from his heavy jowls. He opened his mouth to speak, but Clare said quietly, "Yes, that's right. You're too late. I've seen him. Talked to him."

Mark heaved his bike off its stand, got on and started the engine noisily. "Are you coming?" he said to Clare.

Roger Fletcher looked at them. Sweat was glistening along the line of his forehead. He pointed a shaking hand at her. "I'm warning you . . . If you go with this misbegotten vermin, I'll make it my business to tell Mr Aylward. He will be very angry, very angry indeed. He doesn't like Mark Winters or his mother. If you want to stay here I advise you to have nothing more to do with him."

Mark said, "Come on, Rosie, let's go."

Clare hesitated, looked at Mai and James, and back at Roger Fletcher, then made up her mind. She crossed the yard and slid on the bike behind Mark, holding on firmly as he accelerated away through the archway and up the drive under the yellow lime trees.

That evening her mother said, her eyes on the television, "You didn't tell me that the boy you were with on Saturday was Mark Winters."

Clare's heart gave an uncomfortable jump. "I didn't know you knew him."

"He came up to the House this morning."

"I know." The colour was burning under Clare's skin.

147

"He collected the prescriptions and the nursing supplies," Frances said. "He went all the way over to Salisbury to pick them up. He apologized. Said it was a misunderstanding, and that it was all his fault."

She turned around. "Do you like him, Clare?"

Clare's flush deepened uncontrollably. "He got the prescriptions? He didn't say."

"Apparently he had a confrontation with Roger Fletcher. Roger came in raging, demanding to see Mr Aylward."

"Have I got to start packing?"

"*Packing?*"

"I went off with Mark. Roger Fletcher said Mr Aylward would throw me out."

"That's not very likely, is it?" Frances said, dryly. "In any case he didn't see him. Mr Aylward wasn't well enough to see anyone."

"Why doesn't he like Mark? What's he done?"

Frances turned away, staring blankly at the television. "Nothing. Nothing at all. He's just . . . a victim of circumstances." She banged the arm of the sofa, angrily. "It's not fair."

"What's not fair?"

"Oh . . . *everything.*"

Clare laughed. "You sound like me. I'm making coffee. Do you want a cup?"

"All right. Thanks. What have you been doing?"

"Riding on Mark's bike."

At the main gate he had stopped and made her put on a helmet and an old leather jacket which he had brought in his pannier. The helmet fitted all right but the jacket was huge and studded, hanging down all over her, and it weighed a ton. Giggling she could hardly keep her balance when they started off again, but it had smelled of leather and Mark, and it had kept her warm in the slip stream of wind. It was upstairs now, hidden in her cupboard.

"Where did you go?"

"Wells."

He had bought her cheeseburgers and chips and a Coke, and they had wandered about the ancient city holding hands. They had stood together in the Archbishop's magical garden, where the seven sacred springs which had given the town its name still bubble up and flow away, as they have done for centuries.

"It's so peaceful here. A holy place," Clare said. "It feels like Ravensmere." She could feel his hand shaking suddenly. "What is it? What's the matter."

"I don't know . . ." His hand felt icy cold. He put his arm around her and pulled her close, as though he needed comfort. She leaned her head against him and hugged him back. "Come on, let's go home."

He had driven her back right to the stables, even though she had tried to make him leave her at the main gate, in case Roger Fletcher was around with his shotgun. He had laughed. "Don't worry, he's been threatening to shoot me for years." And he had kissed her forehead, and then her mouth, and neither of them had laughed.

Clare said to her mother defensively, "Well, aren't you going to tell me off? You've always told me to stay away from boys like Mark."

Frances did not rise to the bait. She looked at Clare searchingly, gravely. Clare's cheeks were still flushed, her eyes brilliant and shining. She seemed to be burning with energy and excitement.

"Would it make any difference? You've fallen in love with him."

Clare lay awake, unable to sleep, going over every minute of the day.

It wasn't true, she thought, panicking. Of course she hadn't fallen in love with Mark. It was just a sex thing. Raging hormones. Just because she couldn't stop thinking about him, wanted to see him again, wanted him to touch her, kiss her, it didn't mean it was anything important and serious, like falling in love. It might even be in reaction to Adrian, or exam stress, or . . . well, anything.

She shifted uncomfortably. Her body had never felt like this about Adrian. She lay staring at the circle of brilliant moonlight on her bedroom floor, and heard the stable clock chiming midnight.

She got up and went to the bathroom, and coming back stood at the little window looking down into the cobbled yard. Nothing moved. It was bright and still.

Nothing moved, and yet beneath this surface calm it seemed to Clare that everything was moving. There was a buzzing tension in the air, a tightening. Something was going to happen. There was a calling, a sense of urgency.

She saw a slight movement across the yard. Tabitha slid from under the door of the old blacksmith's forge and flowed across the cobbles, her tail held straight up, and sat down under the window, looking up at her, waiting.

Clare moved away irresolute. She should get back into bed at once and stop imagining things. This place was sending her crazy. But even as she pulled back the covers she knew she would never sleep. The tension and the pulling had increased. She would have to go. She groaned with irritation and pulled on her jeans and sweater.

Tabitha was still waiting patiently and greeted her with a satisfied miaow when she let herself noiselessly out of the front door, but when Clare bent down to stroke her she slid away and went quickly ahead along the route she had taken before and Clare knew that they were going to the China Garden.

The cat was already there when Clare arrived, sitting motionless between the guardian lion-dogs, her tail wrapped around her.

Clare stepped up and through the First Moon Gate, followed by Tabitha, and swung the iron gates closed behind her.

She saw at once that Mai and the boys had been working very hard. They had finished scything the centre of the Garden, and the tall grass was gone, leaving the ground uneven, broken by strange swelling hillocks and ridges.

They had tidied up the Pavilion, propped up the balustrade and taken away the fallen spars, and she saw, with the hair lifting on the back of her neck, that the Third Moon Gate too was open now. They had cut back the great climbing red rose which had blocked it, fastening its trailing branches to the wall. *Red rose for love*, she thought, and looked through the Gate, half-fearfully, expecting to see the Market Cross, but there was only a view of two magnificent oaks in the park.

"Well," Clare said, turning to Tabitha, "you've brought me here, what am I supposed to do next?"

Tabitha looked at her and deliberately turned her back in disgust, ignoring her. Clare laughed and wandered away, following the raised path to the centre Pavilion. The sense of urgency and pressure had gone now.

She sat down on the steps, her arms around her knees, relaxed and a little sleepy, watching the moonlight lapping across the ridges and banks, sculpting them into a pattern of silver and grey. They were like the sea, she thought, as the moonlight flowed and shimmered, throwing the dark groynes into relief. No, more like pillows, a huge feather bed billowing up and down. A quilt, machined into patterns.

Patterns.

There was a kind of rhythm to the shadows in the turf. She could follow the dark lines inwards until they turned right, moved inwards again, turned left, moved inwards, before swinging right once again . . . looping . . . like a maze.

At that exact moment she saw Tabitha calmly weaving her way backwards and forwards along the curved ridges.

Of course it was a maze. *The* Maze. The lost Maze of Ravensmere. Not the kind of maze she and Mai had imagined, with tall hedges like Hampton Court, where you got confused, but a maze cut into the turf. The kind of maze that had been old even in Shakespeare's time, which had a single way to the centre, and a single way back. What did they call it? *A Troy Town.* The words jumped into her mind without difficulty.

Once, long ago, on a Bank Holiday, they had taken a casual drive out into Essex, and had come across an ancient turf maze on the village green at Saffron Walden. Delighted, Clare had started to run the complicated pattern, but her mother had been strangely upset, walking away instantly, refusing to wait, refusing to have anything to do with it, and Clare had never been able to complete the run.

Could her mother know about *this* maze? It had been here a long time. The Puritan Earl had tried to cover it up and had stopped the traditional Maze Dance.

She stood up and stared at the patterns. She could see the way, a depression between two ridges, bending back on itself. The impulse to follow it was too strong to resist.

She started from the First Moon Gate and began to move cautiously along the narrow track. After four metres or so it moved back on itself, retracing the curve but going in the opposite direction, and then bent back again. Backwards and forwards.

Clare counted seven switchback curves, all on one side, moving outwards, getting larger, but disappointingly not circling round to the rest of the Garden. Perhaps it wasn't a maze after all, just the remains of a curling path or old flower-beds. Everything was overgrown, changed. It was at least twenty years since the Garden had been open.

There was an almost hypnotic rhythm to the curving way. She felt her body sway and lift, sway and lift, like a dance. She drifted into a dream-like trance.

Then, suddenly, she realized the path, having led to the centre, had swung right out, up and around the four circular banks at each corner, and she was now circling the whole Garden at an increasingly dizzy pace, like a spring unwound, the flashing patterns of the moonlight and darker shadows confusing her eyes.

When the path stopped at the Fifth Moon Gate she was unprepared. She must have made a mistake somewhere. It had brought her to a different place. And surely only the First and Third Moon Gates had been cleared. Hadn't this one been blocked by a vine of some kind—a thick old fig tree, impenetrable like Sleeping Beauty's castle?

But now the Fifth Moon Gate was framing, like a huge circular painting, the majesty of Barrow Beacon Hill, its lower levels furred with dark trees, its summit open and floodlit by a golden moon hanging directly over it. And there, reflecting from some large dark shapes, was an unearthly haze of light.

What on earth was up there that she had never noticed before? Clare stood on the Moon Gate step, screwing up her eyes, trying to see. What could produce that kind of strange light? But the next moment a cloud sailed across the moon, and the objects, whatever they were, disappeared.

For a moment she went on scanning the hill, but now there was nothing to see, and suddenly she felt shivery and cold. Tabitha was curling around her, pressing warm fur against her legs, forcing her to stumble away towards the First Moon Gate.

Clare turned back once, to take another look at the view through the Gate, and saw, almost without surprise, that it was once again filled by the twisted fig tree.

Chapter 16

"Mr Aylward would like you to take his elevenses, miss, if that's all right," said Mr Bristow, coming into the kitchen the next morning. After the complete bed rest Frances had ordered, he was on his feet again, and anxious to take up his duties, but still not strong, Clare thought.

She was helping her mother wash the dusty Wedgwood china from the Dining Room, terrified she would let slip one of the precious plates, designed for the Tenth Earl in 1771.

"Is he . . . annoyed?" she asked cautiously, drying her hands.

"Oh no, miss. He enjoyed his conversation with you. He said that you have something to tell him and something to ask him."

Clare felt a prickling sensation in her scalp. It was true she wanted to see him again, ask him questions, tell him she had found the Maze—but how did he know? Suddenly she was sure he knew about the Maze, and that she had been there last night.

"How did Mr Aylward know I was looking at the China Garden the other day? Is he psychic too?"

Her mother turned away, but Mrs Anscomb chuckled. "Well, of course he is. All the Guardians have the gift. Runs in the families, don't it? That's why they were chosen to be Guardians in the first place. They know what's going to happen. They have the powers. They can guard the Benison better."

"Just old stories," said Frances, dismissively.

"*True* stories," said Mrs Anscomb, firmly. "Here's the tray, Clare m'dear. Mr Aylward is in his study today. Next to his dining room."

The big room overlooked the terrace too. Book-lined and scattered with files and papers, it was obviously the room he used most. There was a huge desk, and surprisingly an array of state of the art computers with modems and fax machines and Clare realized that he must still be involved in his business interests. The screens were glowing, but he was sitting in his wheelchair by the window, staring out. Surely he wasn't working? Yesterday he had been too ill to get up.

He turned his head. "Well?"

Clare put the tray down on a side table, and poured his cup of China tea, bringing it to him.

"The China Garden is open. Mai Lee and the boys have cut the grass. It's terribly overgrown."

The sharp eyes watched her carefully. "You've been inside?"

"It's the Maze, isn't it? The lost Maze of Ravensmere. Only it's not lost. It was deliberately hidden."

He grunted with satisfaction. "You have done the Maze Dance?" Then there was that ironic, croaking laugh. "Of course you have. Which Moon Gate did you open?"

Clare took a deep breath. "So it *is* the Maze. And the Maze Dance opens the Moon Gates."

"Rather say it heightens the power to . . . see beyond. What have you seen?"

"Last night, the Fifth Moon Gate was open. There was a view of Barrow Beacon Hill. And some dark shapes glowing with light. I couldn't quite make them out."

"The Fifth Gate." His eyes focused on her and seemed to deepen in colour.

"The Third Gate is open too. It was kind of accidental. I saw the centre of the village and the Market Cross." And

Mark and his friends, but she couldn't tell him that. He didn't like Mark.

"Where the youths meet. Two Gates already. They are working fast." His eyes seemed to film over.

Clare sat down abruptly, feeling her knees shaking. "I . . . don't like it much. I don't understand. What is the Maze? Why did you close the China Garden?"

He sipped his tea, carefully. "You must understand that the ability to sense things, to read the future, has saved the Benison many times. It mostly runs through the female line here. Nobody knows how or when the Maze was made, but from the earliest times the Maze Dance was used to discover the most psychic of the women of the area to be the Guardians of the Benison. Certainly the Abbesses were always chosen in this way, forbidden though it must have been.

"Even the Romans must have chosen Guardians for the Benison. They laid a magnificent mosaic in a Temple to the west of this house."

Clare remembered the snaking line of women she had seen dancing in the green bowl before ever there were buildings at Ravensmere. "But who started it? How did they know?"

"My grandfather spent his life trying to find out. He believed that there were women here doing the Maze Dance as long as thirty thousand years ago."

"It sounds too . . . fantastic, crazy even."

"He had evidence. He found a bone scratched with a line of nine dancing women *beneath* a stalagmite flow."

Clare stared. "Thousands of years, anyway."

"Exactly. The Dance is a very efficient method. The females dance, and those that can see beyond—see. I suppose it could even be explained scientifically. You must know that flashing, flickering light can effect changes in the brain. And there is the movement of the dance. The Whirling Dervishes of Turkey dance into a trance state. Perhaps it is a combination of the two."

Clare said, hesitating, "Since I came here I've seen . . . things . . . not in the China Garden. From the past, I think."

"You have a powerful gift. More powerful than your mother. Much stronger than Caroline. They know what will be needed. A strong woman in difficult times."

"You always talk about 'they'. Who are 'they'?"

He shrugged. "A force? Energies? I don't know. I have never seen them. I only know they are there, looking after Ravensmere and the Benison. They are very powerful. Disobey them at your peril."

Clare shivered involuntarily. "What about the China Garden?"

"The turf maze was there in medieval times, covered up briefly by the Puritan Earl, then reinstated by Rosamond the Strong. But by the eighteenth century it was becoming dangerous. Ravensmere was no longer concealed and isolated. James Edward, the Travelling Earl, was an extraordinary and farsighted man. He made a fortune with the East India Company, and undertook diplomatic missions to China and the East before he inherited Ravensmere. I think he realized that there were great changes coming, new machines, a different world. Ravensmere could not remain hidden in its obscure backwater. People would come. More and more of them from the world outside.

"So, with the help of his son, Edmund, he landscaped the gardens and the park as other landowners were doing. The valley of the Raven was dammed to make the Great Lake, the Upper Lake, and the Pool of Poseidon. And he employed Henry Flitcroft to design the island Temple of Demeter and Persephone and other garden follies."

"He made the China Garden?"

He nodded. "His problem was the Maze, you see. He had to find some way of protecting and concealing it. The best way to conceal something is to put it in an obvious place and pretend it's something else. Chinoiserie was fashionable, so James Edward had a China Garden constructed. He brought over real Chinese gardeners. They built a wall around the Maze. Planted suitable trees and shrubs and put a Pavilion in the centre. Of course, Chinese gardens do not have mazes in them, but many have winding paths and bridges."

Clare said, "Why did you lock it up, let it go to ruin? And you bricked up the Fourth Gate."

He was silent, looking out of the window. He said, at last, heavily, "I believed there would be no more Guardians. No one to dance the Maze. I thought it better to let nature cover it."

But he had given the key to her so she could open the China Garden again and do the Maze Dance.

Clare could feel a clammy perspiration breaking out all over her body.

She was Rosamond, Protectress. Did he really think she was the next Guardian? She was too frightened to ask.

The Guardians weren't allowed to leave Ravensmere.

She took a deep breath, trying to hold down her panic. They couldn't make her do anything she didn't want to do. It was just a legend. Her mother had refused to be Guardian, had left Ravensmere, and she had survived. I ought to go now, Clare thought, before I get in any deeper. But Mark was here. She realized suddenly that she badly did not want to leave Ravensmere, at least not yet.

She said abruptly, "Have I got to go? I've made friends with Mark Winters. Mr Fletcher says you don't like him and I'll have to leave."

His green eyes flickered coldly over her and she was sure he understood everything. A slow blush burned up her neck and cheeks.

"Mr Fletcher is mistaken. Of course you will stay at Ravensmere. Is there more tea?"

"What? Oh yes, of course. Sorry." It was cold, but he

didn't seem to mind. He drank it slowly, the long veined hand trembling on the cup.

"What else have you been doing?"

Clare told him about her visit to Salisbury Museum and the model of the dig at Ravensmere. "They said they found a crystal goblet. I've looked in the Etruscan Gallery and asked about it, but no one knows."

He smiled. "Over there, next to the fire."

There was a small cupboard partially concealed in the square panelling. Clare opened it and took out a round object wrapped in a silk cloth. It was surprisingly heavy.

He said, "Here."

She put it on his knees, and he unwrapped the cloth, revealing an irregular, shining shape.

"It's a skull!"

"One of the great treasures of Ravensmere. Carved rock crystal. Of unknown age and provenance. Buried in the barrow on Barrow Beacon Hill over five thousand years ago." He lifted it into her hands.

"They couldn't have made it then, surely? It must have come from somewhere else."

The surface of the crystal had been polished to an exquisite finish, reflecting and re-reflecting endlessly. The top had been hollowed into a shallow bowl. At the bottom of the bowl were carved three joined spirals.

Clare stared at the reflections within each spiral. There were tiny segmented pictures as clear as a photograph—Mr Aylward, the books on the shelf behind him, a huge dark statue, Barrow Beacon Hill crowned with a double stone circle . . .

"What do you see?"

She blinked and handed it back to him hastily. "Nothing. Nothing at all. This is the Benison?"

He croaked into laughter. "No. Certainly not." He cradled the skull, stroking its surface. His green eyes stared at her as translucent and reflective as the crystal he was holding. "Not the Benison. That is a different matter altogether. As you will discover."

The days began to fall into a pattern. Every morning she helped in the House, or the garden centre, or drifted dreamily about the park and the gardens. She tracked down, with the aid of the old pamphlet she had found in Salisbury, the Great Cascade, the Obelisk dedicated to King William and the Glorious Revolution of 1688, the Hermit's Grot in the Wilderness, the Gothick Bathhouse, and Merlin's Cave, where life-size statues of King Arthur and his Knights lay sleeping, the walls wonderfully studded with glittering amethysts.

She climbed to the delightful Temple of the Zephyrs, and one day let herself through the pointed arch that led to the original Abbey. The Cloisters were silent and deserted, the dust motes dancing in the sunlight. She sat on an arched stone seat in the Chapter House, feeling peaceful and curiously at home, and thought, *I have been here before.*

Every afternoon Mark rode his motor bike into the stable yard, and Clare went with him. She was determined not to get involved, but no matter how many resolutions she made, when he came, somehow, suddenly, there seemed no good reasons for *not* going.

He took her to Glastonbury, and they wandered around the ruined Abbey, and climbed the spiral way up and around the great hill called the Tor, trying to pick out the figures of the terrestial zodiac reputed to be laid out in a vast circle below. They went to elegant Bath. They climbed Bratton Hill to the giant white horse cut in the hillside. And in the evenings they rode home in the sunset with the sky flaring gold and geranium red, and he kissed her until she was wild and trembling.

Sometimes it was too hot to move and they lay in the cool

shade of the ring of trees on top of Raven Hill, overlooking Ravensmere dreaming in the sun.

"All this." Clare waved her hand at the House and garden. "It's so beautiful, it's like living in a painting. I keep forgetting that it's all temporary for me."

Mark rolled over and stared at her. "You're not staying? You're going back to London?"

Clare realized that he was angry, although she didn't understand why. He must have known she couldn't stay here permanently.

"Well, eventually, I suppose. I've got into Sussex University. I'm just waiting to see if I got my grades."

"What are you studying? History? English Lit?"

She said stiffly, "Economics and Computer Science."

He laughed and rolled on to his back again and stared at the sky. "Yeah, I can see you with a document case under your arm getting into a Porsche. I bet you'll even have a boyfriend called Jonathan or Adrian or something."

"Adrian," said Clare, tightly. "Present tense." She got up and brushed down her jeans. "It's better than not having a proper job, just bumming around the countryside on a bike."

He said angrily, "Who do you think does all the heavy work at Kenwards? You think my mother mucks out?" He laughed. "You don't know my mother."

"You live at the farm?" Somehow she had got the idea that he lived in the village near his mates.

He stared at her. "Of course I do. Where d'you think? My mother runs it as stables."

"Mrs *Carlton*-Winters," Clare said, remembering.

"My stepfather's name. I don't like double names."

There was a long silence. Into it, he said reluctantly, "Are you still with him, Clare?"

For a moment she didn't understand. "Who?"

"This Adrian."

She shook her head. Surely he knew she couldn't think about anybody but him?

He put his arm around her and pulled her into the side of his body, just holding her. They leaned against a tree, looking down into the valley, glowing like copper in the evening sun, each leaf outlined in glistening gold.

"I don't know why we're having a row," she said.

"Don't you?"

She moved away restlessly, and sat down again. "You'll go on working with horses?"

"No. I'm leaving. Quitting. Getting out. I want to farm. In Australia or Canada maybe."

Clare took a deep, unsteady breath. She had always known there was no future for them, hadn't she? She tried to keep her voice even, unemotional. "I don't understand. You've got a farm already. If you want to farm why go all that way? What's wrong with Kenward Farm?"

"It doesn't belong to us. It's leased from the Ravensmere estate. My mother moved in on the tail end of a lease three years ago and set up the riding stables. The lease runs out soon. Most of the land is farmed, if you can call it that, by the Ravensmere estate. Taking the heart out of the land. Ripping up the hedgerows. Intensive farming of animals. Very profitable." He picked up a stone and smashed it into a rocky outcrop half-way down the hill.

"You have to make a profit, don't you?"

"Not that way."

"Couldn't you ask Mr Aylward to renew the lease, let you take on the whole farm again?"

He laughed bitterly. "You have to be joking. He hates my mother's guts. And me. When my mother moved into the farm Roger Fletcher came over to frighten her out, but she's a tough nut, and it was all proper and legal and they couldn't shift us. Aylward's just waiting for the lease to expire to chuck us out."

Clare said, puzzled, "But why does he hate you? What have you done?"

He shrugged. "It's all in the past."

"But he's a reasonable person. I'm sure he would listen to you. I like him."

"Reasonable!" He roared with laughter. "We're not talking about the same man. He's a ravening grey wolf. A wounded tiger. He'll tear you limb from limb if you cross him. I don't mind telling you, he scares me—and the rest of the village too. There's not a thing he doesn't find out. It's uncanny. You know he's the Guardian?"

Clare said, uncomfortably, "You don't believe in all that, do you?"

He looked away and shrugged. "They all believe it in the village."

Clare said slowly, "You know a lot about this place, don't you, Mark? You know every inch of Ravensmere, even though you're not supposed to come here. I thought you hated it."

She watched his dark, averted face. "But that's not true, is it? I think you love it. You love it so much the idea of losing the farm is eating you up."

He stood up, and stretched. He stood over her, his hands on his hips. "Quite the little psychologist, aren't you? Clare, I'm not staying around to watch the place turn into a disaster area when Fletcher gets his hands on it. There's nothing to keep me here. Nothing and *nobody!* Come on. Let's go somewhere."

Clare shook her head, dumbly.

He shrugged. "Okay. See you."

Clare watched him leap away down the hill like a great cat. She made no attempt to go after him. She laid her cheek on her knees, and felt a great tide of depression sweep over her. There was no reason she should feel so bad. What did it matter to her that he was going away to the other side of the world? She was going to university. What did it matter to her what happened to Ravensmere?

But it did matter. It mattered horribly.

Chapter 17

Most days Clare took Mr Aylward's tray to him and stayed to talk. She had no illusions. She thought that Mark was probably right, that he was a ruthless and dangerous man. Certainly he was mysterious, with strange powers, but somehow she was not afraid of him.

In fact her visits were increasingly precious to her. She had never met anyone so well-read, so worldly wise, so widely travelled, so full of interesting ideas. She enjoyed his black humour, and felt she could talk to him about everything. They understood each other on some deeper, unexplained level.

He told her stories about the Aylwards and the Kenwards which Mrs Potts-Dyrham had discreetly avoided, like the Black Sheep Sixth Earl who had run away with Jenny Barleycorn, a pot-maid at the Sun and Moon Inn, and had been found murdered in a ditch six months later.

Clare shivered. It was surely coincidence that so many had died suddenly when they had refused to be a Guardian.

He said, "And then there are all the extraordinary women of the family. The wife of the Travelling Earl, who went with him to Tibet, disguised as a yak herder. Or the Regency Rosamond, an early feminist, who at seventeen went about the slums of Bristol vaccinating women and children against the smallpox—whether they liked it or not, I suspect. Her book, *Concerning the Subjugation of Women*, is in the Library."

Mr Aylward's eyes gleamed with amusement.

"And there was Rosamond the Strong, who had the Tower

rebuilt so that she could see all the approach roads to the House and be warned in advance of any marauding soldiers. She would be found innocently embroidering bed curtains in a virtually empty house while Royalist troops searched every nook and cranny, and meanwhile the servants and villagers melted away into the woods and hills with the valuables."

Clare laughed, remembering Rosamond's portrait, with the smiling, intelligent eyes, and thought perhaps she had enjoyed outwitting all the men.

"Her grandson's bride, Clarissa Rosamond, was another Kenward, of course. People came to see her from miles around. She was a skilled healer, and her Herb and Physick Garden is still one of the glories of Ravensmere. There are many rare plants here."

"Mai is very proud of it."

"Ah yes. Mai Lee has done well." He gave his croaking laugh. "Roger was somewhat . . . disturbed . . . when I appointed a woman. But she will be needed here."

Mr Aylward lifted his long bony hand, pointing, sweeping it around the bowl of hills.

"There. That's the Trust, Clare. Ravensmere. The valley and hills beyond. And further still, I suppose. The Earth. Gaia, they're calling it now. In my time we called it Mother Earth."

"But . . ." she stopped, remembering Mark's bitterness at the way Ravensmere was being farmed.

"Go on."

"Did *you* accept the Trust?"

"Oh yes," he said softly. "In the beginning I accepted, with idealism and love. But they betrayed me. They took my Caroline and then I cursed the Benison. I cursed Ravensmere and I renounced my title. I went away and I fought them. All my life I have fought them. At terrible cost. And now at last I know they are too powerful for me." He closed his eyes.

Clare waited patiently. She knew he wasn't sleeping, only deep in his mind, in the past. She wondered what Mark was doing.

"What have you been doing?" The green eyes were open, staring at her.

"Exploring the gardens." She remembered then the Salisbury pamphlet she had brought along to show him.

"*An Account of a Visit to the Pleasure Gardens . . .*" He smiled, thumbing through it. "This one must have escaped. Edmund Aylward was obliged to buy up the entire edition in 1805. Keep Ravensmere out of the public eye, well-hidden, unpublished. That's always been the golden rule."

"A low profile—but not so low that it becomes suspicious," Clare said, remembering the lack of postcards, the strange tour arrangements, the mis-direction the village had given Joan and her friend.

"Correct."

"To protect the Benison."

"To protect the Benison."

She looked into the glittering green eyes, and saw that he was daring her, willing her, to ask.

"W-Wh . . ." *What is the Benison?* The question stuttered on the edge of her tongue.

A trap.

Suddenly she could feel his tension, the buried excitement. If she asked he would tell her, and when she knew the secret she would never be free of Ravensmere.

She drew a deep, unsteady breath, looked away from the hypnotic green eyes. She said instead, lightly, "In the pamphlet they call the Upper Lake, the Moon Lake. And the bridge is the Elysium Bridge."

"A bridge to Heaven. An eighteenth-century joke." The excitement had gone. She could hear the weariness in his voice. "You cross into the Land of Beulah, and take the Sublime Walk—they used to call it the Eleusinian Way—

to the Moon Lake and the Temple of Demeter and Persephone . . ."

He was staring at the book unseeingly, retracing the old walk. "Then you . . ." He could not go on. Perspiration was standing along his upper lip and he fumbled out his box of small tablets, and lay back, breathing heavily.

"Is he all right?" Clare said.

"Of course he's not all right." Frances was standing in their kitchen in the stables, making herself a cup of tea. It was nearly nine o'clock and she had just got home.

"There's no need to snap. I'm worried about him."

Frances sat down wearily. "Sorry. I am too. He's getting weaker all the time."

"But can't they do anything? A bypass or something?"

"He's too weak. He'd never survive the op." She put her head on her arms. When she looked up there were tears in her eyes.

"You love him too," Clare said.

"Always. Since I was a little girl. More than my own father. He used to put me up on his big horse. He was so happy when Bran and I were getting married. He arranged this enormous wedding. Afterwards . . . I thought I hated him. I blamed him for making Bran into what he was, reckless and selfish. But somewhere along the way I must have forgiven him because now . . . now I only wish I could put the clock back and make him well and whole again as he used to be."

Next day Clare said to Mr Aylward. "Did you know my grandfather? My mother's father?"

He looked at her under his brows. "Oh yes, I knew John Kenward. He was my friend. But I am bound to say that he was a hard man. Hard on himself and hard on all those around him. Unforgiving."

"He never forgave my mother for running away to London, did he? He wouldn't see her."

"He never forgave her. And he never forgave me either. He said I had brought devastation to his house, and he would never speak to me again, and he did not. In a bad year I bought Kenward Farm out from under him. He had extended himself too far. I wanted to frighten him into sense. To make him bring Frances back. But it made no difference. I don't think he cared any more. He died lonely and bitter. I went to his funeral and laid a wreath for old times' sake, but *that woman* took it away. Unnecessary."

Clare could hear the hurt in the bleakness of his voice. As so often, she didn't know what he was talking about, but she wished she hadn't asked about her grandfather. As soon as you scratched below the surface in this place, she thought, you found a festering abscess of hurt and unforgiveness.

"Unforgiveness, yes," Mr Aylward said, suddenly, into the silence. "That's where we all went wrong. We did not forgive. In our own petty hurts we forgot the greater trust. We forgot the Benison."

The weather was very hot. When the sun went down it seemed even more oppressive, not a breeze stirring.

Clare could not sleep. She lay awake thinking of Mark, her body restless, wanting him. She went often to the China Garden at night. Threading the Maze seemed to calm her, tiring her so that eventually she could get a few hours' rest. Always Tabitha went with her, sitting on the steps of the First Moon Gate, a small guardian.

It was important to get the Maze exactly right. It needed concentration to thread the narrow paths in the right order. It was easy to stumble into another line and lose the pattern completely. It needed moonlight and shadows to carve the path.

Often she fancied she could hear music, a strange archaic

pipe music, and she found it was easier to let her body flow to its rhythm. At first she had felt self-conscious, but there was no one to watch, except Tabitha, and she could dance now with a glorious sense of freedom.

Invariably the Maze wound her to the centre and released her for the return, her feet flying faster and faster, swinging out at last to the Fifth Moon Gate. Always she saw the dark shapes near the top of Barrow Beacon Hill glowing with unearthly brilliance. She knew there was something she must do there, but every day she put it off.

"What's up there?" she asked Mark. They were lying out of sight of the House, in the water meadow where the Great Lake turned into the River Raven again, and wound away broad and shallow. "There is something, isn't there? Apart from the Barrow, I mean."

He rolled over on to an elbow and looked at her, chewing on a grass stalk. His eyes were dark, expressionless. "I'll take you there if you like."

"When?"

"When you're ready."

"How far is it?"

"A stiff climb. Forty minutes, say a couple of hours, there and back."

She laughed. "Not today then, it's too hot."

He lay watching her, his eyes moving over her body, possessive and caressing. He was imagining he was touching her, Clare thought. She blushed and looked away.

"You kept your temper very well with Roger Fletcher." There had been another shouting match, in the stableyard this time.

He lay back, his arms behind his head. "When you're as big as I am you have to learn to be careful. I got expelled from two schools for fighting. Then I realized they were just jerking me about to enjoy the explosion." He looked at her. "Besides, I damn near killed someone."

"Another boy?"

"My Housemaster."

Clare's silent disapproval stung him.

"He always had his hand up my backside. Then he called my mother a trollop, and I hit him. He was a big bloke, but I hit him too hard. Broke his jaw and his nose. He crashed back and hit his head on the corner of the desk. Blood all over the place. He wanted to bring in the police, but it was a top school. Bad publicity. They smoothed it over, but I got the chop."

"They didn't let you take your A-levels?"

He sat up, grinning. "That was my next school. I got thrown out of there as well. It wasn't so much climbing up the tower, it was the banner about the unemployed they didn't like. On Founder's Day."

Clare laughed helplessly. "That's terrible."

He lay back. "Yeah. A waste of time. The story of my life. They let me go back to take the exams."

"Didn't you want to go to university?"

He shook his head.

Clare hesitated. "Mark, what's the matter? I mean, you're not happy, are you? Why are you so fed up, so . . . restless and angry? It's not me, is it?"

He closed his eyes. "No, not you. You're the best thing that's happened to me."

He was silent, and she thought he wouldn't say any more, but he was thinking, trying to work it out. "I was away at school, hating it. My mother got divorced again, and we came back here, and then everything just seemed to fall apart. I've been . . . blocked . . . in all directions. Nothing's been *right*. It's as though I've been forced to wait. I was supposed to go to the Agricultural Institute to study farm and estate management. Roddy Carlton-Winters, my stepfather, was paying, as usual, but I dropped out. I just felt . . . bad when I was away from Ravensmere. It sounds crazy, but it's the truth. I didn't want to be here, but I couldn't stay away either." He banged the ground with his fist.

"There's some money due to me from my grandfather. I said I'd take it and go but until I'm twenty-one my mother is my trustee and she won't hear of it. I've got to stay, she says. We're not exactly friends at the moment. I'm *bored*. Frustrated. Nothing helps. Girls, biking—nothing."

"Girls?" Clare said.

He looked at her, his eyes dark. "No good. None of them. I knew I was waiting for someone."

His long fingers traced the line of her lips. She jerked her head away, blushing, feeling the instant heat between her legs.

"Clare?"

"No."

"Why not?"

"I said *no*!" She was trembling, wanting to give in, wanting to lie in his arms.

"You're driving me mad, you know that?"

"I . . . can't. I'm not ready."

He slid his hand up her thigh, under her shorts and briefs, delicately touching, and kissed her on the mouth as her body reacted against him. He laughed softly against her mouth. "I won't hurt you."

She pushed him away and sat up, turning her back. She was still shaking. "I'm not ready in my *mind*. We're not animals. It's got to be more than just . . . physical. More than just lying down and doing it in a field."

He rolled on to his stomach and laughed.

"It's enough for me—to start with anyway. You could come up to the farm if you're fussy."

"Look, I said no." Clare was angry. "If you're going on like this I'm going home. I'm not getting involved. I'm *not*. We're getting in too deep. You're going to Australia, and I'm going to university. I've worked hard and planned my career."

172

He laid his hand around her head and turned it to him, kissing her slowly, gently, almost sadly, as if he was saying goodbye. Then his arms tightened and they were kissing wildly, holding on desperately.

After a while his arms slackened their hold and she rolled away and lay with her back to him, trembling, trying not to cry. He did not touch her and there was silence except for the sound of river water running over pebbles.

At last he said huskily, "Clare, this is something different. You know that, don't you? I've never been like this with anyone before."

She swallowed her tears, unable to answer.

"It's for ever, Clare. You know."

She sat up, pushed her fingers through her hair and began to plait it tightly.

"*Don't you?*"

"No. Because it's not true. It can't be true. We've only known each other a little while. It's just . . . sex. *Lust.* I'm not getting involved. I'm going to Sussex."

He dragged her round to face him. He was pale under his tan. "Okay. Look me in the face. Tell me that you don't want me, that you're not in love with me."

She jerked away. "There's no future."

"You could come with me. Australia, Canada, anywhere you choose. We could get married . . ."

She sprang to her feet, staring down at him, horrified. "You are out of your mind. Stark raving mad."

He shook his head, tearing at the turf between his knees, his shoulders hunched. "Run as much and as far as you like, Rosie, it won't make any difference. You're *mine*. We're locked together. One day you'll have to admit it."

Chapter 18

The weather grew hotter, a stifling, damp heat which left them all drained and irritable.

"We need a storm to clear the air," Clare said, lying flat out in the copse of trees on Raven Hill.

She was living from day to day, trying not to think of the future. Mark was longing to be gone, and she had worked and dreamed of university for three years. She couldn't give that up. There was no way they could have a future together.

Despite all her attempts to keep a cool distance, not get involved, there was an explosive tension between them, like a parcel of Semtex. Clare wondered how long it would be before it went off and blew them both to pieces.

Mark, his nerves screwed down, wouldn't or couldn't leave her alone. He seemed to crackle with an electric tension that threatened to burn everything it came in contact with.

He was watching her. He watched her all the time now, and touched her too, unclipping her bra, moving his long fingers over her breasts under her T-shirt, and beneath her shorts, stroking until she was wild in his arms, exchanging desperate kisses. Ashamed. Out of control. She had imagined that only boys felt like that. No one had ever told her that girls could feel like that too.

Mark was propped up on one elbow. He had taken off his shirt. His broad, muscular shoulders and chest were deeply tanned and smooth, except for the line of dark hair disappearing into his jeans, low on his narrow hips. His dark hair was falling across his forehead, and his eyes were alight with reckless laughter.

Clare looked away. She pushed the hair back from her forehead. "It's so hot, and getting hotter. I'd give anything for a swim. Where's the nearest swimming pool?"

He laughed derisively. "City girl. We swim in the Raven."

"We haven't got towels or swimsuits."

He looked at her sideways. "I know somewhere. A pool. Hidden in the trees and rocks. Nobody goes there."

Clare went red, but she was tempted. She felt hot and sticky and longed to plunge into fresh cool water under green trees. She could swim in her bra and briefs and the sun would dry them. Or she could go topless. People did, on the Spanish beaches, all the time. Nothing in it really. Except she would be alone with Mark and he would touch her, kiss her . . .

"I . . . don't th . . ."

"You're chicken," he said softly.

Once she was in the water it would be all right, away from his eyes and hands.

He held out his hand and pulled her up. "Come on, I'll show you."

They walked around the Great Lake, past the Great Cascade, and the formal elegant pools with statues of the River God and Poseidon. They crossed the Elysium Bridge and took a curving path, deep between mossy rocks and giant ferns and overhanging trees. It was gloomy, almost frightening, Clare thought, and realized it must be the Eleusinian Way that Mr Aylward had talked about.

She began to hang back uneasily. For some reason she had always avoided this part of the gardens.

"We're not going to the Temple, are we?"

Mark did not answer, but strode on, holding her hand firmly.

They came out suddenly into brilliant sunlight, on to the

banks of the Upper Lake—the Moon Lake her pamphlet had called it.

It was surrounded by cliffs and thick trees, beech, lime and sweet chestnut, and the hanging woods that climbed the lower slopes of Barrow Beacon Hill. At one end the Raven, trapped in a wild, miniature ravine, tumbled in a double waterfall through rocky outcrops and overhanging stone, into the head of the lake.

But Clare hardly noticed. She was staring at the centre of the lake, where an island floated like a vision from paradise.

The dreaming island seemed to be the centre of an enchantment. The bright stillness was upon everything. No breeze stirred the overhanging branches of the surrounding willows and flowering trees. Only the water moved a little between the thick carpet of water-lilies and reeds near the island. There was the perfume of roses and wisteria climbing the column of the statue of Ariadne, holding her ball of twine, and pointing across the water towards the Temple of Demeter hidden among the trees.

Clare moved forward slowly until she stood on the edge of the water. Suddenly she wanted, *needed*, to go across to the island, but there was something there, some danger. She could feel her heart pounding in her chest.

Mark said, "What's the matter?"

"Can you go there?"

"The punt's rotten."

Disappointed, she saw the old boat floating among the reeds, inches of bright green water lapping in the bottom.

"Swim?"

"Mmm . . . if you know what you're doing. But dangerous. Tangled roots and weed underwater. It needs clearing out. Neglected like everything else round here."

"Is it deep?"

"Two or three metres maybe. Come on, we can swim further along. The waterfall keeps it clear."

Clare did not move. "Have you been there?"

"Once." His voice sounded too casual.

"What's on the island?"

He shrugged. "It's overgrown. Remains of a garden. Trees. Funny rocks. The Temple ... Look, let's go." He turned away.

Clare went on looking at the island. You could hardly see the Temple and yet she knew there were broad steps up to the entrance. That four life-size classical statues in deep niches guarded it, gods of healing and nature: Apollo, Artemis, Asclepius, Pan. Their names were carved in the stone under their feet. And in the grotto beneath the Temple, Demeter and her re-born daughter.

"Are you coming?"

Mark had walked back to her.

"No," she said, "I don't want to swim here." Despite the heat of the day she was shivering.

"Okay." He shrugged.

He kicked off his boots, peeled off his jeans, and dived into the clearer water, swimming strongly to the waterfall where he pulled himself on to a flat rock and stood under the spray. His head was thrown back, arms outstretched, unselfconsciously enjoying the water streaming over his face and down his naked body.

Clare watched him. Despite his size his body was lithe and very beautiful, she thought. Wide, powerful shoulders tapering to narrow hips. That intriguing line of dark hair, spreading out around his manhood.

Her stomach clenched and reacted. A wave of heat spread over her.

"Come on—it's great!"

She closed her eyes and swallowed. She had only to step out of her clothes and into the cool water and she would feel his smooth body sliding against her own in the sparkling cascade. And later they would lie down together in the shadows.

She was trembling. She wanted him so much, beyond sense and logic. But it had happened too soon, and there was no future in it, only unimaginable pain when he went away.

Another trap. A different kind of trap.

They were both of them caught, struggling helplessly, like the crane fly caught in a spider's web Clare had once seen woven across the kitchen window. The more they struggled, the more they were trapped. They were being roped in, lashed down, as surely as the spider had bound the crane fly.

"No," she said, and walked stiffly away.

Chapter 19

Towards the end of August Clare's exam results arrived. She held the envelope, feeling sick, unable to open it, and eventually carried it up to Raven Hill, where Mark was waiting for her.

"Please—you open it."

He took it from her, ripped it open, and glanced over its contents. He began to grin jubilantly. "They're all right. Better than all right. Bloody marvellous, in fact." He grabbed her, swung her round high in the air, and kissed her.

Breathlessly she caught the paper and read it disbelievingly. Biology A, Chemistry A, History B, Maths B. And she had passed the Economics exam she had re-taken at the lower level. She read and re-read it, hardly taking it in. She really could go to university, after all.

She became aware that Mark was suddenly quiet. He was sitting down, his shoulders bent, morosely booting the turf.

"What's the matter now?" she said, impatiently.

"Nothing."

"Don't be stupid."

"All right. I don't want you to go."

"But I've worked for two years for this. *Five* if you count the GCSEs."

"I know that. I've been through it all myself, remember? I know you and your mother have made all sorts of sacrifices. It's been the thing you've been aiming at, and I'm glad that you got such terrific grades. I *want* you to do what you want

... but ... Oh God, Clare, I just don't know how I'm going to ... manage when you're not here ..."

She felt as though a hole had opened in her heart. The reality of the separation hit her. Never to see Mark again.

She had sworn she would never be one of those women who gave up everything for marriage, a baby and a house, and got restless and resentful because they hadn't explored their own potential. Over the years her mother had drummed it into her that she must have a career—must be able to take care of herself and her children, in case her husband, like her own father, died unexpectedly, or there was a divorce.

Clare had agreed wholeheartedly, but now, faced with the loss of Mark, she felt her plans for the future, her ideas and assumptions, shatter into fragments. The way to university was open. She wanted to go on studying, wanted to extend herself, find out how far she could go, but not if it meant leaving Mark. The future looked utterly bleak. How could she let him go?

She laid her head against his back, and held him. Mark was going away too, and even if they both stayed, it wouldn't solve anything. He wasn't exactly good husband material. She had never dreamed of marrying anyone like Mark. He hadn't even got a job, and they were too young anyway.

"We could wait. I could come out to you when I've got my degree."

"*Three years?*" he said derisively. "All those Adrians and Jonathans?"

Clare said hotly, "It's more likely to be *you* going off with girls."

There was a long silence. Clare said, hopelessly, "We'll work something out."

"Right." He turned his head slowly, and looked at her. His eyes were almost black, dilated with a pain which made her catch her breath. As he looked at her his expression changed slowly, went completely blank for a few moments, then changed again. His eyes glittered recklessly.

He leapt to his feet, laughing, pulling her up with him. "Right. We'll work something out. Come on. Let's go." He caught her hand and began to run down the hill.

"Wait a minute," Clare said, breathless and relieved. "Where are we going?"

"To celebrate. I've got something to show you."

"But *what?*"

"Wait and see."

They skirted the other side of the lake, keeping to the trees, and crossed the Elysium Bridge by the Great Cascade. Clare began to hang back, reluctant, but instead of turning to the Upper Lake as she expected, he plunged into the deeper woods that climbed the lower slopes of the big hill.

"We're going up Barrow Beacon Hill?"

They had dropped into a walk and he had his arm around her shoulders, holding her hard as though he was afraid she would run away. He smiled down at her. She smiled back, wordlessly, and unable to resist, put her arm around his waist, feeling the warmth of his bare skin under her fingers, the awareness tingling up her arm. She thought despairingly, when I'm near him now I have to touch him.

The trees closed in. He pushed back some low branches which concealed an overgrown path, which Clare would never have noticed.

The land rose and rose again. They climbed upwards through the woods and came out into open land, tawny with standing corn. The path thinned into a track, and they climbed steeply up again into open grass land.

"Is it much further?"

He grinned at her. "City girl."

She smiled, suddenly carefree because the sun was shining, they were together and he was in a good mood now.

The view stretched below them green and gold and blue,

layer upon layer of distant hills, as far as the eye could see, glowing in the heat haze like a promised land. Clare took a deep breath.

"Worth a bit of muscle?"

"Oh yes!"

The wind blew warm and steadily out of the west. It was utterly quiet, no birds even, just the sound of the wind moving in the grasses, surrounding her with a sense of exhilaration and freedom. Suddenly it seemed there was nothing to worry about, nothing but Mark and herself and the sound of the wind. Everything would be all right.

"Why didn't you bring me here before?"

He shrugged. "The time wasn't right. You have to be ready for this hill. Ready to be free."

She looked at him uneasily, hearing the curious undertone in his voice.

They left the path and turned into a wider trackway of crushed chalk that ran up along the broad top of the ridge of the land.

Clare said, "It's odd, this road."

"Trackway. That's what they're called. All over England. There's a network of them. The old straight trackways. All in the high places."

"It's old?"

"Old when the Romans came. Nobody knows who made them. Maybe the Stone Age people. They were sacred ways. They buried their dead along them. Over there, see that thing like a whale? That's the long barrow."

Clare stared at the barrow, which was over a hundred metres long and four metres high, remembering the pictures she had seen in Salisbury Museum. She wondered again why the excavation had been stopped and where the crystal skull had been found.

Up here there was a sense of timeless peace. Everything in its right place and time. A time for dying. A time for loving.

She thought about lying naked with Mark, and her body flared to life.

He pulled her against him. She could feel his warm strong muscles against her side, and turned her face away, so that he would not see the burning colour in her cheeks. Had he picked up her thought? Telepathy was real, wasn't it, between people who loved each other?

She felt her body trembling and tried to move away, but he held her closer, his thigh brushing against hers.

Had the barrow people walked on the hill here holding each other, five thousand years ago?

Mark let her go, and climbed over the single wire that bounded the trackway, holding it down for her to climb over. "Here we are."

The turf under her feet was incredibly lush, as springy as a mattress. She said, without thinking, "Where is the stone circle?"

"What stone circle?"

"Why, the one I've seen from the China Garden."

He looked at her curiously. She rushed into speech again. "There ought to be a big stone about . . . here. She tapped her foot in a dip in the ground. "And another over there."

Mark was staring at her intently. He moved forward, heeling away the turf with his heavy boots. She heard the studs catch on a harder surface. The turf broke away and a round shoulder of stone glinted through the loose soil where the turf had been.

Clare swallowed and said quickly, "I expect the soil is thin up here and the rock is just below the surface all over the hill."

He shook his head. "This is limestone country. But that's some sort of sandstone, like the other sarsens here. See the quartz in it?"

Clare said, relieved, "There are stones here then? I've not imagined them."

183

"Standing stones. Not a circle. At least not now. Over here."

Hidden from the trackway in a hollow, just below the summit of the hill, there was a group of ancient standing stones, leaning together like a band of drunken men. Beyond, standing apart, was a single huge stone at least three metres high, and broad, with a large hole right through it at waist height.

Clare ran across the turf delighted, wanting to touch the ancient stone. It felt surprisingly warm and alive, and her palm tingled as she moved it over the surface.

"That's the Ring Stone." His voice sounded hoarse and tense. His mood had changed again, Clare thought impatiently. She did not want to be weighed down with his changing moods when she felt so good.

She walked around the other side of the stone and looked through. "Oh, you can see the House from here. It's much higher than Raven Hill, isn't it? You can see for miles."

Framed in the surround of stone, Ravensmere was tiny and perfect, nested in its park and gardens.

"It's like looking through a camera lens," Clare said, fascinated. "You can see the China Garden, and that big Scots pine and Kenward Farm. They're all in a line."

She slid her hands around the opening, feeling the warmth of the stone, as though it held the sun's energy. "It must have taken them a long time to make a hole this size with only bits of flint and horn to chip it away and polish it."

Mark did not answer. He stroked her neck gently and kissed her ear.

"I wonder why they put it here. Are there any stories about it? I mean they are healing stones, aren't they? Does it cure rickets or scrofula or murrain? What *is* murrain? What do you have to do?" Clare realized she was babbling on, trying to dispel the sexual tension that had built up between them. Where had the peace and stillness gone?

Mark was watching her but she couldn't meet his eyes.

She was too conscious of him, wanting him to kiss her.

He gave a hard laugh, suddenly, making up his mind. "All right. Okay. I'll tell you. First you're supposed to run round the Ring Stone nine times—three times three. Come on." He caught her hand, laughing maniacally, and dragged her laughing and screaming round and round the stone.

". . . seven . . . eight . . ."

"You're mad. Crazy." Clare panted, laughing and giddy.

". . . nine!"

He spun her into his arms and kissed her fiercely until they were both shaking and breathless. She felt his body surging against her and tried to pull away, elated, exhilarated, frightened.

"That's it?"

He let her go. "Now you join hands through the stone. Give me your hands through the hole, Rosie."

At once she felt the energy, the electricity begin to flow between them, flowing through her, tightening her stomach, making her body tremble again. She leaned through, laughing at him, and he kissed her again, but differently—a sweet, gentle kiss, almost as though he was promising something. She felt his lips trembling.

"I love you, Clare," he said, and his voice was shaking too. "I love you."

Then he was laughing wildly, and hauling her bodily through the opening in the stone into his arms. She shrieked with surprise and laughter, taken unawares. But he had pulled too hard, taking the weight of her as she came through, and he fell backwards into the thick, sweet grass, shouting and laughing, with her on top of him.

They rolled over and over, and then all laughter had gone and they were kissing, their bodies hot and alive, moving against each other. He pushed up her T-shirt, to kiss and caress her breasts, and when he unzipped his jeans and pulled away her shorts, she made no move to stop him. Then there was only his body plunged deep into her own, the wild rhythm of their bodies and a tumbling into exquisite sensation.

There was a dog barking far away, then much closer.

Clare said, dazed, "Someone's coming." She scrambled on her shorts somehow, and dragged down her T-shirt. "Please, Mark."

He zipped himself unhurriedly and, grinning, stuffed her briefs into his pocket.

And then they were joined by a dog, a joyfully barking red setter with a glossy coat, bouncing around them, tail wagging furiously, an idiotic grin on its face. It was delighted to find Clare, and did its best to smother her with kisses.

She pushed it away, laughing, and knelt up, trying to smooth her dishevelled hair back into some sort of order, her face flushed into wild rose.

An elderly man in tweeds, with a walking stick, came striding over the turf, smiling at them.

"Get off, Rusty. Leave her be, you great fool. I'm afraid he's taken a fancy to you. We always like a walk up to the old stones at this time of year. They say they go down to the river to bathe and drink on Lammas Eve, but I never saw them." He laughed jovially.

Clare buried her scarlet face in the dog's coat, making a fuss of it, taking time to regain her composure.

"I brought a young lady up here once." The man smiled again. "We've been married over fifty years. Well, we would be, wouldn't we? We joined hands through the old Wedding Ring here." He slapped the stone affectionately. "And we did the circling for good luck."

Clare's hand stilled in the dog's fur. She raised her head slowly and looked at Mark. He stared back, his eyes challenging, glittering with some deep excitement.

"This is called the Wedding Ring?" she said to the man, trying to keep the tremor out of her voice.

"The Wedding Ring, and those old stones over there are the Revellers—drunk at the wedding, see? It's a marrying stone. In the old days people got married here. You ran round it nine times for good luck and joined hands through the hole with your true love, and then you were married." He laughed. "A lot cheaper than the church hall and a satin dress, eh?"

Clare's colour had all drained away. She forced a smile and got up. "It's only a superstition."

"Well, I don't know. These old stones have strange powers. I wouldn't play around with them myself. They certainly brought good luck to me and my wife. Well bound for fifty years."

Clare shivered.

Mark put his arm around her shoulders, but she shrugged it off and moved away, not looking at him.

The man called his dog. "Well, I must be off. Good luck to you both. A long life and a happy one." He walked away, the dog racing ahead of him.

"He saw us," said Mark, grinning.

"I suppose you think that was funny." Clare whirled on Mark furiously. "You knew it was a marrying stone."

"I'm not laughing," said Mark. His eyes were brilliant, watchful.

"It doesn't count," she said wildly. "It can't count if one of the people doesn't know about it."

"We joined hands through the stone. We kissed. We circled the stone three times three to do the binding."

"This is *stupid*. I am not married to you. I'm *not*."

"Aren't you, Rosie? It feels like it to me."

"No!"

"It's too late to argue."

"It's stupid, just *stupid*."

"And consummated too."

She said, disgusted, "You tricked me."

"No tricks. You wanted it too."

"I thought you really cared," she said bitterly. "I thought we were friends. That you wanted the best for me, like I do for you. But real friends don't cheat each other. You're playing stupid tricks just for the hell of it. It was all just a game, wasn't it? A game to trap me. Just a bit of sex on the side. I suppose you'll go away and tell your mates all about it and you'll all have a good laugh."

"You've got it wrong. Do I look as though I'm laughing? You think I go blabbing things around the village?"

"I don't care. In future just stay away from me."

He gave a hard laugh. "Listen, it was a gamble. A last throw of the dice. I had to try, didn't I?"

"I don't want to see you again." Her voice broke. "I won't be trapped."

"Rosie . . ."

"*Don't call me that.* Just stay away from me, do you hear? Just stay away." She turned and ran away down the track.

Chapter 20

Mark did not stay away. He haunted the stables and the kitchen at the House, where he was a favourite of Mrs Anscomb and Mr Bristow, and Frances too. Often Clare would walk in and find Mark leaning against the kitchen units deep in conversation with her mother, or lounging in a chair in their sitting room watching television with her.

He went on talking to her as though they had never quarrelled, turning up on his bike, suggesting places to go, but Clare couldn't answer, could not even bring herself to look at him before turning and walking away. She was hurting too much inside, too angry and disillusioned. He had made a fool of her. There had been no need to lie to her and pretend there was something special between them, that he was in love with her. She had been completely taken in.

At first she intended to go back to London at once, and stay with Sara, but Ravensmere seemed to have woven invisible threads about her, and she couldn't make up her mind to go. Not quite yet. Besides, it seemed silly to shift now, when in only a few weeks she would be leaving anyway.

She spent her time working hard in the garden centre, helping to harvest and pack the herbs, or sitting and talking with Mr Aylward, the only place that was Mark-free.

At night, unable to sleep, she lay awake long hours. She did not go to the China Garden, reluctant to do the Maze Dance in case it took her to the Fifth Moon Gate. She had no wish to be reminded of the Ring Stone on Barrow Beacon Hill.

Two days later Mai told her that they had chopped back the fig tree, and that the Fifth Moon Gate had been re-opened.

When the calling came that night, insistent and urgent, she was unprepared. It was so strong she knew at once that it was very important, that she would have to go. *Disobey them at your peril.* Tabitha was already waiting, and they made their way to the China Garden in full moonlight.

The Fifth Moon Gate was indeed open, but there was no unearthly energy-light, and no stone circle, just the ordinary view of Barrow Beacon Hill.

Clare turned her back quickly and began to thread the long path to the centre, feeling the sway of the Dance as she turned and turned again. By the time she began the return, the moon was directly overhead. She moved faster and faster, blinded by the radiance which seemed to engulf her in a pale gold burst of light. She closed her eyes, and found herself stumbling giddily into the Second Moon Gate.

Tonight she had been sure, somehow, that the Maze Dance would reveal something especially important, but the open Gate showed only a misty view of Kenward Farm venerable and ancient, half-way up the hill on the other side of the valley.

As she watched, two small figures came down the farm track. They were the children she had seen before, just the two little girls. This time the younger girl was clinging to a small pony, and the older girl was holding her on protectively. Then the younger girl deliberately broke free, kicked her mount into a gallop, laughing and waving her hand too confidently. Her red hair streamed out behind her. The next moment she had tumbled off, a bad fall, and the older girl was running forward anxiously, picking her up and cuddling her.

Clare too had started forward involuntarily, and found

herself crashing into the great pile of wood logs and cut-down trees which was heaped against and blocking the Second Moon Gate.

In the morning Frances said, worried, "Mr Aylward's very restless and anxious today. He keeps asking for you. Perhaps if he sees you he'll settle. Don't stay too long, though."

He was sitting at his huge desk, legal-looking papers spread before him. He was wrapped in his rug, despite the heat of the morning and the fire in the hearth. He seemed to have sunk into a light sleep. Clare stood quietly and watched him. The bones of his face looked as though they were covered with pale grey tissue paper, spotted with blotches of pale brown like a bird's egg. She felt a sudden flood of anxiety, love and grief that she had found him too late and that they had so little time together.

In her head she begged for healing for him, and felt an answering warmth and tingling in her fingertips as she took his long hand, like a fragile parcel of bones which might fall to pieces at any moment.

The long sunken shutters of his eyes lifted. Hawk's eyes, ages old. But the green was dark, clear, full of sharp intelligence.

"Not long now," he echoed her own thought, but joyfully, as though it was something he looked forward to. He turned his head slowly, staring up at the heights of Barrow Beacon Hill. "I was dreaming about the old days. I was walking on the hill with my Caroline."

Clare felt herself flushing. She turned away and pulled a chair up nearer to him.

"Despite everything, you know, I have always loved Ravensmere. I was brought up here by my grandfather. I ran in the fields and bathed in the pool by the waterfall."

Clare picked at a loose thread on her jeans.

"My grandfather, Eldon Edgar Aylward, was a strange and

rather frightening man. He was very tall. There was a grandeur about him. He was deeply learned in many cultures and esoteric knowledge. He knew seven languages, some of the most ancient—Icelandic, Arabic, Sanskrit, Chinese. He was expert in archaeology, natural history, science, geology. He spent years researching his life's work."

Clare smiled. "Ten volumes. *The Evolutionary History.*"

"Correct. But he was a lonely and unhappy man. He had to wait for his beloved Rosamond to grow up. He married her on her seventeenth birthday. He was thirty-nine, but it was a love match for all that. Three years later she died bringing my father into the world.

"My grandfather never married again. He was reclusive. Yet he made many good friends—William Morris, who shared his love of Iceland, Burne-Jones, who made a memorial window for him in the church, *The Waters of Paradise.*"

"I saw it," said Clare. "It's beautiful."

"And appropriate. He imagined, I think, that he was reincarnated from an ancient, more beautiful age."

Clare said, "Atlantis?"

The green eyes focused on her. "Perhaps. He firmly believed he had evidence of its existence."

"What evidence?" asked Clare, but he was far away in the past, speaking slowly.

"I don't think my grandfather could bear to look at his son. He blamed him for his wife's death. He sent him away to school as soon as possible, thence to Oxford, and made over our great London house in Berkeley Square to him. It was a terrible mistake. He grew up knowing nothing of Ravensmere or the Benison and deeply resented being made to marry my mother, another Rosamond Kenward, on threat of losing his inheritance."

There was a long silence. Clare said, "They weren't happy?"

"He made her suffer for it. He was a gambler and a

womanizer. One of Prince Teddy's circle. He spent vast sums on the jewels of the kept women that he preferred to my dear mother and he gambled away the town house and over a million pounds—a great sum in those days."

Clare took a deep breath. "I saw his memorial in the church. He died at Ypres in the First World War. I thought he was a great hero."

He said, succinctly, "He was a bullying sadist whose greatest pleasure was to beat my mother black and blue and whip me with a cane until I was bleeding."

Clare stared at him, horrified.

"His death came only as a relief to us. My grandfather sent for me and I came back to Ravensmere. My mother refused to come back—who can blame her?—and was one of the first victims of the great influenza epidemic that ravaged Europe after the War."

"You must have been lonely."

"I was not allowed to visit my mother. My grandfather . . . tolerated me. Saw that I was educated. And passed on the Trust."

Clare was appalled. What had gone wrong with all these people? Surely Ravensmere was meant to be a loving and peaceful place. But it seemed there was a long line of pain stretching back generation by generation.

"I hated my father, but I am bound to admit that he was badly treated as a child. He was a victim too. You know, Clare, I begin to see at last that we are indeed all born victims of victims. It is a strange and terrible thing how history repeats itself. I married my Caroline when I was twenty-one. We had only one year together before she was taken from me. I was very bitter. I was determined not to marry again. There would be no more Guardians. Let the Benison take its chances, I thought. Let it all go—what did I care?

"When it was clear there was going to be another war, I joined the Royal Air Force. Your grandfather, John,

Caroline's brother, came to me and pointed out my responsibilities to Ravensmere and the village. If I was killed everything would go to the Fletchers. So I married again to get an heir for Ravensmere. I made a bad choice."

His voice sank into silence. Clare waited patiently. She thought he had maybe dropped off to sleep, and wondered if she should tiptoe out, but suddenly he spoke again, loudly and strongly, banging the chair arm with frustration, startling her.

"I did my damnedest to get killed in the War. Flew the most dangerous sorties, volunteered for lunatic ventures. Offered myself for death in every way—and survived. Other, better, men went down all around, but not me. Not a scratch. My punishment was to survive."

Clare said, "VC, DSC, DFC . . ."

He snorted disparagingly.

"You should be grateful," she said. "You might have been terribly disabled, not killed."

"Oh no," he said, ironically, "they wouldn't allow that. You have to be strong and well to guard the Benison. Well, or dead. Strong in body, strong in mind."

There was a strange look in his eyes. For a moment Clare thought it might be fear. But that could hardly be in a man with medals for bravery and the next moment it had gone.

He took a deep breath. "After the War, Cecily and I patched things up briefly and my son was born. I loved my son, but the marriage was—disastrous. We fought like cat and dog. She was jealous and wild. There is bad blood in that family."

Clare said tentatively, "Perhaps she thought you still loved Caroline."

He looked at her in surprise. "But that was true. Only ever Caroline. She was soft and gentle. She never raised her voice. Here . . ." He fumbled in his jacket pocket and handed her a miniature in a small gold case.

A pale girl with smooth fair hair cut short under her ears smiled hesitantly at her, but there was no smile in her eyes.

Clare handed it back. "She looks sad. What did she die of?"

But he had looked away broodingly across the Great Lake and did not answer. At last he said rawly, "I loved my son but he disliked me. He blamed me for his mother's death. It was an accident, but he thought I had driven her to her death by my neglect and my lack of love.

"I couldn't bear to see that virago in my Caroline's place. I hated to see her walk through the rooms of Ravensmere. And she was no good to me. She could never be a Guardian. I was glad when she broke her neck hunting."

Clare felt cold. Poor Cecily. How would it feel married to someone who could only love a dead woman, and who resented and hated you?

"I was vindictive, inhuman. Taking out on her my anger about the loss of Caroline. But I was punished, Clare. I was dreadfully punished. My son died too. My only son."

He looked deathly tired suddenly, and Clare wondered if she ought to stop him. To her dismay she saw his cheeks were wet.

"Mr Aylward . . ."

"No, I want you to hear. To know the truth. To understand why I wanted Ravensmere to die. Why I refused to do my duty as Guardian.

"I went away from Ravensmere and devoted myself to making money. I am a gambler, Clare, like my father, but I gamble on the Stock Exchange and the international money markets. They say all gamblers do it because they really want to lose and destroy themselves. But I couldn't lose. I have a . . . talent . . . for forecasting the movement of the market."

He gave his ironic croaking laugh. "The Benison looks after its own. But none of it mattered. I'd lost Caroline and then I lost Brandon.

195

"I left him to grow up wild and lonely. I heard from Roger Fletcher that he was reckless and irresponsible like his mother. On the day he died we quarrelled violently.

"I helped to kill my son, Clare. I blamed the Kenwards. Your mother. But mine was the greater blame. I accept that now. I made him what he was."

His voice sounded so anguished that Clare gripped his hand. "It's all over, Mr Aylward. It was all done with years ago. Perhaps he wasn't as bad as you thought. Roger Fletcher was probably telling lies. You've got to forgive yourself. There's nothing you can do about it now."

For a moment he went absolutely still, thinking. His green eyes pinned her with painful intensity. He said, at last, "But I have to put it right. When I came back to live permanently at Ravensmere I tried to pass through the Seventh Gate, but the web would not part."

"What web?" Clare said. "Do you mean the Seventh Gate in the China Garden? But there's only an imitation Gate there."

But he wasn't listening, and she saw that he had that strange look in his eyes that her mother had sometimes. His voice took on the weird chanting rhythm that sent a chill down her spine.

"It has taken me a long time to understand and accept defeat. A long time to acknowledge the wrongs I've done. They will not let me go, whatever my suffering, until there is a new Guardian."

Clare rubbed her forehead. "But if Roger Fletcher inherits Ravensmere, surely he'll be the Guardian too?"

He stared at her with weary amusement. "They would never allow Roger to inherit."

Clare said cautiously, feeling her heart give a great leap of hope, "You mean, you've changed your Will? Roger Fletcher *won't* inherit?"

"The Will was never made in his favour. It suited me to

allow him to believe it was. For a time I sought to use him as a weapon of destruction. Futile. The Guardians are hereditary. I thought you understood that. Brandon was the next male Guardian."

He was looking at her closely, but Clare did not notice.

"Bring him to me, Clare. I said I'd never forgive them. I swore that the son of *that woman* would never set foot in Ravensmere, but I was wrong. God help me, it has taken me twenty years to accept it. I've been wrong all my life. Bring him quickly. I have to put it right."

Clare said, frightened, "But, you know, Mr Aylward, Brandon's *dead*. You just told me . . ."

He said in a more normal voice. "Not *Brandon*, girl. D'you think I'm senile? Go to Kenward Farm and bring the boy to me."

Clare said, incredulously, "You want to see *Mark?* Mark Winters at the farm?"

"Bring him."

"But . . . Well, it's difficult. You see, I'm not actually talking to . . ."

"You must bring him quickly, Clare. There is danger. The time is running out."

Chapter 21

Clare went back to the stables and made herself a cup of coffee, and then a sandwich she couldn't eat, trying to put off the evil moment when she had to go to Kenward Farm. Why couldn't he just telephone, she thought, or send James?

But she knew why. Mark would need to be persuaded to come. She would feel a fool looking for him at his home, and she would have to sink her pride and start talking to him again, and all the pain would come back.

Her mother came in quickly, holding a newspaper over her hair against the heavy rain.

"It's bucketing down. The weather's broken with a vengeance. But after all that heat it's a bit of relief to see rain again."

"What are you doing home at this time?" Clare pushed her sandwich away.

Frances began to drag the vacuum cleaner out of its cupboard. "I've got a few hours free. Mr Aylward doesn't want me—he's got some estate business on hand. Mr Bristow is hopping round making telephone calls for him all over the place. Roger Fletcher and James Kenward have been sent for and his solicitor is coming over from Bath. I just hope he isn't overdoing it."

Clare said, "He wants me to fetch Mark Winters from Kenwards."

Frances stopped dead. "He wants Mark?" Her eyes were shining.

"But *why*? I thought they'd been trying to keep him off the estate. Why does he want Mark?"

"I expect we'll find out."

"But you know already, don't you?"

Frances switched on the cleaner, and Clare pulled out its wall plug with determination.

"Clare!"

"You'll have to tell me sometime. Don't you think I've got a right to know? Everybody else does."

Frances' fingers curled into fists. She stuffed them into her pockets. She said coldly, "Very well. If you must know. Mark is Mr Aylward's grandson. Brandon's son."

"*Brandon's son!* But you said you were engaged to Brandon, and then he died . . . Oh, my God!" she went paper white. "Is Mark my *brother?*"

"Of course not. If Mark was your brother do you think I'd have let it go as far as it has?"

Clare raised her head slowly and met her mother's gaze. She knew about them. Knew she had made love with Mark. A dark flush flooded up her neck and burned over her face.

Frances said, "Mark told me. He was worried he had made you pregnant. He said he wanted to marry you."

"Big of him. He's going away. To Australia or Canada or somewhere. When he gets his money."

Frances said, "It will be too late. He won't get away. He has to stay."

"But . . ."

"He can't accept that yet. Frightened of the responsibility, like his father. He feels angry and trapped. That's why Bran was so wild. Mark's all right. When he finds his purpose he'll be all right. When he accepts. If he doesn't, he'll die."

Clare watched her mother, saw the filmed eyes, and heard the high even note in her voice, and shivered.

She said, hesitating, "Did you love Brandon?"

Frances rubbed her forehead. "Oh yes, I loved him. I loved

him very much. He was like the other half of myself. But before he died I broke our engagement."

"But if you loved him so much, if he loved you, why did you break it off? How could you?"

"I found out . . . something."

"Nothing could have been so important if you *really* loved each other," Clare said definitely, almost accusing, thinking of Mark. If she really loved Mark she would never be able to let him go whatever happened.

"I had no choice."

"You always say that's not true. There's always a choice."

Frances' voice shook. "I found out my sister was having Brandon's baby."

"Your *sister*!" Clare felt the rush of hot blood to her face.

"My half-sister, Vivienne. She's three years younger than me. Mark is her son."

"Mrs Carlton-Winters! Vivienne Kenward that was. I suppose she moved back to Kenward Farm when your father died," Clare said, as another piece of the jigsaw dropped into place. "Why didn't I guess? So what happened?"

"We grew up together, Brandon, Vivienne and me. We used to go to the village school together until Bran was sent away to school."

Clare heard herself say, "You used to meet at the stile opposite the gates and run down the footpath across the field."

Frances looked at her anxiously. Clare said, "It's all right. I'm beginning to get used to it. Go on."

"Well, Bran and I were always close. Then we got engaged. I went to London to shop and get my wedding dress. While I was away they . . . betrayed me."

Clare said carefully, "You mean while Brandon Aylward was getting married to you he got your sister pregnant."

Frances' voice was hard. "You can understand why Vivienne and I don't see each other."

"And Mark—he's really Mark *Aylward?*"

Her mother shook her head. "He's Mark Kenward. Brandon never married Vivienne. Mark is illegitimate. Mr Aylward would never let her use the name. Vivienne eventually married Roddy Carlton-Winters and he adopted him."

Mark the Bastard. Clare understood Pete Anscomb's jibes now. "He's my cousin," she said, dazed.

"Half-cousin," Frances said bitterly. "He could have been my son."

Clare stared at her. The bond, she thought. That's why her mother got along with Mark so well.

"Does he know?"

"Oh yes. There are family photographs. He recognized me." Frances swallowed, and suddenly Clare could see through her calm mask. There was so much pain and anguish there. The betrayal had hurt her so badly perhaps she had never truly recovered.

"He didn't tell me," said Clare, and felt her own hurt bite deeper. "And neither did you. You brought me down here not telling me anything. I feel a complete fool."

"I was trying to protect you."

"I don't need protection," Clare said angrily. "I need the truth. Then I'll know how to deal with things myself."

Kenward Farm seemed to be deserted as Clare trudged reluctantly up the track from the lane. It was very old, sunken into the hill behind it. It was massive, like a fort, the windows deep and small, its roofs sagging, mossy with lichen. It had an immense, deep porch and a door like a church. The outbuildings, barn and stables, forming a square next to it, were too neat and clean to be a working farm.

She took a deep breath and pushed open the barred gate, which said *Kenward Stables*, and closed it carefully behind her. Immediately there was a volley of honking, and a phalanx of geese advanced on her from the other side of the pond across the yard. A barking dog was quelled by a raised female voice and Clare saw there was a woman striding across the yard towards her.

She was tall, with a high-boned face and a great mane of dark red hair. She was wearing jeans stuffed into wellies, and for a moment Clare thought she was young, but there was a streak of white hair in the glorious auburn and fine lines round her eyes and mouth.

Her face riveted Clare. It was her own face grown older, full of bitter experience.

The woman stared back at her, immobile, and then she threw back her head and roared with laughter.

"My God, no wonder she didn't bring you here when she came back for the funeral."

Clare was embarrassed and furious with her mother. Another unnecessary deception. She said, "You must be my Aunt Vivienne. I came to see Mark. That is, I've got a message for him."

"You'd better come into the house before the geese get you."

Vivienne banged the farmyard muck off her boots on the bootscraper next to the door which said 1686 in its ironwork, and thrust her way into a stone-flagged kitchen. She took Clare along a low passage way, with wide boards blackened by age and polish, to a long sitting room with a lattice window set into the wall a metre thick.

Vivienne said, "Visitor for you." And Clare saw that Mark was stretched out in an armchair, staring at a smouldering log in the great open fireplace. A golden spaniel lying next to him with its nose on its paws got up and came to smell her feet.

Mark said, "*Friend*, Flossie." But her tail had already started to wave vigorously. Clare let her smell her fingers and the dog rolled over on her back, paws in the air, to let Clare rub her stomach. Clare tried not to look at Mark. She knew he was staring at her.

"An unexpected pleasure."

Clare straightened and swallowed. "He wants to see you," she said baldly, thrusting her hands into the back of her jeans, trying to hide her nervousness and excitement. "Mr Aylward sent me to get you. He wants to see you at the House."

Two expressionless faces looked back at her.

Vivienne began to smile unpleasantly, then, throwing back her head, broke into laughter.

Mark was on his feet, his shoulders rigid with tension. "No." The spaniel padded quickly back across the oak boards, and whined up at him, worried and questioning. "*No.*"

Vivienne punched the air with her fist. "Justice, by God! Justice after all these years."

"He wants to put things right," Clare said.

Mark smiled. "You can give him a message from me. Tell him to piss off. I'm no bloody serf. He can't issue orders to me."

"Look, I'm sorry. I've put it badly. It's a *request*. He wants to talk to you."

Vivienne, still laughing, pushed back her mane of red hair. "I don't believe it. *I just don't believe it!* It's a massive climb-down. That stiff-necked old monster has given in. I never believed he would."

"I'm not going," said Mark.

Clare said, evenly, trying to keep the hurt out of her voice. "My mother says you're his grandson. Brandon's son. Why didn't you tell me, Mark?"

He looked at her impatiently. "It would have done me a lot of good with you, wouldn't it? You think I'm proud of it? He's never recognized me. He's never even spoken to me."

"He wants to talk to you now."

"He could have done that any time in the last twenty years. It's too late."

"Why do you hate him so much? He's old and ill. He wants to put things right."

"He should have thought of that before. Listen, he hounded my mother out of the village. He ruined our grandfather. He bought up our farm and its loss killed Grandfather. When we came back three years ago Roger Fletcher came over and told us to get out. Some nasty accidents happened to our horses until my mother brought in the police. And he's destroyed our business. Warned off the local people, so they're too frightened to come here."

Clare said, "But that was Roger Fletcher. Are you sure Mr Aylward sent him?"

"I'm not even supposed to go on Ravensmere land. You heard Fletcher threaten me with a shotgun. He's tried to keep me out since I used to bike over from Roddy's place." He smiled mirthlessly. "You think we're all going to kiss and make up?"

"Mr Aylward is admitting he's wrong now." Clare looked at Vivienne helplessly, and back at Mark. "You're Brandon's only son. You're the next Guardian. You must be. Doesn't that mean anything to you? Suppose he wants you to have Ravensmere? You'll throw it all away and let Roger Fletcher take over?"

He was furious. "He thinks he's only got to wave his money and I'll come running. *Wrong.* I don't want that place like some bloody great albatross hanging around my neck all my life. I'm getting out. Starting a life somewhere else, where I can build something new, without all this garbage from the past choking me."

"You'd let it all go to Roger Fletcher? Turn Ravensmere and Stoke Raven into a nuclear dumping ground?"

"Why should I care? The people here have never done

anything for us except shout insults at my mother. Most of the villagers won't talk to her and they won't even serve her in the village shop."

Clare looked desperately at Vivienne. "Can't you tell him? We're not playing sulky baby games."

Vivienne flung herself into an armchair and lit a cigarette. She shrugged. "He makes his own decisions. If he wants to chuck it all away—House, estate, money and *girl*—that's his choice. I think he's out of his mind. But he's never taken any notice of my opinions in the past, so he's not likely to start now."

There was a stain of colour across Mark's cheek bones. He looked at Clare, his green eyes brilliant and reckless. She saw suddenly the likeness to Mr Aylward, wondering how she could have missed it before.

"Is that right, Clare? Am I chucking the girl away too? If I accepted, would you be in it with me?"

There was complete silence. None of them moved, then Clare looked away. She said awkwardly, "I don't come into this. I'm just a messenger. It's you he wants to see."

Her voice sounded false even to her own ears. She couldn't do it. The responsibility was too heavy, too big. She wouldn't be blackmailed. She wouldn't give up her future.

She said stubbornly, "You are the Guardian."

"So are you. The daughter of the daughter."

She said desperately, "*No.* I don't believe that. There's been some mistake. It must be someone else. It can't be me. Anyway, it's just a story, a myth."

"Sure," he said, and smiled grimly. "That's what I think. It can't be *me*." He got up and opened the door for her with exaggerated courtesy. "They baited the trap nicely, didn't they? And we took it. But that's it. We're off the hook. Goodbye, Rosie. It's been nice knowing you. Take care of yourself."

She trailed to the door miserably. "Please, Mark. *Please*

think about it. Please come and see him. Just *speak* to him. That's not asking much."

"Too much. I'm already packed. I'm on my way tomorrow. You came in time to say goodbye."

Chapter 22

"What happened?" Frances looked up as Clare let herself in and slammed the door angrily.

"Nothing. He won't come." She kicked off her soaked trainers and threw her wet rain-jacket on a hook.

"You told Mr Aylward?"

"I gave him Mark's message—'Tell him to piss off. I'm no bloody serf'."

"Clare!"

"That's what he said. Mr Aylward didn't seem surprised. He gave a snort and that funny laugh of his. Then he said I was to tell Mark he was only making it hard on himself, and that he hadn't got any choice now. But Mark is going away tomorrow. All he thinks about is getting away."

Frances said, worried, "He's the Guardian. He can't go. It's his inheritance. The whole future of the valley. He has to stay."

"*You* tell him—he might listen to you. He says he doesn't owe Ravensmere anything. He's bitter about the way the village treats his mother. He said they won't speak to her."

"They have long memories here. They haven't forgiven her."

"He called Ravensmere a bloody great albatross." Clare's voice cracked.

"What did *she* say—Vivienne?"

Clare shrugged. "She said he makes his own decisions, but I think she wanted him to stay."

"Did she look well? Did she say anything about me?"

"Not much. She looked all right. Like you, a bit, but older and she's got that red hair. She was on edge. She smokes a lot and keeps moving about. She laughed when she saw me. When I said that Mr Aylward wanted to see Mark, she said 'By God, justice at last!'"

"That sounds like Vivienne." Frances went into the kitchen and started to unload their washing from the machine, folding it quickly and unevenly.

Clare followed her to help with the sheets. "You hate her."

"Did I say that? If you want to know, I miss her badly. She was my little sister. I always loved her and tried to look after her. She was so lively and full of energy. And courage. She would even stand up to Father. He never could control her. She brought life into that dead house. There was always life where Vivienne was." She brushed a tear away from her cheek with the back of her hand.

"And Bran was my best friend. It was always Brandon and me, like two parts of one whole. We always knew we would marry. It was like night following day. Bran wanted us to get married when I was sixteen, but Father wouldn't agree. He said we must wait until I was eighteen, and Bran was twenty-one. It was hard, waiting. We wanted each other so much. We tried to keep things cool and low-key but it was very difficult. Bran was angry and wild—doing all sorts of crazy things."

"Did they tell you both you were the next Guardians?"

"We just knew, like everybody else. Everyone knew we would take over and be responsible for the Benison.

"I didn't know what it was, of course. But Bran knew. His father told him about it and what we had to do, but he wouldn't tell me. He said he'd tell me when we were married.

"I only know that summer he was worried and terribly upset about something. He was completely wild. He rode his motor bike all over the county. Came off and broke his collar

208

bone. I was fed up with his moods and we kept quarrelling, arguing about the least thing. I began to wonder if we were doing the right thing. Mr Aylward started to plan a huge wedding, which neither of us wanted, for the late autumn."

Frances took a deep breath. "And then Vivienne decided that she had fallen in love with Bran. She was sixteen then, and beautiful. She made a dead set for him."

Clare said, "Was she jealous about the big wedding? I should think she likes to be the centre of attention."

Frances shrugged. "Perhaps, a little. But I think she genuinely thought she loved him. And Bran played up to her. Later, when it was too late, he told me that he thought he was losing me, that I was cooling off, and he wanted to make me jealous. Perhaps that was true. I don't know. Anyway, I went to London to get my wedding dress. It happened then."

She turned away, stacking the pile of washing in the ironing basket.

"A few weeks later it all came out. There was a dreadful scene in the Library here. Both families. Vivienne said she was pregnant—flaunted it, rather, and said Brandon was the father. She thought he loved her. She was sure he was going to marry her instead of me."

"What did Brandon say?"

"He . . . jeered at her. In front of all of us. He was so cruel. It was as though he hated her and wanted to destroy her. I've never forgiven him for that.

"I was in deep shock. I couldn't believe what they'd done. I felt I'd been deep-frozen. Nothing was real. I looked at him and I hardly knew him. I said that of course he must marry her now. That I would leave Ravensmere. Bran went crazy. *Demented*, like a wasp in a jar. He kept bellowing at me that we were the Guardians. We *had* to marry. That I *couldn't* go away. But I knew that I would never be able to stay while she married Brandon and had the baby that should have been mine.

"I took off my engagement ring and threw it on the library table. I remember it slid right along the length of the table, scratching the polish. It fell off on to the floor and went on sliding. We all watched it. I think it was then that we realized what was happening. I started to feel again, but I was so hurt and angry. And Mr Aylward was . . . terrifying."

Frances filled the kettle and began to make tea. Her hands were trembling.

"Vivienne blamed me, you know, for Brandon's death. They all blamed me. They think he took his bike out and crashed it deliberately—that he committed suicide because we'd broken up."

"What do you think?"

Frances was silent for a long time. Then she said haltingly, "Yes, I think I was . . . indirectly . . . responsible for his death.

"I think he was leaving Ravensmere for good. Trying to escape from whatever it was that was worrying him. Something about the Benison. But the Guardians can't leave for good. They can go for a while—provided they intend to come back. If they leave for good they have refused the Trust and they die."

Clare stared at her. "You really believe that, don't you? But *you* went away."

"That's right. I went away, but we weren't married. I didn't know the secret of the Benison. The Trust hadn't passed. That saved me."

"You went to London."

"I lived in a hostel, and did my nurse training. I loved my work but I was homesick. I couldn't stop dreaming of Ravensmere. Something was trying to drag me back, I know it was, and I got . . . ill. After a while I met your father who was having a heart bypass operation in the hospital. He was quite a bit older than me. I knew our chances weren't very good. But we got married all the same and when you came along I was very happy.

"Your father was a good man, Clare. Deep thinking. Intelligent. Spiritual. He understood me, and I loved him. Not like Brandon. There are so many different ways of loving. It was a terrible blow to lose him. I'm sorry you grew up not knowing him."

"I can remember him a bit," Clare said. "I remember him laughing and reciting something I couldn't understand."

"He wrote poetry in Welsh. He was a Bard. A very high honour." She hesitated. "I ought to tell you, Clare . . . He was psychic too, and a spiritual healer."

"I never stood a chance between the two of you, did I?" Clare said, ruefully.

Frances smiled. "I never told you because you were always so frightened of it."

"I'm getting used to it now, I suppose. A bit. I-I'd just like to be able to control it more."

"You were very psychic as a child, always talking about people I couldn't see and telling me what was going to happen. And then you seemed to switch it off."

"I think Ravensmere started it up again."

Frances stood up. "I'd better get back to Mr Aylward. He'll be exhausted after all the visitors. I've no idea what he's up to."

Clare said, "You didn't want me to come here, did you?"

"I thought if I kept you away you wouldn't get drawn into the old legend. That you'd be free. But you don't know how difficult it's been. For a long time I refused to think of Ravensmere or talk about the past. I tried to forget it—become a different person. Then I had to come back for Father's funeral and after that I began to feel this . . . driving power, insisting I had to bring you home. I had trouble sleeping. It got worse and worse and I know I got irritable and distraught.

I couldn't concentrate and I thought I was losing my mind. Then I knew that Mr Aylward was very ill and the next day a letter arrived from him, begging me to come back. He said I wouldn't have to stay in the House—that I'd have my own home.

"I love him, Clare, and I felt so guilty about the way Bran died. I owed Mr Aylward for that. I *had* to come. I couldn't put it off any longer. And you insisted on coming too. I thought, I can't stand up to them, they're stronger than I am. I was just so tired of it all, and worried. There was a faint hope that you could come for a few weeks and slip away but . . ."

"Roger Fletcher changed that, didn't he?" said Clare. "That day we arrived. You were furious with him."

"I understood just what it meant for Ravensmere if he took over. I was torn to pieces. Your future—my only child's future—against the well-being of the whole area and all the people's lives."

"It was taken out of your hands anyway. Mr Aylward made sure of that."

"Yes. He schemes and plans. He knows about the future. He's too clever for me." Frances pulled her jacket out of the hall cupboard. "I must go."

Clare said slowly, "Are you going to speak to Vivienne?"

Frances went still. "I don't know. I don't know if I can face her. I feel so guilty. I should have helped her through her bad time, given her support and love, but I . . . couldn't. I was so ashamed at Father's funeral. And the village people were so rude to her. I couldn't say anything."

"She ruined your life," Clare reminded her. "Brandon's as well."

"But she was only sixteen, Clare. Younger than you. She was impulsive. She always did things first and thought about them afterwards. She never considered the consequences. I loved her—I almost brought her up—but I let her down badly. I can't forgive myself for that. I was too full of pain, thinking only of myself. I left her to fend for herself. She was sixteen and pregnant and Father threw her out. She must have been very frightened." She brushed her hair back tiredly. "She would have suited Brandon better than me, Clare."

"But he was in love with *you*," said Clare.

"Was he? I'll never know. That's what tears at me still, after all these years.

"Clare, the night he died he telephoned me. I don't know where he was. He didn't say much. He sounded calm, serious. We decided we had to talk, and he said he'd come to the farm.

"I didn't tell him then that I'd made up my mind that I would marry him after all. Accept the Guardianship. Start again. I'd worked out that perhaps we could adopt the baby when it came. I knew Vivienne never wanted a baby. She'd planned to go into show jumping. But Bran never came.

"I didn't tell him, Clare," Frances said, anguished. "That's the point. *I didn't tell him.* And when he died he wasn't coming to see and talk to me. *He was riding away.* If I had told him he might have come back. And maybe he wouldn't have crashed."

They were silent. Clare went over and put her arms around her mother and hugged her wordlessly, and they stood together looking out at the gloomy afternoon. Her mother's reflection in the window glass showed a face looking hardly older than her own.

"You ought to marry again, Mum. You've had too much pain. You deserve something better. There's time to make a new life."

"Chris Stevens wanted to."

Clare said carefully, "That sounds like a good idea." And saw that her mother was fighting back tears. "I'm sorry I've been such a pain this year. I was manic about the exams and trying to make up my mind about the courses. And Adrian didn't help. You were right about Adrian. I can't think what I saw in him. Since I came here things seem clearer somehow."

She took a deep breath, a faint flush of colour in her cheeks. "I've been thinking lately that I was wrong about my university course too. Like you said. I don't want to do a business degree, and I don't want to go away to Sussex."

The expression of relief and delight on her mother's face made Clare realize just how worried she had been. "Oh Clare, I'm so glad. I knew that degree wasn't right for you. What are you going to do?"

Clare said hesitantly, "I thought perhaps I'd ask Dr McKinnon about Medicine."

"But won't the courses be filled for this year?"

"I'll have to wait till next year. I don't mind. I can work and save up. The thing is, it would mean I'd be studying for years longer. I don't know if we can afford it."

Frances kissed her. "You've got to have a good career. Something you really want to do. We'll manage somehow, Clare."

She opened the front door. "We'll talk about it this evening. I'll probably be late back."

"Mum? Write to Chris?"

"I'll think about it."

Clare went on staring blindly out of the window, thinking about her mother's story. She felt cold, angry and depressed. She should telephone Mark, tell him what Mr Aylward had said. Tell him she had decided not to take up the place at Sussex. The coil of anger in her wound tighter. Why did it always have to be her who gave way? He hadn't even apologized for his trickery on Barrow Beacon Hill.

Tomorrow would be soon enough. She would tell him tomorrow when he came up to the stables. She turned on the television.

*　　*　　*

214

In the morning she bumped into James Kenward coming out of the garden centre. He was grinning from ear to ear, his red hair curling wildly over his forehead.

"You look cheerful."

"Top of the world."

"Wait till Roger Fletcher gets at you."

He stared. "You mean you haven't heard? He's gone."

"*Gone?*"

"Sent off yesterday with a flea in his ear and six months' salary in lieu of notice."

"You mean Mr Aylward has sacked him?" Clare could not believe it.

"Sent for us both yesterday. Said that it had come to his notice that Fletcher had been attempting to dispose illegally of valuable parts of the estate like the *Liber Somnium Sanctus* for his own profit.

"Fletcher was livid. He said that Mr Aylward was senile and he'd have him certified and thrown into a private clinic."

"He can't do that, can he?" Clare was horrified.

James grinned. "Not after Mr Aylward produced his solicitor, sitting in the next room with the door open listening, and a list as long as your arm of all Fletcher's nasty little activities over the last five years, with dates, times, corroborative evidence—most of which he could go to prison for.

"By the time he'd finished Roger Fletcher was as white as a sheet and couldn't get out of the room quick enough. My guess is he's on his way out of the country in case Mr Aylward changes his mind and calls in the Fraud Squad."

"But how did Mr Aylward find out? And why didn't he do anything before?" But she knew that. She could hear his voice: *I thought to use him as a weapon of destruction . . .*

James shrugged. "He finds out everything. Just gives people enough rope to hang themselves. Fletcher was a fool to try it. When the old man moves he moves fast."

"But who's going to manage the estate now?"

215

He flung his arms apart dramatically, "*C'est moi!*"

"James!" Clare beamed with delight. "Oh congratulations. How absolutely fantastic! Promise you won't sell Ravensmere to Nuclear Energy."

He grinned. "Not a chance. I can't wait to stop his dubious farming practices too. By the way, we're bringing the wedding forward now. I've been offered Kenward Farm when the lease expires at the end of the month. Mai wants to know if you'll be her bridesmaid?"

Clare frowned. "But what about Mark's mother? Mark wanted Kenwards."

"Mr Aylward owns a racing stable and house over at Wincanton. I think he's going to offer her a partnership. She's a brilliant horsewoman, but the stables aren't paying here. Not in the right place."

"And Mark, what about him?"

James looked surprised. "He gets Ravensmere, of course, the estate, the farms, the whole caboodle."

Chapter 23

Mark had gone.

Clare could not believe it. All day she had expected to see him come riding into the stable yard, when he heard the good news that his old enemy was out on his ear, but he did not come. She telephoned Kenward Farm, but there was no reply. Late in the evening there was still no reply. Clare began to realize, with a cold misery, that he had meant exactly what he had said.

In her mind Clare went over and over her visit to Kenwards obsessively, trying to re-write the script. What she *could* have said. What she *could* have done. If only she hadn't put off making that telephone call.

He did not come the next day, or the next, and then it was nearly a week since anyone had seen him.

She told herself that it was just as well he had gone. She was glad that it was finished. There was no future for them. They were different kinds of people. She would get over it, just as she got over Adrian. But deep down, there was a jagged wound that was not healing at all. Part of herself had been lost. The future looked bleak and empty.

The weather echoed her feelings. Autumn was definitely in the air. Days of cold, driving rain, spinning dark gold leaves off the trees. The lake looked like an iron frying pan under the scudding clouds. Soon she must leave Ravensmere. She would never come back. It would be too painful.

She wished she could see Mark again, just once, just to

tell him ... Tell him what? Something he didn't want to know. That she wouldn't be going to university for a year. *That she loved him?*

She wondered where he had gone. If there were girls there. He wouldn't be long without a girl. If only she knew where he was.

One evening she went down to the village to find his friends at the Market Cross. They were surly and hostile, blaming her for Mark's trouble. Pete Anscomb said he didn't know where he was—they had hardly seen him since he'd met her in Salisbury. Blackhead said he thought he'd passed him on the bypass heading towards London, but he couldn't be sure because he was going too fast. It just looked like his bike.

Clare's last hope died. He had really gone then. Gone for good. He had made a break for it. A last chance to get away.

But he was a Guardian. If the old stories were true he was in terrible danger.

Her fear grew as the days passed. She was restless, unable to concentrate. She climbed Barrow Beacon Hill and sat for hours with the rain running down her face, staring at the mist-shrouded countryside below. Was he all right? Had something happened to him already? She tried to fight down her mounting panic. There was a brooding sense of danger, a premonition which she tried to deny, that death was coming closer to him.

"Why don't you go over to Kenwards?" Frances said, at the end of the week, recognizing her state. "Vivienne must have heard from him by now. Maybe he's come back, even."

But Vivienne had not heard from Mark. She had no idea where he was. She was walking up and down jerkily, and she looked years older, the skin drawn tight over her cheek bones. The ashtrays were piled high and the whole room reeked of smoke. She hadn't eaten. Clare made coffee and sandwiches for her while Vivienne talked about Mark.

"Don't you have anybody you can turn to? Where's your husband?"

Vivienne laughed. "Which one? I've had three—each one worse than the last. I should never have come back here. I hate the place. Too many old, bad memories."

"Why did you? Come back, I mean."

"Oh, any number of reasons. They all seemed good at the time. The farm was here, and I always wanted to run a stables. Mad about horses always. I wanted to get away from Number Three. And besides I kept feeling that Mark should be here." She looked sideways at Clare. "Stupid, wasn't it?"

"He's a Guardian."

Vivienne shrugged. "I suppose. If you believe all that. But the main reason I came back— this will really make you laugh— I hoped your mother would come home one day, and that we could be friends again." She lit a cigarette from the stub of the previous one. "Stupid, like I said. How is she? Did she say anything about me? Well of course she did." She laughed harshly. "I suppose you heard all about how I ruined their lives."

Clare said evenly, "I've heard her story. Do you want to tell me yours?"

"It's so long ago. I don't rake over old ashes."

"But it's not forgotten, is it? It's affecting everything now. I want to know what happened. What went wrong."

"Okay. I suppose you might as well hear it. To start with you have to understand I adored Frances. But I was jealous of her. I always felt our father loved her more than me. And that he loved her mother more than mine. Frances' mother died from complications after Frances was born. He married my mother a year later. But she took off with an agricultural salesman when I was ten. I didn't blame her really. Father was a lemon. Rigid, joyless. The only thing he cared for was his land and the family history. He was more stiff-necked than the Aylwards themselves. He swore the Kenwards were the original owners of Ravensmere, and the Aylwards were upstarts who came over with William the Conquerer and pinched our land." She shrugged, grinning. "The only person he had any time for was old man Aylward himself."

Clare said, "Who looked after you when your mother went?"

"Frances more or less took over, even though she was very young. She was the nearest to a real mother I ever had. We had a daily woman, but Frances had to do most of the cooking and had to learn how to run the house. She got told off if it didn't run like clockwork. I suppose it was very unfair, but that's what Father expected.

"When she could get away for a few hours she was always off with Brandon Aylward. Father never seemed to worry about that. Sometimes I tried to tag along, but they didn't want me. It was always Frances and Brandon together, never *me*. I was always crazy about Brandon, right from a little kid, and I was furious when they got engaged. I was sick of hearing about this fantastic wedding they were going to have. I couldn't understand why it was taken for granted by everyone.

"They seemed so laid back about it all. They never seemed to kiss or hold hands. I convinced myself somehow that they didn't really love each other. They were just going along with what was expected of them—something arranged by the families. Frances always seemed so quiet and cool, she didn't seem to be that involved. I really thought Bran would be much happier with me.

"He used to tease me, cuddle me. I thought he had a thing about me. He was in a state that summer, smoking cannabis with his mates in Bristol, generally going crazy. There was something he was upset about. I thought it was that he didn't want to marry Frances. It's so easy to deceive yourself.

"One weekend when Frances was away we had a few drinks, got a little worked up and ended up having it off together.

"Men have always come easy to me, but Bran never really wanted me, you know. He wanted Frances. But she was frightened of getting pregnant. It was different in those days. Not easy to get contraceptives for women if you weren't married. And Bran would never have bothered.

"Instead it was me. I got caught nicely. It only happened the one time with him too." She gave her slightly hoarse, attractive laugh. "Ironic, wasn't it? Serves me right, I suppose. But I was young. I thought you could have everything if you wanted it hard enough. I wanted Bran and I was going to be the world's greatest show-jump champion. Fate clobbers you, you know."

Clare said, "Not fate. *You* made it happen. You brought it on yourself."

"Straight for the jugular. You're your mother's daughter all right."

"You could have had an abortion," Clare said.

Vivienne blew out a stream of smoke, watched it disappear into the ceiling and shook her head. "Not Bran's baby." And Clare realized with a jolt that she had really been in love with Brandon, and maybe still was.

Vivienne got up and poured herself a glass of whisky from the decanter set out on a carved oak cupboard.

"When he found out I was pregnant Father dragged me over to Ravensmere. God, what a scene! I'll never forget it. Brandon was there. Old man Aylward was there. Frances was there. She was like marble. I suppose Bran had told her. He looked dreadful. I could see he hated me. I think it was then that I began to understand what I'd done." She drew on the cigarette. Clare saw through the smoke that she had tears in her eyes.

"Mr Aylward was angry?" Clare prompted.

Vivienne choked with laughter. "*Angry?* He was like an Old Testament prophet, with his fists raised, shaking with rage. I tell you I have never before or since seen such rage. I was absolutely petrified. I thought he was going to strike me dead.

"He was shouting that I had shattered the lives of five people, that I didn't understand the great harm I had done, that I'd killed my father and sister's love for me. He said I was a whore who had tempted his son and he would see me grovelling in the mud.

"My father didn't say a word. Brandon didn't say a word. They just stood there. It was Frances who saved me. She wasn't frightened of him. She seemed taller, and very thin. I remember she had on a pale grey dress, and her eyes were glittering like stars. She stopped Edward Aylward. I don't know if she frightened him, but by God, she frightened me. Every word is engraved on my memory.

"She said, 'Don't you call my sister a whore. It takes two to make a child. Your son has lied and betrayed. The Aylwards have broken the Trust. *You* are to blame for Brandon's wildness. You neglected him while you went after money and power, wallowing in self-pity, never showing him love. Always sneering, criticizing, blaming, listening to his enemies.' She was pointing at him, like they do in horror films, and she was almost chanting."

Clare shivered. She knew the sound well.

"I'd never believed in this business of the Guardians before, but this was like some sort of cosmic battle. I've never been so frightened in my life, Clare. Even my father looked like death.

"Frances said 'I'm going now, and don't think, Edward Aylward, I will ever come back. I swear now, upon my mother's grave, that I will never sleep under the roof of Ravensmere. The Guardianship hasn't passed yet, and I'm free to go. You will carry the burden alone. I will never open the Seventh Gate for you.'

"I'll never forget his eyes. Green daggers of glass. Then they dilated, went out of focus and rolled up. I thought he was having some kind of fit, but he chucked his head back and ... well, *howled*. 'You are the Guardians. You have broken the Trust. My son is a dead man.'"

Clare took a deep breath, horrified.

Vivienne said dully, "The next morning we heard that Bran was dead. My father told me to pack my bags and get out. I was crying and hysterical, but when I went to find Frances she'd already gone. Just walked out without saying goodbye even. I couldn't believe she'd leave me just like that. And it must have hurt Edward Aylward. He loved Frances. When we were young he sometimes put her up on his horse for a ride. He had this marvellous grey stallion that I worshipped, but he never put me on the horse."

She lit another cigarette and coughed into the smoke. "The old man was right, of course. It was all my fault. I did ruin their lives. But honestly, Clare, I didn't understand. It all seemed like a game to see if I could get Bran off Frances. The great love of my life, I thought. It was just a silly game.

"I never expected Frances to act the way she did. I thought she'd forgive me and we could all be friends again, and maybe Bran did too. But she was like iron. Like our father. And Bran was absolutely frantic. I'd never seen him like that. When he realized he'd lost her, he committed suicide. Crashed his motor bike deliberately. It was all down to me. I've had to live with that for twenty-one years."

She put the glass back on the tray and poured another drink from the decanter.

"What about Brandon? It was his fault too," Clare said.

"Bran?" Vivienne smiled. "Nobody ever blamed Bran for anything. Except his father, and he always listened to that lying toad Roger Fletcher, putting in his poison. We all loved Bran. He was ... an enchanter."

Clare said, impatiently, "He was as much to blame as you, and he was older, so he should have known better. What did you do afterwards? How did you manage?"

"Oh, I went to Bran's mother's family, the Carlton-

Winters. I knew they would take me in, if only to spite Edward Aylward for what he'd done to Cecily. He just ripped her to pieces, you know."

"Mr Aylward said there was bad blood in that family."

Vivienne laughed. "Pot calling the kettle black. I'm bound to say they're a bit wild. But they know how to live and enjoy themselves, and they've all got hearts as big as the Bank of England, which is more than you can say for the Aylwards. When I was seventeen Roddy Carlton-Winters married me, but we were divorced seven years ago."

"Didn't Mr Aylward help at all?"

Vivienne laughed bitterly. "After I had Mark, I went to see him. I didn't want anything for myself, but after all, the baby was his grandson and I thought he ought to do something for Mark, like pay for his education. He told me to get out of his sight and out of the village too. He told me he wouldn't acknowledge any misbegotten whelp of mine. He said if I stayed he'd see me off with a riding whip—and he meant every word. I never asked him again."

Clare stared at her. A harsh, beautiful, wilful face. The skin was taut around her mouth, laughter lines around her eyes. Life had marked her more than it had marked her mother.

"When my father died I came back here. He left what there was in trust for Mark when he's twenty-one. Frances was at the funeral. I went to speak to her, but she just walked past me and got into her car and drove away."

There were tears in her eyes again. "What I did was unforgivable. She's never going to forgive me, is she?"

Clare got up. She felt ill. Never mind the nuclear waste, Ravensmere was already buried in layers of guilt and blame, unforgiveness and pain, all swept away under a carpet of silence and left to rot and smell. Who could you blame? They were all victims of victims, as Mr Aylward had said. Somehow it had to be cleansed and healed. The cycle stopped.

She said aloud, "She loves you. She misses you. She thinks she let you down when you needed her most. She felt so guilty she couldn't talk to you at the funeral. Why don't you come over sometime and tell her how you feel?"

Vivienne stared at her. "You're telling the truth? Not conning me?" Her voice broke and Clare saw that the tears were running down her cheeks. All the toughness and sophistication had crumbled away. Clare hesitated, then went over and hugged her, as she would hug her mother.

"I'm sorry," Vivienne said, blowing her nose. "I never cry. It's just digging up the past . . . and I'm worried about Mark. I'm so afraid it's bloody history repeating itself. Just like his father. He's got to stay here and look after Ravensmere, I know that."

"Don't worry. He'll come back," said Clare. "It'll be all right. We're a new generation. We won't make the same mistakes."

But they *were* making the same mistakes. They had quarrelled. They had refused to accept the responsibility of the Benison. They were hiding from their destiny, refusing to admit the truth.

Clare felt the cold seeping into her bones. It wasn't only the burden of looking after Ravensmere either. There was some terror attached to the Benison that only the Guardians knew. She had known it all along in some part of her mind. Brandon Aylward had run scared. Even Mr Aylward had been frightened. And Mark knew it too. That was why he too was running.

Clare felt icy. Her whole body had begun to shiver.

History *was* repeating itself.

Chapter 24

"What's gone wrong at Ravensmere?" Clare asked, abruptly.

She was sitting on a stool in Dr McKinnon's conservatory, watching her repot geraniums, while the rain battered against the windows. "It did go wrong, didn't it? It's so beautiful and peaceful, a special place, and yet the people are all miserable and wrong—every generation since Mr Aylward's grandfather as far as I can see."

Dr McKinnon was silent. She pressed the plant into the pot with her long fingers, and Clare knew that the plant would grow strongly. "You know, don't you?" she said.

Dr McKinnon said, at last, "Theories. I think it may have been the women."

Clare said, cynically, "That's what Adrian was always banging on about. All the fault of the women. But I'm surprised to hear *you* say that."

"Think about it. For centuries it was the women here who protected the Benison. Not the men. The female Guardians have to be strong mentally and spiritually. Stronger than the men. It was only when the Abbey was closed and sold that the men came in. I think Rosamond, the last Abbess-Elect, realized that in future Ravensmere would need additional protection. The status of women was going down. She needed someone out in the world. Rich. Important. Someone with clout at Court. A politician if you like."

"She married the Second Earl," Clare said, remembering the wide eyes under the black veil.

"A clever woman. She saved the Benison from Henry VIII. Produced a bogus gold chalice to throw them off the scent."

"*Bogus*? You mean it wasn't the Benison?"

"Of course not. A Guardian would never hand it over."

"If they threatened to kill her?"

Dr McKinnon's pale eyes pinned her. "The Guardians die for the Benison. Make no mistake, Clare. It's their reason for living—and dying."

Clare shivered. "The Benison—what is it, do you think?"

Her gaze shifted. "Don't know. Don't want to know. Not my business."

"But you must have wondered."

She turned away and began to repot another plant. "The female Guardians have always been strong. Clarissa, a famous medical herbalist. Wrote an excellent treatise. Rosamond who built the tower. Strong nerves, you see. Determined.

"Now compare the recent females. Nonentities, the lot of them. Eldon's wife, a meek Victorian miss, physically weak, died in childbirth."

"She couldn't help *that*," Clare protested.

"It was the tight lacing," said Dr McKinnon. "And Edward Aylward's mother. Cowering and frightened. Think of the disgrace. The Guardian allowing herself to be *beaten*! Shameful. Too frightened to come back even when Edmund died at Ypres.

"They allowed the men to dominate. Isn't good for men. Goes to their heads. They get greedy and power-mad."

"Caroline?" asked Clare, thinking of the sad young woman of the photograph.

Dr McKinnon nodded. "My cousin Caroline, Edward's wife. A twit. A nerd, I think you'd call her. A ninny. No strength of mind or character."

Clare grinned. "You didn't care for her?"

Dr McKinnon snorted. "She always knew she would have

to marry Edward. A nice comfortable life she had too. He was nutty on her. Persuaded herself she was in love with a solicitor in Taunton. Couldn't face up to things. One year after they were married she committed suicide. Found floating in the Upper Lake."

"Suicide!" Clare exclaimed, horrified. "He never told me that."

"Never admitted it. Said it was an accident. And we all know now what that led to. All the trouble with Cecily and Brandon. Caused a lot of our troubles, no doubt about it. She should have done her duty and faced things. We wouldn't have come so close to losing everything. And then there was your mother."

Clare stiffened. "It wasn't her fault."

"Too soft," said Dr McKinnon relentlessly. "Gave in to that spoiled sister of hers once too often. Then she ran away. Failed the Trust."

Clare was silenced. There was nothing to argue about. Her mother had admitted it all.

"You see? The women haven't been strong enough. They put their feelings above their duty to the Benison. Allowed the men to run wild. Men function best in double harness. Like horses."

Clare laughed.

"Equal balance—that's what we need. Women who accept their strength and dignity, and aren't afraid of using it fully. We need a strong female Guardian again. And now there's you."

"*Me?*"

"You know you are the next Guardian of the Benison in the female line. What are you going to do?" There was a long silence.

A sudden squall whipped the rain against the glass panes. Clare said, painfully, embarrassed, "I can't ... I mean, I don't *believe* ..."

"No more dodging, girl. What are you going to do with your great psychic gift?"

"Some gift!"

"There's nothing to be worried about. Be proud. Hundreds of remarkable women through the ages have had the second sight, sixth sense, psychic healing abilities, call it what you like. Cassandra. Pythia, the Oracle at Delphi. Sibyl of Cumae. All kinds of prophetic women in ancient history. Egypt. Babylonia. Persia. Greece. Very highly regarded until we allowed the men with their religions to make us frightened and ashamed of it. Are you going to stay here?"

"I don't know," said Clare. She felt her throat tighten. "I don't know if Mark . . ."

"Never mind about Mark. What are *you* going to do?"

There was another long silence. Clare watched the rain running down the glass. For the first time she admitted to herself just how much she wanted to stay. Ravensmere had invaded her mind and heart, taken her over.

She *was* the Guardian. She knew it. Had always known it deep down. No more dodging. A strange, turbulent mixture of emotions welled up. Embarrassment. Fear. Acceptance. Then a feeling of strength and pride, a sureness that she could look after Ravensmere.

"I didn't want to give up university."

"No need to. You could commute to Bristol from here, or come home at the weekends. Get your training, then come back. You wouldn't be going away for good. Have you thought of medicine? Suit you better than business."

Clare looked at her, her mouth open. "How did you know?"

Dr McKinnon laughed. "Been waiting for someone to take over from me eventually. Let's get down to a serious discussion. You'll want information."

The wind was hammering a loose door somewhere. It woke Clare from her wild dream. The rain had stopped and the moon was bowling swiftly, brilliantly, in and out of the torn and ragged clouds. Over the top of the stable roof she could see the great trees in the park lifting their branches, swirling and bending like dancers.

She felt lost and alone. How was she going to manage on her own all her life? All very well for Dr McKinnon to say, *be strong.* There's a legend, she had said, that when Ravensmere is in particular danger, Rosamond the last Abbess-Elect comes back.

She brushed away the wetness on her cheek and leaned her head against the window, feeling her body still burning from her dream of loving Mark in the deep grass of Barrow Beacon Hill. She wanted to hold him again. She wanted him for ever.

The cat was there in the stable yard, calling loudly and impatiently up at her, its voice clear above the sound of the wind.

Surely she didn't have to go to the China Garden tonight? It would be spooky with moving shadows, the sudden darkness, cold in the wind.

The cat called again, insistent. Clare turned away and pulled on her sweater and jeans reluctantly.

Clare saw, without surprise, that the pile of logs that had blocked the Second Moon Gate had been cleared away, and that the Gate was open.

The Maze Dance was difficult tonight, with the wind tugging and butting her away from the narrow path. On the return, Clare put her arms out to keep her balance and was spun along dizzily like an autumn leaf.

Even before she reached the Fourth Moon Gate she could hear the sound of the motor bike above the crying wind. It was coming very fast, accelerating down Barrow Beacon Hill towards the village.

Mark was coming back!

Joyfully Clare began to run to meet him through the Fourth Moon Gate, through the trees of the park, down to the crossroads. Almost at once she realized that something was wrong. Instead of the bike slowing for the sharp turn at the crossroads, it seemed to increase its speed, and as this thought crystallized she began to run faster, impelled forward, a dread filling her, but before she could even reach the road, there was an explosive bang, a stomach-churning crash of splintering glass and rending metal.

"Mark!" she screamed, bursting forward through the trees. "*Mark!*"

The sharp moonlight lay in silver bars across the white road, and in the shadows she saw the bike, upended, smashed into the Leper Stone, its wheels still spinning, pieces of metal skidding across the road. Its rider had been thrown like a soft leather glove against the Leper Stone, and blood was already running in a dark stream across the road and she knew, without doubt, that he was dead.

"Mark!" she whispered, and her legs were like spaghetti, the world tilting and darkening. Forced to a stop she held on to the stones of the boundary wall, shaking her head violently. She couldn't faint now. She had to do something. Go to Mark. Fetch help.

Then, incredibly, she saw the slumped figure *rising*, standing tall under the shadow of the stone and a pale face turned to stare at her.

"Mar . . ." But the word died in her throat, and she saw that it wasn't Mark.

He had the same build as Mark, tall and broad, and in his black leathers he looked very like him, but he lacked Mark's midnight darkness. The moonlight gleamed on his thick fall of fair hair.

Clare swallowed and licked her dry lips. "A-are you all right?" Her voice came out creakily. How could he be all right? How could he even stand up when the dark pool of his blood was still pulsing across the road, glistening in the silver light?

Her heart seemed to stop beating. She lifted her head slowly, reluctantly, and looked into his shining eyes. The sound of the wind died away. There was absolute silence. Moonlight lapped across the road between them. Time seemed to have stopped.

He smiled, Mark's smile, rueful, charming, devil-may-care, inviting her to share the joke. He raised his hand casually in greeting.

Clare felt her lips lift irresistibly in an answering smile before the darkness came down and she fainted for the first time in her life into the turf of the China Garden.

"I tell you he was *there*, and he looked just like Mark and he smiled like him too. Mum, it must have been a ghost. There's nothing there. No wrecked bike, no body, no blood stains even. Nothing! I went down to the crossroads specially to look. There was nothing there!"

"All *right*, Clare. Don't get so excited." Her mother was pale, sitting on the side of her bed. "I accept you think you saw something strange."

"It was *him*, I swear it," Clare said, stubbornly. Her body ached all over, but her head felt extra clear.

After fainting she had opened her eyes and found herself lying by the bricked-up Fourth Moon Gate, with Tabitha stretched full length on top of her, keeping her warm and licking her face, the rain beating on them both.

All the lights were blazing at the stables cottage when she eventually stumbled through the door. Her mother, angry and frightened, had refused to listen to her excited raving and bundled her into the bathroom for a warm bath to ease out the chills, but now she had to listen.

"I saw the whole thing. I saw Mark's father, Brandon. I saw him die. He was riding his motor bike. He smashed into the Leper Stone and severed an artery, didn't he? It was all over the road, the blood . . ."

Her mother shuddered and hid her face in her hands. "It was my fault. If only I'd told him. He was going away."

"But that's it, don't you see? Brandon wasn't going away. He was coming back. He came *down* Barrow Beacon Hill. His bike hit the Leper Stone and slewed round in the road, what there was left of it. Perhaps they thought he'd been travelling in the opposite direction. But he wasn't going away."

Frances stared at her uncertainly. "Not going away? You're telling me the truth, Clare?"

"Of course I am. Why should I lie? I heard him come down the hill. *Down*—towards the village, or maybe he was going to turn up the lane to the farm or Ravensmere. He was definitely coming back. Don't you see? He didn't die because he was a Guardian who was leaving. He didn't commit suicide. You're all wrong. It was an *accident*. Just an accident. He came too fast down the hill, like we did when we came, and his bike went out of control into the Leper Stone. It was a frosty night, wasn't it? Ice on the road?"

"The first frost of the year," Frances said dully. "Winter came early that year."

The tears were sliding down her cheeks in an unstoppable stream. Perhaps it was the first time she had really let herself cry for Brandon.

"Oh Clare, I've always been so bitter. I thought he didn't care about me any more, didn't want to talk to me even. I thought he loved Vivienne after all. I hated her for so many years. But he was coming back."

Clare put her arm around her and sat silent while her mother cried out the years of loss and hurt. It was odd, comforting her mother. She felt that they had somehow changed places and her mother was the child now. She said aloud, "Maybe you ought to talk to Vivienne. She feels very bad. She thinks you'll never forgive her. I told her to come over sometime."

Frances muttered something and tried to mop up her tears, but they kept coming.

"He smiled, you know," Clare said. "He was grinning like a kid. Like Mark does. And he waved."

Then she went out and closed the door, knowing her mother needed to be alone for a while. She was at the top of the stairs deciding she would go down and make chocolate for them both, when the telephone began to ring urgently, loud in the quiet night.

Chapter 25

Clare gazed at the face on the pillow, somehow shrunken and fallen in, with its unhealthy flush and film of sweat across the cheeks and forehead, heard the harsh, shuddering breathing, and knew without a shadow of doubt that Mr Aylward was dying.

". . . must see the boy. Send for boy. Where is he? Where . . . must tell . . . Fool. Left it too late. *Fool*. Must come soon . . . Wrong! Wrong! Wrong!" The voice, hoarse and breathless, subsided into incoherent mumbling, as the old man moved his head restlessly on the pillow.

Clare, wide eyed, bit the inside of her cheek and clenched her hands trying to keep control. There would be time for crying later, but now she must try to keep as calm and competent as her mother, standing next to her, who was holding the thin wrist, taking the pulse rate once again.

It was like a scene from the past—the firelight leaping from the huge marble fireplace to the oak four-poster bed, and the richly patterned carpets and curtains. And outside, the wind blowing in the dark night, the rain beating at the windows.

The hoarse voice had started again. "Bran, my boy . . . Bran? The Mother must drink . . . The Mother . . . No good. Gone. No time . . . Mark! *Mark!* Hurry!"

The anguish in the old voice was too much. Clare clenched her hands. She couldn't take much more. Surely something could be done to ease him?

Her mother glanced at her. "Clare, go and see if Mr Bristow has managed to contact Dr McKinnon yet. She may have got back from her call-out. You're doing no good here."

Clare looked at the figure under the heaped blankets, now unnaturally still. Frances pulled the covers a little higher. "It's all right. He's fallen into a light doze. It won't be yet. Go on. I can manage."

Clare was glad to escape, despising herself for her eagerness. But as she reached the door it crashed back and a figure stood in the doorway, huge and dark against the lighted corridor.

Clare caught her breath, unable to believe her eyes. "Mark," she whispered, and couldn't move.

He stared at her. The rain was running down his leathers, and his long hair was plastered to his head. The firelight gleamed on his cheek bones, throwing his eyes into shadow like a skull. He looked taller. Bigger. *Older.* A stranger.

She said nervously, trying to hold down her joy. "You came back."

There was an aura of wildness and desperation about him. He looked all over her. "You're all right?"

She was confused. "All right?"

"Earlier. What happened to you?"

She stared at him. "What do you mean?"

"You screamed—'Mark? Mark!' A terrible scream that nearly knocked me off my bike, and then *nothing.* Blackness."

Clare remembered then hearing her own voice screaming his name, as she saw the motor bike smash into the Leper Stone.

He pulled her into his arms and held on to her. "Oh God, Clare. I thought you'd died. I couldn't hear you any more."

"I'm all right. I'm fine."

His arms tightened until they hurt. She felt him draw in great sobbing breaths. They stood there holding on to each other. Not kissing. Just accepting that they were together and well.

Across the other side of the room there was a hoarse cry, and Mr Aylward was struggling to sit up. Frances hastily propped pillows behind him.

"*Mark.*"

"You can't see him now, Mr Aylward. You have to rest. Tomorrow, perhaps, when you feel better." Frances was worried.

"Fool woman. No time left. Must talk." His face was flushed and his breathing was getting worse.

Mark let Clare go and strode further into the room. He stood at the end of the four-poster and stared at the old man. "Well, I'm here. You sent for me. What do you want?"

The old man's head rolled on the pillow, and Clare saw the tears in his eyes. "Wrong," he said. "Wrong. Regret all . . . Forgive me."

Mark's eyes flickered. He looked at Clare and back to the figure in the bed. He was shaken. Always he had thought of Mr Aylward as powerful, invincible, dangerous. He hadn't expected to see his enemy so weak and broken.

"You never acknowledged me or my mother."

"Forgive. *Must* forgive. No time left."

Mark hesitated. "I've come, haven't I? What do you want?"

"Tell about Benison. Clare stay. Frances . . ."

Mark said to Frances, "Wait outside."

"No," Clare protested. "She has to stay. He's very ill."

Frances said uncomfortably, almost fearfully, "I don't want to hear about the Benison. He won't settle until he gets this business done. Ten minutes, Mark, no more." She went out and closed the door, and Mr Aylward weakly motioned Clare and Mark to come closer.

"You and Clare . . . next Guardians. No choice, boy. You're next or you die."

Clare felt her throat tighten with fear.

Mark said impatiently, "We know that. Tell us about the Benison."

"Guard Benison. Must guard Benison. Promise."

Clare met Mark's eyes. "*Promise.*"

"I will guard the Benison," Mark said evenly, staring into the old man's eyes. "Clare?"

"I promise to guard the Benison."

The old man drew in a rattling, harsh breath. "Not enough. Guard the Benison with *my life. Promise* . . ."

Clare hesitated. How could she make such a promise, when she had no idea what the Benison was? Was she really prepared to sacrifice her life for some miserable old bowl, even if it was gold? But Mr Aylward was gripping her arm painfully, his eyes begging and frantic.

She said, "All right—*with my life*, if you think the Benison is worth it."

"Thirty thousand years." She felt his hand drop away.

"I'll guard the Benison with my life," said Mark, without hesitation. "Tell us what it is and where it is."

There was another appalling rattling noise as Mr Aylward fought for breath. "Must go quickly. Urgent. Hurry . . . hurry . . ." His voice fell to a hoarse whisper.

Mark bent over him, holding his hand. "I can't hear, Grandfather. What . . . ?" He put his head closer to the desperate whispering. Clare, further away, could not make out any of the words. She hoped Mark was having better luck.

Mr Aylward's face became suffused with dark colour. It sagged and twisted. His tongue hung helpless between his lips unable to form the words.

"What is it?" Mark said, desperately, "Where is it? Come on, Grandfather, you've got to tell us! *Where is it?*" He seized and shook the flaccid shoulder, but it was too late. The exertion had been too much for the old man. Mr Aylward had had a stroke.

*　　*　　*

238

Clare and Mark sat at the table in the big kitchen, numbly drinking coffee while the sky lightened outside. The wind and rain died away, leaving the world rainwashed and tousled. They were waiting for Dr McKinnon and Frances to come down to give them news, too exhausted to make the effort to go to their beds.

"Have you phoned your mother?" said Clare.

He shook his head. "I came straight here."

"She's going crazy."

"I'll phone later. She sleeps in."

Clare thought that Vivienne probably hadn't slept much at all since he'd walked out, but she said nothing. Vivienne would be coming over to see Frances later anyway.

"What happened last night, Clare? When you screamed?"

Clare flushed. "I thought you were dead. I fainted." Hesitantly, she told him about seeing Brandon's crash, waiting for him to make some derisive comment, but he was silent. "You believe me?"

"Why not? The villagers say the Guardians are always psychic."

Clare stared at him. "*You?*"

He looked away. "Maybe. Sometimes."

"You *heard* me?"

"A terrible scream, then blackness. I nearly went under a tanker."

"Where were you?"

"On the motorway."

"Your grandfather has been calling for you too."

"I know."

Clare took a deep, steadying breath. "Telepathy?"

"Or something." He shrugged. "Strong with you. When you let me in."

There was silence. Clare picked at the wood grain. "You came back. Are you staying?"

Their eyes met.

"I've stopped running," Mark said. "I'm back for good. I've had time to think. I can't let Ravensmere die. I can't let Roger Fletcher take over."

"He's gone. Mr Aylward threw him out the day he sent for you."

Mark grunted with surprised satisfaction. "That's one job I won't have to do then."

They sat silent, remembering. Mark said quietly, "That day—I waited for you to come back, you know. I couldn't believe you'd really walk away from me."

Clare flushed painfully. "I'm sorry . . . It's not that I don't . . . I mean, I didn't understand. I didn't believe you would leave Ravensmere."

"I'm sorry too. That day by the Ring Stone, I shouldn't have tricked you. I wasn't playing games, Rosie. I just couldn't bear to lose you. It was my last chance. I had to try everything."

There was another silence. Clare could feel his tension. "Clare, what about you? What are you going to do?"

She swallowed and looked into his eyes. "I'll stay too." They were brilliant green now. "I accept that I'm the female Guardian." As she said the words she felt the strange mixture of relief, pride and *fear*. "We promised."

Mark said, slowly, "I think it's going to be very hard. There's something . . . wrong. Bad."

"I know."

"To do with the Benison."

"Yes."

"Clare, we've got to find the Benison and find it quickly. Where is it? *What* is it?"

"A needle in a haystack. It must be well hidden. Could be anywhere. We don't know what size it is even." Clare yawned, widely. Her brain felt like a soggy sponge. "Why is it so urgent anyway?"

"That's what he said. Urgent. You know this house. Where do we start?"

"I've only been here a few weeks," Clare protested. "I haven't even been into all the rooms." She tried to think. "The old Abbey part, maybe. The Cloisters and the Chapter House. It's all closed off. Rosamond's Tower. That's where all the old documents are kept."

"We'll start there," Mark decided. He sounded wide-awake and energetic.

Clare yawned again. "I've got to get some sleep. We've been up all night."

Mark grinned at her. "Little cat." He put his arm around her shoulders, hugging her, and kissed her ear. "Missed me?"

He would never know how much, Clare thought. She leaned on him and rubbed her head against his neck. "You don't sound tired at all."

"I'm waking up. It's my birthday."

Clare sat up. "You're joking."

"Twenty-one today."

Clare stared at him, feeling her heart turn over. He'd come back—but only just in time. She said, slowly, "Many happy returns."

Dr McKinnon came in, looking very tired. Clare made tea for her and she drank it gratefully, standing up, holding the cup between her hands. For once she looked her age and Clare saw that there were tears in her eyes.

"He's still alive. Can't speak. Can't move." She looked at Clare's tense face. "Go home, Clare. Nothing you can do. Nothing any of us can do. He might die at any time. It might be days or weeks. I'll get a specialist down from London."

They prepared a breakfast tray for Frances and Mr Bristow, and Mark carried it up while Clare washed up.

Mrs Anscomb came bustling in from the stable yard, unbuttoning her raincoat. "That were a fair old wind last night. Blew off the new thatch those foreigners paid so much for. Brought down the peach tree by the China Garden too."

Clare said, blankly, "Peach tree?"

"What's the matter with you this morning, Clare, m'dear? You'm like a zombie. I said, the peach tree came down. Bashed out all the old bricks from one of the Moon Gates. Mr Aylward will be annoyed. A fair old view there, down to the crossroads. I never understood why he had it bricked up."

Clare stared at her. The Fourth Moon Gate was open. She knew now why Mr Aylward had bricked it up. He had bricked up the memory of the smash, and his son's death.

She said, tired, "Mr Aylward won't mind. He's too ill," and broke the bad news to Mrs Anscomb.

Chapter 26

Clare ran a grubby hand through her heavy hair and looped it behind her ears, staring with frustration at the ever-growing piles of books and ancient documents covering the long library tables. For three days now they had been scouring the Library, trying to find clues to the Benison.

Incredibly Mr Aylward hung on to life, unable to move or speak. Only his green eyes moved, glittering with a desperate question. Clare knew what his question was. Had they found the Benison? But she could only shake her head and watch his despair, as he tried once again to talk.

They had hunted unsuccessfully through the bare stone rooms of the old Abbey, tugging at knobs and carvings, hoping to find secret rooms.

They had climbed to the Muniment Room in Rosamond's Tower, and stared in horror at the ancient records of the estate. The walls were covered with oak shelving from floor to ceiling and crowded on to the shelves were thousands of rolled parchments with seals, documents, maps, files, boxes, and account books of all shapes and sizes. It seemed that Ravensmere had kept everything, even down to the receipts for wax candles. It all looked orderly, properly arranged, although the dust of many years lay thickly.

"This is no good," said Mark. "We haven't got the time to go through all this. We can't just pull stuff out at random. We might be mucking up the system. We need to know where to look."

"The Library," Clare said. "There must be a catalogue somewhere."

The Library yielded another avalanche of material. Books on Somerset and Wiltshire. More maps. Ancient histories of Raven Abbey, and Ravensmere. Old photo albums, sketch books, watercolour portfolios. Household books full of recipes and household hints. Victorian scrap books. They found the Elizabethan Earl's *Treatise on the Benefits of Clear Water* and Clarissa Kenward's herbal healing book. There were memoirs, diaries, bundles of letters.

"This looks more promising," Mark had said. "Let's start with this lot."

Clare longed to linger over the diaries full of exquisite, copperplate handwriting, but they had decided to look only for references to the Benison or the China Garden or the Maze.

"There's a connection," Mark had said. "There must be. All the female Guardians, including the nuns, have danced the Maze right back to the Middle Ages. Maybe even before."

Mark was going to be worse than useless, Clare had decided early on. He kept getting sidetracked in the farming and estate records, fascinated by the numbers of mangel-wurzels grown in 1566 or the breeding of a horse called Demophoön which nearly won the Derby in 1786. She sent him a hostile look and went back to Elizabeth Kenward's household book of 1615.

To cure Pain in the Bone also Gripe in the Belly, take three leaves of Comfrey and steep in Holy Well Water ...

To ease women's monthly courses also childbirth take raspberry leaves ...

It was slow work. Some of the handwriting and printing was difficult to read, the old paper fragile, the parchment and vellum stiff. The documents all needed careful handling.

They hadn't been able to find the records for the year 1539 when the Abbey had been sold and the golden chalice, supposedly the Benison, handed over to Henry VIII's Com-

244

missioners. And so far, references to the Benison were conspicuously absent.

She pushed the book away, sighing. Three days and all they had was a receipt dated 1204 for 'Ye re-cutting of Ye Abbey Maze . . . ten pence', and a box of plans and letters about the construction of the China Garden in the eighteenth century.

There was a copy of a letter dated 1766 from James Edward, the Travelling Earl, to his son Edmund, living in London, telling him about building work in progress in the Garden: *We are hard at work without doors. The turf in the China Garden has been recut. I am well pleased with my Dragon Wall and little T'ing or Pavilion. More so with the delightful Rock Pool over the Holy Well . . .*

So that was what the pile of tumbled stones and masonry blocking the Sixth Moon Gate had once been, Clare thought. A rock pool. Another concealment. Why had he needed to hide the famous Holy Well? And who had destroyed it?

My Huayuanzi, (flower garden men), are all now returned to Suchow. They will be glad to see their families after so many months, but I will miss my conversations with Mr Wu Cheng Ming, a most scholarly and erudite Gentleman. The Garden will protect those who, not understanding, would use the Maze for casual games to their injury.

The work on Flitcroft's Triumph goes on apace. Four Deities of Healing, Light and Nature—Apollo, Artemis, Asclepius, and Pan—now guard the entrance. Within we are out-doing Hannibal and working through rocks more obdurate than the Alps. Sam Kenward and his three sons work as fifty men and have accomplished much, but the last part must fall to me alone, and I ask you to come in all haste to lend me your younger strength. My bones ache and I feel my years. Later, the damming of the Raven to isolate the Island will be your task.

> *Your loving Father,*
> *James Edward Aylward*

Clare rubbed the coldness from her arms. She had been right about the statues on the island. But what did he mean "the last part must fall to me alone"? And why on earth would he need his son to help him when he already had four strong men? Clare sighed with frustration. Just more and more questions. She put the letter aside. Mai would be interested to read about the Chinese gardeners.

They found other references to the Maze and the China Garden. William Stukely, the antiquarian, had visited the Maze on a day trip from Avebury in 1724. He had done a pen and ink drawing showing the Revellers and the Wedding Ring on their hill above the Maze which the Eighth Earl had promptly purchased for forty guineas, promising at some unspecified date in the future to allow Stukely to investigate the "poor remains".

There is no doubt in my mind, wrote Stukely, *that as Abury doth far exceed Stonehenge, so might Stoke Raven exceed Abury, were proper investigation made.*

But he gave no details, and as far as Clare could see the Eighth Earl had never kept his promise to allow antiquarian research.

In fact, Clare realized, turning over papers, there were copies of letters from every period refusing, with a variety of polite and specious excuses, to allow any archaeological digging on the site.

But why should they all be so concerned to stop people digging, or even caving, she thought, finding yet another refusal dated 1863 addressed this time to the Derbyshire Caving and Underground Exploration Society.

"Mark," she said, slowly, "I think you'd better find a way of stopping that dig over the hill. What we're looking for could be buried somewhere."

Mark had been given Power of Attorney by Mr Aylward's solicitor, and was now virtually in charge of Ravensmere.

He glanced at her impatiently. "I already have." Her mouth

dropped open. "James and I have stopped pretty well everything authorized by that greedy slug, Fletcher. You can bet that anything he started would be to line his own pockets."

"Or to destroy Ravensmere. He always hated it."

Mark shrugged. "You could be right. The archaeologists have packed up and gone anyway."

He grinned and stretched, his strong muscles moving silkily over his bones under the cotton shirt he was wearing. Clare looked away, flushing.

"I promised a substantial donation to the Professor's university. Enough to take his team to Egypt. The Professor is an Egyptologist. Money talks loudly, Clare. Simple. When you have it."

Kevin from the House tour would be spitting tacks, Clare thought, amused.

She said, "Mark, we've been working for days now and what we have could be written on one page in a Filofax. We're not even sure that there is a connection between the Maze and the Benison."

She sat on the end of the table. "We know that there are legends of something incredibly *holy* about Ravensmere. This book here," she hooked it out from under the pile, "definitely suggests that Ravensmere may be the resting place of King Arthur's Holy Grail."

"All the old abbeys and ruins like Glastonbury are supposed to have the Grail. And if it isn't the Grail it's some other holy relic—a phial of the blood of Christ over at Hailes, a piece of the True Cross . . . They were just trying to get the last groat out of the pilgrim's pocket," Mark said, cynically.

"But they didn't have pilgrims here. The people only came for healing. And the Romans put up a temple and the Neolithic people put the stone circle on the hill. They all thought it was a sacred place for some reason. So that must mean the thing we're looking for is something older than Christianity. The Benison is *not* the Holy Grail. But we haven't found any plans, maps, or clues to where or what it might be. It's not even mentioned. They covered up well."

"There must be clues somewhere. It can't be the first time in all these centuries that the Guardian has died without passing on the information," Mark said, frustrated. "And why is it so urgent?"

"Mr Aylward is frantic, Mark. You can tell he is. I can hardly bear to go to see him. He just lies there looking out of his body, like a prisoner. He's desperate to know. We've got to find it. We can't be the generation of Guardians that ruins it all. We *can't*."

"Why not?" Mark said, sardonically. "We're the generation that's going to destroy the last bits of the rain forest, and the whales and the dolphins and the coral reefs and the elephants and the birds and the seas. Maybe even the air."

Clare shuddered. "Oh, don't. It's not our fault. We didn't start it."

"The question is, are we going to stop it?"

"We can't do much. But we can do something about *here*. Our place." Clare flushed suddenly. "I mean, *your* place."

It had occurred to her that he was responsible for all this now. All Mr Aylward's immense fortune, Ravensmere and its treasures, the land, the farms and a good part of Stoke Raven too, and yet he looked relaxed and confident, nothing like the driven and angry young man who had lounged in the chair at Kenward Farm.

"You were right first time. *Ours*. We're married, aren't we?"

"Oh shut up. How can sticking your hand through a stone mean you're married?"

He looked at her, his eyes dark and amused. "It was a bit more than that."

Clare looked away. The colour burned deeper in her face.

"We're in this together, Clare. Don't try to wriggle away.

248

You heard what the old man said, 'You're next or you die'. Just remember that—whatever you feel about me. I know you think you're trapped, but just try to make the best of it."

"Mark, I-I don't ... I mean ..." Clare stammered, her tongue wrapping itself around the words as she tried to explain.

But he had wandered away, casually, scanning the shelves. "Maybe we should start again in a different way. Go back as far as we can go. Back to the Abbey records. Nine nuns. A few lay sisters. No fixed rules. They must have been isolated here. According to this old history, they had some unorthodox ideas. When the old Abbess died they elected a new one by dancing the Maze Dance."

"The Guardian," Clare said.

"Right."

Mark moved restlessly, looked out of the window, then came back and flung himself down in the Hepplewhite armchair next to the big open fire, stretching his long legs in front of him. He was wearing black jeans, a black denim shirt and heavy cycle boots. As a concession to the warmth of the room he had dumped his heavy leather jacket with its studded decoration on the floor. He looked an incongruous figure against the background of the white and gold elegance of the Library.

"Are there any books from the early days of the Abbey here?"

At that moment his outline blurred, the colours softened. Clare felt the shift, and for a moment there was another young man lounging there. He was thinner than Mark, with a narrow, clever face, which grinned across at her. His ruffled shirt gaped open, and his breeches were tucked into tasselled hessian boots, lifted carelessly on to the brass fender. He was holding a small, slim book with a peeling leather cover, one long finger keeping his place. He smiled at Clare again and flipped open the cover so that she could see its title: *Liber Somnium Sanctus.*

Clare closed her eyes and took a deep breath. When she opened them Mark was there again, watching her carefully.

"What is it?"

She shook her head, trying to breathe properly.

"Tell me."

"A man, sitting where you are, holding a book, grinning at me." She tried to laugh. "Your age. A Regency rake. This place is haunted. Do you think I'm going crazy, Mark?"

He looked at her. "What was the book called?"

She stared back. "The *Liber . . .*" In a second she was on her feet, racing to the small room off the Library that contained the chained library. Mark followed her curiously.

"The oldest books are here," Clare said. "The *Liber Somnium Sanctus* is very valuable. Roger Fletcher was trying to sell it to a book collector from London. It must be here somewhere." She trailed her hand along the chains hanging from the books, setting them swinging.

Some of the books were very large, but her hand stopped of its own accord at a small slim volume bound in peeling brown leather squashed almost out of sight between two larger volumes. It opened easily when she took it from the shelf and Clare was looking at a most beautiful, handwritten illuminated manuscript, glittering with gold and jewel-like colours. The black letter script was as dark as the day it was written, a thousand years before.

There was no doubt it was the same book. The title was on the first page, opposite a maze-like pattern, with a small figure dancing happily on the top. There were letters underneath.

"'*Rosamunde daughter of Cynward made me*'," Clare read aloud.

"Try pronouncing it as a K," Mark said, looking over her shoulder.

"Kynward? *Kenward!*" Clare gave a yelp of pleasure. "She must have painted it herself."

On each page there were borders of intricate interlaced spirals in gold and blue, with tiny flowers, birds and beasts peering saucily around them.

"It's in Latin," Clare said, disappointed. "Did you do Latin at your posh school?"

"Only enough to read the title—*Book of the Sacred Dream.*"

They turned the pages. Every few pages half the space was taken up by an elaborate gold capital letter. Inset in the centre of each was a small picture.

The first showed a collection of stone buildings—a farm, perhaps, half-way up a hill.

"That looks a bit like Kenwards," Mark said.

The second showed a tiny hamlet of wooden houses nestling in a valley, followed a few pages later by a picture of two trackways crossing by a great mottled stone.

"The Leper Stone!" Clare exclaimed. "These are all pictures of Stoke Raven."

"Right. And look." Mark turned another page. "Here's Barrow Beacon Hill." The hill was crowned with a stone circle.

"So there was a circle there once," Clare said. "Why did they bury the stones?"

"To stop them being destroyed maybe? Or moved?"

The next scene was Barrow Beacon Hill again, but at night. The sky was alive with stars and the moon reflected in a pool curling around its base.

Finally there was a figure bent double beneath a heavy load, in what looked like a landscape of tumbled rocks.

"It could be Christ carrying the cross," Mark said doubtfully. "Or somebody burying something? Clare, if you had something very valuable to hide in bad times, where would you hide it?"

Clare thought aloud. "Probably not in the House. It would

have been searched too many times. They must have had a fit when King Henry's men came, and later in the Civil War."

She looked at the painting of Barrow Beacon Hill and a memory stirred. "Kevin said the archaeologists thought there might be caves there."

"Why not? It's limestone. There's a twenty-mile system over at Wookey. But I never heard of any here."

They stared at each other.

Then Mark slammed his fist on the table. "If it's there, it's no bloody good. We'll never find the Benison. I've done some caving, Clare. Big caves, small caves, above, below, next to each other. Fissures, cracks, tunnels, underground rivers, rock falls . . ."

Clare said, "Mr Aylward's grandfather found bone fragments scratched with drawings of dancing women. Beneath a *stalagmite*. Where do you find stalagmites?"

He stared at her, and then groaned. "That's it then. And it's hopeless. The Benison could be anywhere. And where the hell is the entrance, anyway?"

Clare turned the pages of the *Liber* again, and sat looking into space. There was no further doubt in her mind. She had seen these scenes before, Kenward Farm, the village, the Leper Stone, the circle on Barrow Beacon Hill, all framed in the Moon Gates in the China Garden—and all exactly in the right order. The Second Gate had showed Kenwards. The Third Gate, the village. The Fourth Gate, the Leper Stone. The Fifth Gate, Barrow Beacon Hill.

All the Moon Gates were open now—*except for the Sixth Moon Gate.*

There might still be a way of finding the Benison. She wondered why she hadn't thought of it before.

Chapter 27

They sped across the deer park, Clare and Tabitha, two swift silver shadows. The air was clear and cold after the recent rain, the night sky brilliant with stars. The grass was frosted with moonlight so deep that Clare felt she was wading through it.

The China Garden seemed to shimmer with an extra brilliance. For a moment she hesitated, afraid and reluctant. Since she had seen Brandon's crash, she had avoided the Maze. And there was this other fear—a forewarning which shivered through her, and made the sweat stand out on her forehead. But there was no alternative. They had to find the Benison.

The Maze Dance came so easily now that she did not need to look at the pattern. Her body turned and swayed, instinctively, following the pattern in her mind. Tonight the music was very clear.

The return unwound her dizzily to the Sixth Moon Gate, blocked by the rock pool masonry. But now it was open, and she saw without surprise that it was framing a picture of the Temple of Demeter on its island, the dome gleaming above dark close-clustering trees, a mirror image in the moonlit water surrounding it.

The moon slipped behind a cloud. She took a deep breath, stepped through the Gate and began to run down the grassy slope.

She skirted the Great Lake, went unhesitatingly across the Elysium Bridge by the Great Cascade, took the Eleusinian Way, through the frightening darkness of the sunken path, with its overhanging rocks and trees and smell of decayed vegetation, and emerged into the open where the statue of Ariadne pointed across the Moon Lake to the Temple.

The island seemed to be floating in silver light like a great swan. She stood on the bank, longing to cross the water. The Temple was there, waiting for her. Why had she been so frightened of coming? Almost she expected a boat to be there for her, but there was only the shimmering path that the moon had laid across the water, a bar of silver so solid she felt she could walk across it.

Could she wade to the island? Perhaps the water was not as deep as it looked.

She slipped off her trainers and, holding them, stepped forward cautiously. The water was almost warm, and to her surprise she felt smooth stone, not mud, under her feet. She saw then that it was a causeway, built up beneath the surface of the water with large flat stones—a secret pathway.

She followed the silver path without difficulty to the other bank and the water never rose above her ankles.

There was an overgrown track between the trees winding up to the Temple, set on a mound, its pillars and dome luminous, rising like a dream above her into the dark sky shot with stars.

Flitcroft's Triumph, Clare thought, and there were its guardian statues, almost alive in the flooding moonlight. There was no sound or movement, not even the usual night sounds. Everything seemed to be frozen into stillness.

She climbed the steps to the tall double doors, carved with ravens in roundels, and pushed them open. The moonlight flowed ahead of her across the marble floor to the steps leading down to the Sanctuary where she knew the beautiful statue of Demeter bent forward gracefully, arms outstretched, welcoming Persephone back through the waterfall from the Underworld.

"I am here," Clare said. "I have opened the Moon Gates and the Temple."

For a second nothing happened, and then she felt a strange sensation, a flow of energy, as if she was being lifted up and spun like a snowflake. She struggled to regain her balance, feeling exhilarated, but scared too because it was so strange and unexpected.

There was a rushing sound in her head like a huge wave about to break. She staggered and fell, banging her knee painfully on the rough pile of masonry blocking the Sixth Moon Gate in the China Garden.

The next morning, looking for Mark, Clare found a portrait of the young man who had grinned at her from the library chair.

Edmund Edward Aylward (1784–1856). The son of the Revolutionary Earl, husband of the feminist Rosamond who had treated smallpox in Bristol. He was leaning on a table looking inscrutable and surprisingly neat, with an uncomfortably high cravat. Under his elbow were the architectural plans for his new Library and a familiar, small leather book with a peeling cover.

"What are you looking at?" Mark was standing behind her. He put his arms around her waist and rested his chin on her head.

"The man who was sitting in the chair in the Library." Clare ducked and twisted away from him.

"Listen, Mark. Last night I opened the Sixth Moon Gate. I know where the Benison is. It's behind the waterfall in the Sanctuary in the Temple. The entrance to the Underworld."

Mark was silent, thinking. "It's possible."

"Clever old James Edward. I expect there's some sort of tunnel. In his letter he said they were 'working through rocks more obdurate than the Alps'. That's why he needed his son. He couldn't let even Sam Kenward know where he was putting the Benison. He had to do the final digging himself."

"One problem. No waterfall."

"But there must be."

He shook his head. "Not now. The water dried up or maybe the mechanism has gone."

"You've been there?"

"Of course I have. I swam out from the bank one night when I was about thirteen. I biked over from Roddy's place. I don't know why. Ravensmere was always an obsession. They couldn't keep me away from the place." He grinned wryly.

"And?"

"Overgrown. Needs repair. Oh, all right, it's kind of . . . eerie. There's an odd feeling. I can't explain. Something big, like when you walk into a cathedral. It spooked me. I cleared off pretty quick.

"Tom Longman, the Gamekeeper, caught me on the bank and gave me the worst thrashing of my life. I never tried it again." He stopped suddenly. "Tom Longman. He must have known something."

"They all know something. All the village people. It's a giant conspiracy to protect the Benison."

"We'll go this afternoon," Mark decided. "Get it over with."

Clare felt her heart seem to stop beating and then start again twice as heavily. She felt sick.

"We'll need to prepare."

"A couple of hours. Compass, rope, food, hot drinks, first-aid stuff, thick sweaters. It may not all be necessary but we'll go prepared."

"What about lights?"

"I've got a couple of really powerful flashlights over at the farm. They last for hours, and we'll take extra batteries. There may be some of those flare things we had for a barbecue. Will you try and find the keys? I bet the place is all locked up."

"Mark . . . couldn't we leave it a while?"

He put his arm around her. "We don't know why it's so urgent. Grandfather isn't the kind of man to panic for no reason. Besides, we promised."

They had promised, accepted the responsibility. Clare only knew it was going to be the hardest thing she had ever done.

The keys were on Mr Aylward's key-ring lying forgotten on a side table. She waited until Frances had left the room, and held the keys up for his permission to take them.

She said, "We're going to the Temple, Mr Aylward." And saw the blaze of hope in his eyes. She nodded. The heavy eyelids sank down, and tears ran along his cheek. She wiped them away with a tissue, and kissed his hand.

"Wish us luck." And felt a faint pressure from his fingers in hers.

Chapter 28

It was late in the afternoon before everything was assembled, and they were ready to start out. They found the causeway in the Moon Lake, invisible in the daylight under the surface of the water and the waterlilies, exactly in line with Ariadne's pointing finger, and waded across to the island.

Clare could hardly believe she was really there at last. The Temple glowed above the flowering trees and rambling roses, alive with bees in the late afternoon sun, and they climbed the overgrown path to its entrance where the four guardian gods of healing and nature looked down, as Clare had always known.

Inside, the Temple was circular, paved in pink and white marble tiles. Tall pillars divided the walls and arched upwards into a painted dome. Opposite the door, a flight of curved white marble steps led downwards to the Sanctuary. There was a protective iron grille with double gates, patterned with spirals, and beyond the grille Clare saw the white marble statue of Demeter, bending forward lovingly, her draperies carved so delicately they looked as though they were fluttering free, just as she had seen her in her vision. But there was no shallow pool of water in front of her. No concealing and protecting waterfall. Persephone could be seen clearly, gleaming white in the dark grotto beyond, arms outstretched, smiling joyously as she climbed from the Underworld into new life, Spring reborn again.

Mark found the key for the gates and unlocked them.

Clare hung back. Suddenly she could not go forward. She could feel her heart beating irregularly in her throat, her hands shaking.

"... Mark ..."

He heard her and turned, holding out his hand. He looked pale under his tan. "I know. But it's something we have to do. It's all right. We'll be all right."

The wall behind Persephone was dark and shadowed, framed with a collection of precious minerals glinting brilliantly in the light.

"So, where's this entrance then? I can't see anything."

They climbed across the dry pool and moved under the lintel, where the water should be falling, stopping inquisitive visitors from approaching too closely.

Clare caught her breath. At one side, concealed behind the false front of the glinting minerals there was an even darker shadow, and the faint outline of narrow steps leading down.

Mark's flashlight played over them. "You were right. Here it is." He shrugged on his rucksack. "Let's go."

"Mark ... be careful. Please."

He smiled and ruffled her hair. "You're making me nervous."

But Clare could not share his amusement. She could feel the sweat cold on her forehead.

There were forty steep steps curving down before they were standing on the floor of a second chamber, with roughly hewn walls, and a floor set with a design of pebbles.

It was completely empty. There was no sign of anything that could be the Benison.

Clare tried to laugh. "I was *sure*... I mean ..."

"Over here," Mark said. Unnoticeable in the far corner was a narrow fissure in the rock—just wide enough for a grown man to get through. The flashlight showed a roughly-cut tunnel, very narrow, running downhill.

They slid through the gap, and walked along quietly, expecting at any moment to come to its end, but the tunnel ran on, oppressing them with the weight of the rock over and around them.

"This must be James Edward's tunnel," said Clare. "I wonder what excuse he gave the men for making it?"

"He wouldn't need to. Sam Kenward was his wife's father. They would know it was to protect the Benison."

Ahead of them another tunnel appeared, but it was clearly a natural opening in the rock, and they kept to the man-made one. Nevertheless Mark took a piece of chalk from his pocket and drew an arrow on the wall. "We'll take no chances about finding the way out."

The tunnel grew narrower until it became hardly more than a slit in the rock, and then suddenly they were in a small natural cave with tunnels leading off in all directions.

"Now what? Which way, Rosie?"

Clare looked around slowly. "I think this might have been the original entrance, before James Edward and his son made the new garden and dammed the lake."

"So, make a choice. One's as good as another. None of the tunnels look man-made."

"All right. Downhill, because we've been going downhill all the time, and north-west by the compass. Let's try this one."

"Okay, but why?"

"I think we're heading for Barrow Beacon Hill. The Neo-lithic people put a sacred stone circle on the hill. I think the Benison may be hidden under the hill. Anyway, it just feels right to me."

"Okay. Let's go, then."

They plunged into the chosen tunnel which was wider than the one they had left, and at first it seemed as though they were walking through a natural tunnel formed in the living rock.

Behind her, Clare heard Mark say, "This is odd."

"What?" She tried to keep her voice light and even, but she was beginning to feel very strange, as though she was floating, with snatches of distant pipe music in her ears.

"This rock. It's not limestone any more. Stop a bit, I want to look closer."

They shone the powerful lights across the surprisingly smooth walls and overhead, following the line of the cracks in the stone.

"See that glitter? It's some sort of granite. A pink granite, for pete's sake! And it's got these chunks of quartz in it. Like the buried stones on the hill. How did that get here?"

Clare looked at the narrow crack between the rocks and the shape it enclosed. She licked her dry lips. "Mark, it's man-made. Look at the joins. They're massive cut stones."

"Can't be. They never had the technology in the eighteenth century."

"James Edward didn't make this part," Clare said, with certainty. "He just made a new entrance and tunnel to hide and protect the Benison better. This part is *ancient*. Look at the size of the stones. Like Stonehenge. Even the Roman Guardians couldn't have cut these." In her mind she heard Mr Aylward's voice gasping, *Thirty thousand years*, and felt at once the strangeness of immense age around her.

Once again they came to a division of the way. The pink granite continued in both directions.

"Left," said Clare, unhesitatingly, and wondered how she knew.

There were more and more tunnels now, all identical, made to confuse.

Right. Left. Right. Left. Right. Right. Right. Each time she knew automatically which choice to make. It felt almost as though they were turning back on themselves. Could she hear a faint drift of the pipe music?

"Are you sure we're right?" Mark sounded increasingly uneasy. "We could get lost. It's a bloody maze."

Clare stopped so abruptly that Mark cannoned into her. "You're right," she said, understanding at last. "It is a maze. A huge maze. The true Ravensmere Maze. It's one of their little jokes, don't you see? A maze within a maze. A Chinese puzzle. You tread a maze to find a maze."

"Some joke," said Mark, banging his head on the low roof, and swearing. "How far have we got to go?"

"A long way. We haven't done a quarter of the maze yet. And there's the return too."

"The return?"

"We have to come back from the centre."

Mark swore again. "You mean all this is unnecessary? We come back to where we started?"

"We come back but not to where we started. It's different. And it's not unnecessary. Don't you see how clever it is?" She had worked it all out now.

"The Maze in the China Garden picks out the girl with psychic abilities to be the next Guardian, but it's also a *training ground*. You have to keep doing the Maze Dance to open the Moon Gates, so you learn the Maze too, then you can find your way through *this* Maze. That's how I knew I was choosing the right tunnels. It's a marvellous way of protecting the Benison. A stranger would get lost in all these alternative passages."

"Just so long as *we* don't," Mark said grimly. "I just hope you're right."

"There'll be seven doors or gates too. We've already passed five—the Temple door, the iron grille to the Sanctuary, Demeter's waterfall might be another when it's working, the entrance in the underchamber, and the entrance to this maze system."

The maze continued to wind down and around. They stopped talking and pushed along silently. Clare knew that

Mark was really hating it, feeling trapped and confused by the constantly changing directions, entangled in the coiling passages.

There was no obvious sign when they reached the centre and began the return, but Clare became aware that they had begun to move faster and more freely. She could hear the pipe music clearly now, and her body fell into the familiar pattern of the Maze Dance, lift, sway, turn and turn again.

Mark was following her with difficulty, his large bulk, carrying the rucksack, only just making it through the narrowing passages.

Just as he began to give up hope, sure they had taken a wrong turn somewhere, the passage swung out in a long curve and straightened, heading westward according to the compass.

They stepped through a huge stone with a square hole cut through it.

"Six," Clare said. "One more."

Beyond the holed stone, the walls of the passage had been carved into huge triple spirals curling over the whole surface.

"Impressive," said Mark.

But Clare was uneasy. Her stomach had tightened, and the strange floating feeling had come back. "It's a lot of trouble to go to just to bury an old bowl." She stopped, shocked. "We can't go on. Look. We've come to the end."

The way ahead was blocked by another great stone covered with deeply carved lines which resolved into a series of joined spirals and a great bird with outstretched wings forbidding entry.

Mark pushed past. "Let's have a look. See if we can shift it."

Clare said, doubtfully, "Maybe somebody's buried behind it. This bird is meant to be a raven, I think. It's a symbol of rebirth or death. It's to stop people."

"Not us," Mark said. "We're the Guardians, remember?

One of us put that stone there in the past. I know how you feel, Clare, but we have to go on. The Benison is behind that stone."

He ran his fingers along the edge of the stone which fitted so closely to the side walls that even a penknife could not penetrate the crack. He grunted with satisfaction.

"It's a blocking stone. We roll it or push it out of the way, somehow."

Clare laughed. "Move *that?*"

But Mark was right. Under their combined effort, the stone pivoted slowly, grating, allowing enough room for them to squeeze through.

Behind was an immense dark space.

Chapter 29

Their flashlights could not penetrate the darkness, but they were conscious of the overarching space around them. There was something about the quality of the sound that suggested distance and vastness, and something else, beyond the silence. Something waiting.

At the far edge of Clare's hearing there was soft movement.

"Water?" she whispered.

"A spring maybe. An underground river."

"Where are we?"

"At a guess, directly under Barrow Beacon Hill. I think we've hit a cave system."

"It's like a great womb under the hill," Clare said, awed.

"Don't move. There's a sheer drop." Mark swung his flashlight urgently, and Clare saw that they were on a ledge, very high up.

"Can we get down?"

"I think . . . yes, there are steps here, cut out of the rock, and hand holds too. I'll go first. For God's sake hold on tight, Clare. It's a long way down."

The steps were steep, but cut smoothly into the rock face. They climbed down carefully, taking their time.

It was almost as though they were stepping down into a clear cold pool of sparkling water, Clare thought, and shivered as the clarity spread over her, filling her body, filling her mind. She gripped Mark's shoulder.

"What is it?"

"Can't you feel it?"

"Feel *what*?" Mark sounded irritable, nervous almost. "For God's sake, let's get on."

"It's different . . . There's a difference."

They had reached the cave floor of rippled white flowstone.

"We need more light." Mark shrugged off his rucksack, and lit a barbecue light. He moved forward impatiently, holding the light high. It flared extravagantly, like white phosphorus, as the air took it and transformed it.

The flame lengthened and spread upwards, incandescent, illuminating glittering white walls of towering stalactites and stalagmites joined together, lace-like curtains of them hanging from high spears of rock, forests of pencil-thin spines, delicately coloured blue and amber. Along the floor of the chamber, a dark river moved stealthily, almost imperceptibly, reflecting the splendour.

"Rats' bellys!"

Clare stared at the leaping light. "I told you. Can't you feel it now?"

Mark did not reply. He could feel it. Feel the strangeness, the clarity. His whole body tensed.

Clare had moved on almost in a daze, wandering among the stalagmites staring at their shapes and colours. She was desperately trying to hold on to herself. She was beginning to feel even more disorientated, as though her feet were several inches above the ground, and that she was being sucked forward into a vortex.

She looked up and in the flickering light of Mark's torch thought she could see a pair of horns. Not just horns—two great bulls' heads in the stone above swung into focus, and disappeared as she moved her head, and she could not find them again. Imagination. Who would have carved such a thing? She felt sick and giddy, and her head had begun to pound.

As she moved her flashlight, another shape crystallized,

and she cried out in alarm seeing the massive figure, four metres tall and very thin, like a stick man towering over her. The image of a hideous bird like a great vulture with a wing span of three metres flew down at her until she jerked away and saw it flatten into an overhang of rock.

There were sounds now, too. She could hear the pipe music, getting louder and higher all the time, shrilling, an agonizing high-pitched screaming in her ears. It was in her head, filling the cavity until she was stumbling, losing her balance, nauseous.

A life-size herd of mastodon flickered along in the distance. How did she know they were mastodon? And a great leopard crouched on a ledge to her right, snarling, and seemed to leap at her, arching over her. She screamed and twisted away into a tall figure with pendulous breasts and a beaked head, her arms and neck wreathed with snakes. A thousand Valkyrie voices were rising up, crystalline, unearthly, swelling into a scream at the edge of her hearing.

She dropped the torch, holding her ears, but the sound was inside her head. The floor seemed to be heaving under her feet and her brain felt on the the point of bursting. Her stomach churned with sickness. It was difficult to breathe.

She crouched, groping for the flashlight, and found it still alight. But even without the torch she could see now. The whole place was glowing with a ghostly phosphorescence.

Mark had not stopped. He was moving ahead slowly, bent forward as though he was walking against a high wind. She went after him, tugging at his arm. "Mark, we've got to get out of here. It's terribly dangerous. It's too powerful for us. *Mark!*"

But his eyes were fixed and blank. "Find the Benison. The Mother must drink."

They were being tossed in a high wind, an electrical storm, driven along with no way of regaining control, like children with their fingers in an electrical socket, being jerked about like rag dolls.

"Mark! We can't stay here." She caught his arm again, but he shook her off angrily.

"The Mother must drink . . ." His face was ashen and he was weaving from side to side, stumbling on through the labyrinth of stalactites and stalagmites. "The Mother must drink. He said so. The Mother must drink."

He had gone mad, lost control, Clare thought, panic-stricken. His voice sounded mad, with that high-pitched chanting that made her blood run cold. "The Mother must drink, the Mother must drink . . ."

"What Mother? What are you talking about? There's nothing . . ."

But there was something. Through a glistening white tracery of calcite she could see another, smaller chamber glowing gold under their lights. Covering most of the floor of the chamber was a pool of shining water, bubbling with springs rising from the living rock. To one side, set on a low block carved with running spirals, there was a great stone, bigger than Mark. It was irregularly faceted, like a piece of quartz, roughly the shape of a huge pregnant woman. Its surface was iron black, matt and dull. Surrounding it there was a faint sparkling haze.

The Mother. The words slid into her mind with a sudden knowledge of immediate disaster.

"Mark don't!" She shouted the warning, but already he had his arms wrapped around the stone and appeared to be trying to lift it.

Her eyes on the stone, Clare began to back away. The noise was screaming through her brain, and shaking her limbs violently out of control. She turned and ran.

But Mark did not follow her.

In the big cave Clare got a grip on her terror, and forced herself to stop and look back.

Mark had gathered all his great strength. His muscles bulged and lengthened as he once again tried to lift the stone from its base. It did not move. He dropped to his knees gasping.

"Mark," Clare cried. "Please leave it. It's no good. You'll hurt yourself. *Please*..."

He would never move the stone. It was impossible.

Mark got to his feet. He took off his leather jacket and his shirt. He seemed to be attempting to balance himself carefully, his legs wide apart. Then, as she watched disbelievingly, he threw back his head and began a strange wild chant, half song, half shout, in a language she had never heard spoken.

Then he bent to the stone again, and this time she could see that the stone moved fractionally. Mark was on his knees again, gasping for breath, his face and body running with sweat and blood where the sharp stone had cut his skin.

Surely he wouldn't try again? He would kill himself. Reluctantly she started back, her feet dragging, her heart pounding. She must go to help. She couldn't leave him in this crazy, deranged state.

Mark had climbed to his feet again. He bent his knees, and wrapped his arms completely around the stone. His muscles flexed, strained, and now, suddenly, the big stone came loose, swung towards his chest and was in his arms. He hefted it, and in a mad access of strength, swung it round and gave a great shout of exaltation and triumph, which turned instantly to a scream of utmost agony.

For a moment Clare saw the stone was glowing a dark and angry red, like a coal, and Mark's arms and hands holding the stone were glowing too, like a living X-ray. She saw the bones of his spine and ribs dark in the glowing flesh, saw the flesh darken, grow black and crack.

He staggered the few steps to the pool and with a last surge of strength hurled the stone away from him into the centre of the bubbling springs. He shouted words in the language she had never heard, and then fell screaming, rolled, and was still.

Clouds of hissing steam rose from the stone in the pool.

Clare stumbled back to him through the vapour, sobbing, frantic with terror and horror. There was a high sound like a rusty screech, continuous, which only afterwards she recognized as her own voice.

Some still-sane part of her mind told her that she must try to get him into the pool. She knew it was the way to treat burns, to exclude the air and reduce the heat, but he had staggered and fallen his length away from the water.

Close up, with the steam thinning now, she could see the full extent of his injuries. Everywhere the stone had touched his body had burned—his arms, shoulders, chest, stomach, thighs—the skin was blackened and peeling, cracked like ancient leather gaping open redly.

Gagging, she spat away the bile in her throat. Panic clawed at her. She wanted to run, leave this charred horror.

The women have to be strong—stronger than the men.

She couldn't leave him. Sobbing for breath she began to push and tug him nearer to the pool. She was frightened of pulling at his arms in case they came away from his body, they were so badly burned. He was bigger and heavier than she had realized, a dead weight, and she could move him only inch by inch.

When he was near enough, she waded into the pool, pulling his feet, and managed to drag him down the slope of the smooth flowstone into the clear green-gold water, so that only his head rested on the higher slope above the water. Then she collapsed in the water beside him, bathing his face with her hands. There was no sign of breath.

She took a deep, shuddering breath, and began to breathe into his mouth, giving him the kiss of life she had learned in a first-aid class. But she knew already it would do no good. His injuries were too great. He was dead.

She went on trying for a long time, unable to accept the truth. Then she lay there next to him in the water, exhausted, unable to cry, unable to move. There was a deep unearthly silence. All the screaming sounds had died away. The springs in the pool lifted gently, bubbled and died away.

At last she sat up shaking, and cupping her hands drank deeply. The water tasted—strange. Colder and clearer and fresher than any water she had ever tasted. It was faintly golden in her cupped hands, prickling on her tongue with tiny bubbles. She drank again. Her mouth was parched.

She didn't look at Mark. It was all over. She knew he was dead. She had done her best and it was not enough. She felt empty of emotion.

She dragged herself wearily out of the pool and propped herself against the base of a great stalagmite. Soon she would get up and make the long journey back through the caves and tunnels. Bring help to take his body home. There was no other way. For the first time in uncounted centuries the sacred chamber would be exposed. She would have to betray the Trust.

She understood now that flash of fear she had seen in Mr Aylward's eyes, and why just the memory of this place had brought on an attack. She understood too why his Caroline had committed suicide. Not because she was in love with her solicitor, but because she could not face the terror of this sacred chamber.

It must be nearly sixty years since Mr Aylward had been here. No good to come alone. It needed both Guardians. But how had he and the other Guardians escaped alive? What had gone wrong?

Sixty years since the stone had been taken to the water. Too long. Too many Guardians had failed the Trust. At least she and Mark had tried.

She sat on, reluctant to leave him. Now, when it was too late, she knew how deeply she loved him. He was the other part of herself. Why had she been so frightened to admit it? Why hadn't she told him she loved him?

There was nothing left. She felt hollow, blank. She closed her eyes and sat on and on. Strangely, although she was soaked through she wasn't cold. The cave was not cold, and now she became aware of a gently glowing warmth on her skin, as though she were sitting in a chair in the garden on a sunny day.

The warmth increased and she realized it was coming from inside her, flowing through her veins and arteries, covering her entire body. Her jeans and shirt were steaming gently. Indeed it seemed suddenly that she was in a golden stream of sunlight flowing up and over and around her. The stream was carrying away all the blackness within her. All the pain and fear. She felt the darkness streaming out from her head, flowing from every part of her like a sooty liquid smoke.

She let it all go. The pain from her knee, the despair in her heart, it all flowed away into the brilliant light until she was clear and translucent, like the light itself. She was part of the light, flowing upwards in the stream, flowing upwards to a greater white light which fused with the gold and expanded, scintillating and glistening.

She was flooded with a powerful energy revitalizing her mind and spirit. She opened her eyes. Her body felt incredibly strong and well. She stood up, taller and straighter, stretched, and felt her muscles moving together in a way she had never dreamed possible. It was a dream. It must be a dream. But her eyes were open and she could feel the flowstone under her feet.

It was obscene to feel so marvellous when Mark was there, lying dead. Before she left she must move him out of the water. It would do him no good now.

She put her hands under his shoulders and pulled him up the slope, out of the water. It was easy now with her new-found strength. She laid him down carefully and knelt to wipe his poor white face with her shirt, and then suddenly she sat back on her ankles, her body shuddering from head to foot, dragging in each breath.

All the blackened skin had gone. The gaping wounds closed. Where the burned flesh had been there was clear perfect skin and muscle, unscarred. Only the tattered remains of burned jeans remained to give testimony that she had not dreamed the whole dreadful experience.

Tentatively, incredulous, she put out her hand and touched his chest where the deepest burns had been. She could feel his heart pulsing strongly beneath the sculptured muscles. His naked body was firm and beautiful.

He groaned and opened his eyes, staring around. His head fell back and he groaned again.

"Water?" he croaked.

Clare quickly got him a scoop of water from the pool with her hands. He drank greedily. "More."

It seemed as if his thirst could never be satisfied. She brought him scoop after scoop and still he drank.

After a while he pulled himself up and put his head in his hands. "What happened?"

"You were dead," Clare said evenly. "Burned to death by the stone. I dragged you into the water and it healed you."

He shuddered and she saw it was all coming back to him. "I remember the pain. Some of it. And then I passed out."

"You were shouting something in another language."

"Words that came into my head. It was like holding a woman."

"You can hold me, instead," Clare said, shaking with nervous reaction. She put her arms around him. "You were dead. You were *dead*, Mark. I love you so much." The tears ran down her cheeks. "I never realized how much until you were dead."

He hugged her. "What took you so long? I knew as soon as I saw you. You saved my life, Clare."

273

"It's the water. We've found the Benison, the Blessing, after all. Not a chalice or a treasure or even the Mother. We might have known it was something more important. People guarding something for thousands of years with their lives."

"Did I get the stone into the springs?"

"You heaved it into the centre. I don't know how you carried it. It's huge."

"Look," he said, pointing, his hand shaking.

The stone had landed on its side in the full flow of the centre of the springs, washed by the golden green waters. It had changed too. Once it had been matt and dull, like lead, but now it was wonderful. A huge, transparent crystal, glittering in the golden flashlight, plane upon plane of light inside it throwing off rainbows.

Clare said, "The crystal has been healed too."

He stretched. "I feel marvellous. I've never felt like this."

Clare swallowed and said gruffly, "You really are all right? No pain or anything?"

He caught her hands in his and pulled her into his arms, holding her tight. She hid her face against him.

"I'm fine, Rosie, my darling. I feel great, fantastic, stupendous . . ." And then he was kissing her.

"I thought I'd lost you for ever, Mark."

"Instead you've got me for ever." He laughed, and they were rolling over and over down the flowstone into the shallow water of the sacred springs, kissing and loving in a wild celebration of life and the great spirit, while the crystal shone incandescent and threw its rainbows into the golden water.

Chapter 30

It was near dawn when they closed the great blocking stone, climbed back through the underhill labyrinth, and up the stairs into the temple. To their astonishment they found that Demeter's waterfall had begun to flow again, bringing the healing spring waters from underground up into the Raven, where it would spread, diluted, through the whole valley and out into the surrounding countryside.

Outside it was dark. Hours had passed. They had been below ground all night. Mark put his arm around her shoulders and they walked slowly, unhurriedly, down the steps, breathing in the fresh earth smell, not speaking, glad to be alive under the stars.

Clare looked at her watch, but it had stopped long ago when the energies had screamed around their heads.

She had given Mark her jeans, which he had managed to get into by slashing the leg seams with his penknife, and she was wearing his big shirt, which came down to her knees.

Before leaving the caves they had taken the great crystal from the water and carried it back to its base. There was no danger; the burning, the radiation, had gone. It felt cool to the touch, and weighed much less. It stood upright, flashing and scintillating with breathtaking beauty.

On the ground in front of the carved base they found offerings; ancient pottery bowls that might have once held food, a crystal skull like the one in Mr Aylward's study and three clay figures joined together: a slender young woman with a pure face, a mother with a swollen belly holding her breasts, and, strangest of all, an old woman with a serene face, with one of her arms turning into a bird's wing. At the side of the skull was a large gold chalice, marvellously decorated with the figures of dancing women. The last Abbess-Elect had got it back from King Henry's men after all.

The moon had gone and there was that strange hush before the sky lightens into dawn. There was an eerie white mist shifting over the ground waist high. Hand in hand they drifted like long-ago ghosts across the Elysium Bridge, and up through the trees to the China Garden.

They sat on the steps of the Pavilion waiting for the dawn, exhausted.

A small grey shadow, Tabitha, joined them, purring delightedly, weaving patterns of eight around their legs before curling up on Mark's knees. He stroked her ears gently.

Clare said quietly, "How often do we have to go back?"

"Every year."

There was a long silence. She said at last, "I can't do it, Mark. I can't go through that again and again." She gagged. "*I can't*. It's too hard."

He said, bleakly, "We're the Guardians. We have no choice. Maybe it won't be so bad next time. There was a tremendous build-up of power and energy in that cave. I've been thinking that if the crystal is carried to the water *every* year there won't be so much danger. The spring dispersed the energy somehow."

"It will build up again," Clare said.

"But don't you understand? Look, when was the crystal moved last? It's supposed to be done every year, Grandfather said. When did he do it last? My guess is nineteen twenty-eight when Caroline committed suicide. And what about the Guardian before him? He was eighty-six, holding on so he could hand over to his grandson. I bet he didn't go heaving rocks around."

"How could he? His wife died young too. There was nobody to do the Maze Dance. He couldn't find his way through the tunnels. Could *you* find your way through the tunnels, Mark?"

She felt the involuntary shudder that ran through him. "You see, you need the two Guardians. Two ways of thinking."

"No wonder the whole place was jumping. It's been closed nearly seventy years, and sixty or so years before that."

"Mr Aylward must have been burned too," Clare said, realizing. "He was frightened. He knew what he was sending you to do. What sort of energy can turn a crystal black?"

Mark shrugged. "Who knows? Some sort of electro-magnetic radiation? An energy natural to that particular cave?"

"Perhaps somebody put the crystal there as an accumulator or earthing material."

"There are quartzite stones on the hill above the chamber as well, remember. They could be collecting the energy maybe. Channelling it down."

"What energy? I don't understand."

"Join the club."

"Crystals are funny things. Mysterious. They conduct electricity. Didn't they use them in the old radio sets? You can disintegrate things with sound vibration." Clare shuddered.

"We could have been killed by the sound alone in that cave. Never mind the radiation."

"I just wonder what would have happened eventually if we hadn't found it. It might have blown the hill apart. Or worse. That must be why Mr Aylward was so frantic. He must have been worrying about it for years. Waiting for something to happen."

"Maybe the whole cave is a giant crystal resonating to the wavelength of the smaller crystal. There's a theory that the whole Earth may be a crystal."

Clare said inconsequentially, "Did you know that the oldest tombs were built with a facing of white quartz crystal? And there was Atlantis. They were supposed to have destroyed their continent with crystals."

"But who put it there? Who *knew* . . ."

The mist grew thicker. Clare shivered. They would never understand the ancient, awe-inspiring power in the cave under Barrow Beacon Hill.

She said, reluctantly, "Mark . . . the pool . . . those springs . . ."

There was a long silence before he answered. "It sounds crazy."

"Maybe the energy the crystal discharges in the water alters its composition. Gives it . . ." She hesitated.

"Go on, say it: life-giving qualities."

They looked at each other.

Clare said desperately, "I really don't believe what happened to us. It could have been some sort of hallucination."

He shook his head. "You know it wasn't. Believe it, Rosie. Every single thing. It wasn't imagination. Look at it honestly. Don't run. You think I wouldn't like to push it away too? It happened and we've got to accept it. We're responsible for it for the rest of our lives."

She was silent, watching the trailing mist.

"We drank the water, Clare. Lay in it. *Soaked* in it. Say it straight: If you drink the water you go on living. It's the water of life. Raven's mere. The water of rebirth. That's what we've been guarding here for thirty thousand years. The Great Blessing. The Benison."

"But I don't want to live for ever, Mark," Clare wailed. Panic swept over her. "It'll be awful. We'll be freaks. Everybody we know will be dead, all our children and friends. We'll be alone and worn out like Mr Aylward . . ."

He pulled her close and held her head against his chest. "Maybe you have to keep drinking the water."

"Mr Aylward hasn't been near the place for years but he hasn't died, has he?"

"The others did."

"They got killed accidentally. Or they refused the Trust . . ."

"You can choose," Mark said. "There must be some way."

"The Seventh Gate!" Clare closed her eyes, and took a deep, shuddering breath, feeling her heart rate slow down. "I'd forgotten. Mr Aylward said he'd tried to go through the Seventh Gate and they wouldn't let him."

They looked across the mist-shrouded Garden. The Seventh Moon Gate was solid, built as part of the wall, with its outline traced in dark marble, and its inscription marking the place.

"It was all here," Clare said, exasperated. "So many clues and we missed them all. All the garden is one big clue to the Benison. All the statues are about healing or going into the earth or about being reborn and healed. Apollo, Aesclepius. All the names. The Raven symbol. The triple spirals. Even the church window, *The Waters of Paradise*. We just didn't understand.

"Mark, what are we going to do about the Benison? Do we just hide it and guard it for another hundred years? What's the point of guarding selfishly something that only the Aylwards and the Kenwards can use?"

"What do you want us to do then? Tell everybody? Get the scientists in?"

The vision came spontaneously. The devastated Earth, the frantic grabbing people, the greedy companies siphoning away the water into great tankers, the hedgerows broken down, great earth dredgers scooping away Barrow Beacon Hill to get at the water first. The breaking down of the great cave, so at last there would be no healing water for anyone at all. Greediness killing the goose that laid the golden egg. Again.

Clare said, "No. No, of course, that's no good. We have

279

to find our own way to share it. That's the problem all the Guardians have had to solve. It was all right when it was an Abbey. People came and were healed miraculously from the Holy Well, and nobody questioned it.

"And clever old James Edward and his son Edmund, they dammed the Raven to make the lake to dilute the spring water, and then landscaped it so the water flowed out into the countryside to make it fertile. No wonder the people here have always lived a long time."

"Mangelwurzels," said Mark. "I knew that crop was extraordinary. I bet the other crops were marvellous too. Now the springs have started to flow again. We can clear out the passage. Make sure it flows into the Raven again, so the animals and fields get the benefit."

"And rebuild the Holy Well in the China Garden." Clare was following her own train of thought. "The women all used the Holy Well water for their remedies. And Clarissa Kenward made her Herb and Physick Garden. I bet she used the spring water to grow them and make her medicines. And there's Rosamond who treated the smallpox.

"Mark, there are still so many terrible diseases. Cholera, cancer, motor neuron disease, AIDS. All the poor sick people of the whole world. There must be a way we can use the water to help in some way."

Mark rubbed his forehead thoughtfully. "We could farm the herbs, of course. Make special medicines. But we don't know what the water can do. Maybe it could develop new disease-resistant strains of crops and healing plants. Animal foods. Make herbal fertilizers to regenerate the earth . . ."

"The trouble is, we don't *know* enough," said Clare, frustrated. "I'm definitely going to university to read Medicine. Oh don't look like that, I'm not leaving Ravensmere. I'll just commute each day to Bristol or Southampton."

Mark said slowly, "And I need to know more about agricultural research and estate management."

She turned to him, excited. "Mark! We could go together!"

He laughed and kissed her nose. "We'll talk about it."

They sat on, watching the mist thicken and rise, dissolving the walls of the China Garden. Tabitha sat up, alert, staring into the mist, her ears bent forward.

Clare said quietly, "It's not just the water. It's the place too. You can feel the difference. The water heals your body, but the place heals your spirit and mind. We could have a healing sanctuary here again. There's plenty of room."

She thought of the healing secret she had been given in the cavern. She could teach it to everybody. Even if you hadn't got the spring water you could still imagine it. You could remember to let go of all the darkness in you, all the pain, anger, fear, anxiety, hatred, so that it flowed away from you like a dark stain dissolving in the light. The golden light flooding over and around you, so that you became part of it, golden and transparent yourself, flowing up and fusing with the greater white light of the universe.

She must remember to tell Mark, or maybe he already knew. It was something everybody could do to help themselves. You only had to imagine.

There was a stirring, a movement. The ground mist swirled and parted, and looking up Clare saw, disbelieving, Mr Aylward, sitting in his wheelchair.

"I came to see the China Garden again," he said. He looked better, Clare noted with relief, well wrapped up in his rugs. His voice sounded stronger too.

"I think, if you gave me your arm, I might be able to walk to the Pavilion."

Astonished, she helped him from the chair. Once he was on his feet he seemed to gain strength, and although they stopped several times along the path to the centre, he grew stronger all the time, and eventually lowered himself slowly to the top step.

"Are you warm enough?" Clare asked. "Do you want me

to fetch the blankets? This really is absolutely crazy. My mother will murder me."

He gave his harsh croaking laugh. "I think not."

She saw that he was staring at the Fourth Gate. Could he see the Leper Stone shining iridescent, as she could? There were tears in his eyes.

She said, "I saw Brandon. He smiled and waved to me."

He turned his head slowly and looked at her. "You have opened all the Moon Gates?"

Clare said firmly, "The past is healed. All the Gates are open."

"All the Gates except one. Do the Maze Dance for me, Clare. You found the Benison and survived. I'm free to go. Open the Seventh Moon Gate."

"But we can bring you water from the cave."

"Do the Maze Dance. Open the Gate."

"You're *sure?*"

She looked at him uncertainly. Looked into his shadowy eyes, shining in the starlight like a cat's, and understood.

She stood up stiffly, reluctantly, the tears running down her cheeks uncontrollably. The pipe music came. It was very clear tonight. Her body swayed into the Maze Dance.

Mark watched her. *Who was she talking to? What could she see?* He felt himself shuddering with a cold terror. She was moving weightlessly, like a shadow through the silver mist swirling and wreathing her. *Who was dancing there?* Clare, or some strange goddess, aeons old, weaving her labyrinth web?

She turned and turned again, ever nearer the centre, then spun into the return, swinging outwards to the Seventh Moon Gate, the imitation Gate that had been no more than a patterning in the stones of the wall.

The Gate was open now, but stretched across the space were almost invisible filaments, a cobweb, strong and flexible. She pushed at the silken strands, trying to force them away, to part them, but they merely gave to her touch like elastic before springing back.

Beyond the web the sky shone deep blue and silver, shimmering with ice blue and green shot with violet. And hanging in the sky in line were three glowing moons.

She realized then that Mr Aylward was standing next to her, leaning on his stick, staring through the Gate.

"You can't go through," she said. "There's a web or something."

But he wasn't listening. His eyes were fixed on the glory of the central moon.

The web was parting—she could see it now, shining, throbbing with its own internal light—the golden cobweb was unravelling. Mr Aylward moved forward and suddenly the Moon Gate was dark and long, like a tunnel, rather than a gate. He seemed a long way away.

There were lights on the moons. A rich, comforting ruby on the right, a green light, soothing and peaceful on the left. But the centre shone with splendour, a diamond-bright effulgence.

Clare took a deep breath, her eyes fixed on the explosion of light, and took a step forward.

"Wait for me," she said, and took another step. Freedom was there. No responsibility.

"*No!*" Fierce hands clamped to her shoulders, dragging her back, while she fought to be free to go to the white moon.

Mark held her against him convulsively, hurting her with his strength and fear. "For God's sake, Clare. You can't go yet. We're the Guardians. We've got work to do. It isn't the time."

Mr Aylward had turned at the end of the tunnel and they heard his croaking laugh. He raised his hand in a gesture like the figure on the stable clock. A blessing. Then he turned and walked on energetically, like a young man.

Clare drew a deep, sobbing breath, and felt under her

hands the rough garden wall. The Seventh Moon Gate had faded back into the stone. Closed. She felt the tears wet on her cheeks.

"We get another chance," Mark said. "When we want it. When we've done our work."

Clare looked ahead, down the years of her life, years of learning and work, of love and achievement, of guarding the Benison with Mark. She thought of all the uncounted generations of female Guardians, women who had created and danced, birthed and healed and felt a sudden strength and pride. She was a woman too, like the clay figures in the cave, inheritor of all their intelligence and knowledge. She was strong and powerful. She would experience life as fully as she could and one day she would be like the wise old woman turning into spirit, and the Seventh Gate would open for her again.

A strange wind blew through the China Garden, invigorating, sharp with the scent of lavender, mint, herbs. The sky lightened, reflecting the glow of the rising sun.

Mark took her hand. "Come on. Let's get some breakfast. There's a lot to do today."

They walked back through the First Moon Gate.

A single bird started to sing.

Author's note:

The reader may be interested to know that the ideas in this book came from actual customs and legends in the English countryside. There is, alas, no Ravensmere (that I know of), but there are numerous healing stones and standing stones that are reputed to go down to the water to drink at certain times of the year. There are customs like Turning the Stone (the whole village takes part) and Washing the Stone in holy well water, which continue to be done each year. And there are, of course, many stone circles, healing springs, mazes and strange and enchanting gardens and houses, like Stourhead, Studley Royal at Fountains Abbey, Lacock Abbey and Calke Abbey—all National Trust properties, which I visited when researching this book. There are also China Houses—but the octagonal China Garden with its Moon Gates is my own invention.

The reader is recommended to any of the books by Janet and Colin Bord, in particular, *Sacred Waters* and *Mysterious Britain*, and *Labyrinths* by Sig Lonegren.

This book is dedicated to
my Readers—
the new generation of Earth Guardians

and to
Debbie Lewis
who went through the Seventh Gate as I completed
this book